Praise for Robert Crais

'[An] adrenalin-fuelled outing' *Time Out*

'A nerve-wracking, switchbacking tale of guilt and redemption. It's so good it gives you goosebumps'
Evening Standard

'It's a simple enough plot but Crais packs it with terrific action and dialogue. He gets better and better'
The Times

'Crais knows his way around a wisecrack and a narrative sucker-punch . . . enormously appealing'
San Francisco Chronicle

'This is a novel of suspense, and it keeps racking up the tension until the very end. Crais is an old-timer at this kind of thing and *The Watchman* is him at his very best'
Irish Times

'Robert Crais is shooting for the big time with all guns blazing' *Guardian*

'The story moves along at top speed in typical Crais fashion, with lots of ultraviolence, gallows humour and great writing. A must from first page to last' *Independent*

'Robert Crais is a major crime-writing talent, exciting and thought-provoking' *Sunday Express*

'Crais tells a compelling tale that glints with wit, intelligence and expertise' *Literary Review*

By Robert Crais

The Monkey's Raincoat
Stalking the Angel
Lullaby Town
Free Fall
Voodoo River
Sunset Express
Indigo Slam
L.A. Requiem
Demolition Angel
Hostage
The Last Detective
The Forgotten Man
The Two Minute Rule
The Watchman
Chasing Darkness
The First Rule
The Sentry
Taken
Suspect

Robert Crais is the author of nineteen novels, including the international bestsellers *Taken*, *The Sentry*, *Demolition Angel* and the Edgar-nominated *L.A. Requiem*. He has two additional Edgar nominations as well as Anthony and Macavity awards for his series as Elvis Cole and Joe Pike crime novels. Crais has also written for acclaimed television shows such as *L.A. Law* and *Hill Street Blues*. *Hostage* has been made into a major motion picture featuring Bruce Willis. He lives in Los Angeles. Visit his website at www.robertcrais.com

chasing darkness

ROBERT CRAIS

An Orion paperback

First published in Great Britain in 2008
by Orion Books
This paperback edition published in 2009
by Orion Books, an imprint of The Orion Publishing Group Ltd
Orion House, 5 Upper St Martin's Lane,
London WC2H 9EA

An Hachette UK company

7 9 10 8 6

Reissued 2012

Copyright © Robert Crais 2008

A CIP catalogue record for this book
is available from the British Library.

ISBN 978-0-7528-8283-3

Printed and bound in Great Britain by
CPI Group (UK) Ltd, Croydon, CRO 4YY

The Orion Publishing Group's policy is to use papers
that are natural, renewable and recyclable products and
made from wood grown in sustainable forests. The logging
and manufacturing processes are expected to conform to
the environmental regulations of the country of origin.

www.orionbooks.co.uk

for Shelby Rotolo
because rope ladders and
Christmas tree forts last forever

ACKNOWLEDGEMENTS

The publication of a book requires many hands. My thanks, as always, to:

My editor, Marysue Rucci, and publishers David Rosenthal and Louise Burke.

My copy editor, Patricia Crais. Thankfully, one of us can spell.

Aaron Priest, Lisa Vance, and Lucy Childs for their wise counsel and zealous representation; and Carol Topping and Clay Fourrier for creating the wonderful worlds of our websites and newsletter at RobertCrais.com. Our family of readers now extends around the world, with numbers in the millions.

PROLOGUE

BEAKMAN AND TRENCHARD could smell the fire—it was still a mile away, but a sick desert wind carried the promise of Hell. Fire crews from around the city were converging on Laurel Canyon like red angels, as were black-and-white Adam cars, Emergency Services vehicles, and water-dropping helicopters out of Van Nuys and Burbank. The helicopters pounded by so low that Beakman and Trenchard could not hear their supervisor. Beakman cupped his ear.

"What did you say?"

Their supervisor, a patrol sergeant named Karen Philips, leaned into their car and shouted again.

"Start at the top of Lookout Mountain. Emergency Services is already up, but you gotta make sure those people leave. Don't take any shit. You got it?"

Trenchard, who was senior and also driving, shouted back.

"We're on it."

They jumped into line with the fire engines racing

up Laurel Canyon, then climbed Lookout Mountain Avenue up the steep hill. Once home to rock 'n' roll royalty from Mama Cass Elliot to Frank Zappa to Jim Morrison, Laurel Canyon had been the birthplace of country rock in the sixties. Crosby, Stills, and Nash had all lived there. So had Eric Burdon, Keith Richards, and, more recently, Marilyn Manson and at least one of the Red Hot Chili Peppers. Beakman, who banged away at a Fender Telecaster in a cop band called Nightstix, thought the place was musical magic.

Beakman pointed at a small house.

"I think Joni Mitchell used to live there."

"Who gives a shit? You see that sky? Man, look at that. The frakkin' air is on fire!"

A charcoal bruise smudged the sky as smoke pushed toward Sunset Boulevard. Beginning as a house fire at the crest of the Hollywood Hills, the flames had jumped to the brush in Laurel Canyon Park, then spread with the wind. Three houses had already been lost, and more were threatened. Beakman would have plenty of stories for his kids when he returned to his day job on Monday.

Jonathan Beakman was a Level II Reserve Officer with the Los Angeles Police Department, which meant he was armed, fully sworn, and did everything a full-time uniformed officer did, except he did it only two days a month. In his regular life, Beakman taught high-school algebra. His kids weren't particularly interested in the Pythagorean theorem, but they bombed him with questions after his weekend ride in the car.

Trenchard, who had twenty-three years on the job and didn't like music, said, "Here's how it goes down—we get to the top, we'll leave the car and work down five or six houses on foot, me on one side, you on the other, then go back for the car and do it again. Should go pretty quick like that."

The Fire Department had been through the area, broadcasting an order to evacuate over their public-address system. A few residents already had their cars piled high with clothes, golf clubs, pillows, and dogs. Others stood in their front doors, watching their neighbors pack. A few were on their roofs, soaking their homes with garden hoses. Beakman worried the hosers might be a problem.

"What if somebody won't leave?"

"We're not here to arrest people. We have too much ground to cover."

"What if someone can't leave, like an invalid?"

"First pass, we want to make sure everyone gets the word. If someone needs more help, we'll radio down or come back after we reach the bottom."

Trenchard, ever wise for a man who didn't like music, glanced over.

"You okay?"

"A little nervous, maybe. One of these houses, you watch. Some old lady's gonna have fifteen pugs waddling around. What are we going to do with fifteen pugs?"

Trenchard laughed, and Beakman found himself smiling, though his smile quickly faded. They passed a little girl following her mother to an SUV, the girl dragging a cat carrier so heavy she couldn't lift it. Her mother was crying.

Beakman thought, This is awful.

When they reached the top of Lookout Mountain, they started the door-to-door. If the inhabitants weren't already in the act of evacuating, Beakman knocked and rang the bell, then pounded on the jamb with his Maglite. Once, he hammered at a door so long that Trenchard shouted from across the street.

"You're gonna knock down the goddamned door! If they don't answer, nobody's home."

When they reached the first cross street, Trenchard joined him. The cross street cut up a twisting break in the ridge and was lined with clapboard cabins and crumbling stone bungalows that had probably been built in the thirties. The lots were so narrow that most of the houses sat on top of their own garages.

Trenchard said, "Can't be more than eight or ten houses in here. C'mon."

They split sides again and went to work, though most of the residents were already leaving. Beakman cleared the first three houses easily enough, then climbed the steps to a run-down stucco bungalow. Knock, bell, Maglite.

"Police officer. Anyone home?"

He decided no one was home, and was halfway down the steps when a woman called from across the street. Her Mini Cooper was packed and ready to go.

"I think he's home. He doesn't go out."

Beakman glanced up at the door he had just left. He had banged on the jamb so hard the door had rattled.

"He's an invalid?"

"Mr. Jones. He has a bad foot, but I don't know. I haven't seen him in a few days. Maybe he's gone, but I don't know. He doesn't move so well, that's why I'm saying."

Now she had the irritated expression of someone who wished she hadn't gotten involved.

Beakman climbed back to the door.

"What's his name?"

"Jones. That's all I know, Mr. Jones. He doesn't move so well."

Beakman unleashed the Maglite again. Hard.

"Mr. Jones? Police officer, is anyone home?"

Trenchard, finished with his side of the street, came up the stairs behind him.

"We got a holdout?"

"Lady says the man here doesn't move so well. She thinks he might be home."

Trenchard used his own Maglite on the door.

"Police officers. This is an emergency. Please open the door."

Both of them leaned close to listen, and that's when Beakman caught the sour smell. Trenchard smelled it, too, and called down to the woman.

"He old, sick, what?"

"Not so old. He has a bad foot."

5

Down on the street, she couldn't smell it.

Beakman lowered his voice.

"You smell it, right?"

"Yeah. Let's see what's what."

Trenchard holstered his Maglite. Beakman stepped back, figuring Trenchard was going to kick down the door, but Trenchard just tried the knob and opened it. A swarm of black flies rode out on the smell, engulfed them, then flew back into the house. Beakman swatted at the flies. He didn't want them to touch him. Not after where they had been.

The woman shouted up, "What is it?"

They saw a man seated in a ragged club chair, wearing baggy plaid shorts and a thin blue T-shirt. He was barefoot, allowing Beakman to see that half the right foot was missing. The scarring suggested the injury to his foot occurred a long time ago, but he had a more recent injury.

Beakman followed Trenchard into the house for a closer look. The remains of the man's head lolled backwards, where blood and brain matter had drained onto the club chair and his shoulders. His right hand rested on his lap, limply cupping a black pistol. A single black hole had been punched beneath his chin. Dried blood the color of black cherries was crusted over his face and neck and the chair.

Trenchard said, "That's a damn bad foot."

"Suicide?"

"Duh. I'll call. We can't leave this guy until they get someone here to secure the scene."

"What about the fire?"

"Fuck the fire. They gotta get someone up here to wait for the CI. I don't want us to get stuck with this stink."

Trenchard swatted futilely at the flies and ducked like a boxer slipping a punch as he moved for the door. Beakman, fascinated, circled the dead man.

Trenchard said, "Don't touch anything. We gotta treat it like a crime scene."

"I'm just looking."

A photo album lay open between the dead man's feet as if it had fallen from his lap. Careful not to step in the dried blood, Beakman moved closer to see. A single picture was centered on the open page, one of those Polaroid pictures that develop themselves. The plastic over the picture was speckled with blood.

The flies suddenly seemed louder to Beakman, as loud now as the helicopters fighting the flames.

"Trench, come here—"

Trenchard came over, then stooped for a closer look.

"Holy Mother."

The Polaroid showed a female Caucasian with what appeared to be an extension cord wrapped around her neck. The picture had been taken at night, with the woman sprawled on her back at the base of a trash bin. Her tongue protruded thickly from her mouth, and her eyes bulged, but they were unfocused and sightless.

Beakman heard himself whispering.

"You think it's real? A real woman, really dead?"

"Dunno."

"Maybe it's from a movie. You know, staged?"

Trenchard opened his knife, then used the point to turn the page. Beakman grew scared. He might have been only a reserve officer, but he knew better than to disturb the scene.

"We're not supposed to touch anything."

"We're not. Shut up."

Trenchard turned to the next page, then the next. Beakman felt numb but excited, knowing he was seeing a darkness so terrible that few people would ever imagine it, let alone face it. These pictures were portraits of evil. The mind that had conceived of these things and taken these pictures and hidden them in this album had entered a nightmare world. It had left humanity behind. Beakman would have stories for his kids when he returned to school, but this story would not be among them.

"They're real, aren't they? These women were murdered."

"I dunno."

"They look real. He fucking killed them."

"Stop it."

Trenchard lifted the album with his knife so they could see the cover. It showed a beautiful sunset beach with gentle waves and a couple leaving footprints in the sand. Embossed in flowing script was a legend: *My Happy Memories*.

Trenchard lowered the cover.

"Let's get away from these flies."

They left the album as they had found it, and sought comfort in the smoky air.

Part One
LOOKOUT MOUNTAIN

I

OUR OFFICE was a good place to be that morning. There was only the tocking of the Pinocchio clock, the scratch of my pen, and the hiss of the air conditioner fighting a terrible heat. Fire season had arrived, when fires erupted across the Southland like pimples on adolescent skin.

Joe Pike was waiting for me to finish the paperwork. He stood at the French doors that open onto my balcony, staring across the city toward the ocean. He had not spoken or moved in more than twenty minutes, which was nothing for Pike. He often went soundless for days. We were going to work out at Ray Depente's gym in South-Central Los Angeles when I finished the grind.

The first call came at nine forty-two.

A male voice said, "Are you Elvis Cole?"

"That's right. How can I help you?"

"You're a dead man."

I killed the call and went back to work. When you

do what I do, you get calls from schizophrenics, escapees from Area 51, and people claiming to know who killed the Black Dahlia and Princess Diana.

Pike said, "Who was it?"

"Some guy told me I was a dead man."

Pike said, "Smoke."

I glanced up from the work.

"Where?"

"Malibu, looks like. Maybe Topanga."

Then Pike turned toward the door, and everything that had been normal about that ordinary morning changed.

"Listen—"

A stocky man with a short haircut and wilted tan sport coat shoved through the door like he lived in Fallujah. He flashed a badge as if he expected me to dive under my desk.

"Welcome to hell, shitbird."

A woman in a blue business suit with a shoulder bag slung on her arm came in behind him. The heat had played hell with her hair, but that didn't stop her from showing a silver-and-gold detective shield.

"Connie Bastilla, LAPD. This is Charlie Crimmens. Are you Elvis Cole?"

I studied Pike.

"Did he really call me a shitbird?"

Crimmens tipped his badge toward me, then Pike, but talked to the woman.

"This one's Cole. This one's gotta be his bun boy, Pike."

Pike faced Charlie. Pike was six-one, a bit over two, and was suited up in a sleeveless grey sweatshirt and government-issue sunglasses. When he crossed his arms, the bright red arrows inked into his deltoids rippled.

I spoke slowly.

"Did you make an appointment?"

Crimmens said, "Answer her, shitbird."

I am a professional investigator. I am licensed by the state of California and run a professional business. Police officers did not barge into my office. They also did not call me a shitbird. I stood, and gave Crimmens my best professional smile.

"Say it again I'll shove that badge up your ass."

Bastilla took a seat in one of the two director's chairs facing my desk.

"Take it easy. We have some questions about a case you once worked."

I stared at Crimmens.

"You want to arrest me, get to it. You want to talk to me, knock on my door and ask for permission. You think I'm kidding about the badge, try it out."

Pike said, "Go ahead, Crimmens. Give it a try."

Crimmens smirked as he draped himself over the file cabinet. He studied Pike for a moment, then smirked some more.

Bastilla said, "Do you recall a man named Lionel Byrd?"

"I didn't offer you a seat."

"C'mon, you know Lionel Byrd or not?"

Charlie said, "He knows him. Jesus."

Something about Crimmens was familiar, though I couldn't place him. Most of the Hollywood Bureau detectives were friends of mine, but these two were blanks.

"You aren't out of Hollywood."

Bastilla put her card on my desk.

"Homicide Special. Charlie's attached out of Rampart. We're part of a task force investigating a series of homicides. Now, c'mon. Lionel Byrd."

I had to think.

"We're talking about a criminal case?"

"Three years ago, Byrd was bound over for the murder of a twenty-eight-year-old prostitute named Yvonne Bennett, a crime he confessed to. You produced a witness and a security tape that supposedly cleared him of the crime. His attorney was J. Alan Levy, of Barshop, Barshop & Alter. We getting warmer here?"

The facts of the case returned as slowly as surfacing fish. Lionel Byrd had been an unemployed mechanic with alcohol problems and a love/hate relationship with prostitutes. He wasn't a guy you would want to know socially, but he wasn't a murderer.

"Yeah, I remember. Not all the details, but some. It was a bogus confession. He recanted."

Crimmens shifted.

"Wasn't bogus."

I took my seat and hooked a foot on the edge of the desk.

"Whatever. The video showed he was here in Hollywood when Bennett was murdered. She was killed in Silver Lake."

Behind them, Pike touched his watch. We were going to be late.

I lowered my foot and leaned forward.

"You guys should have called. My partner and I have an appointment."

Bastilla took out a notepad to show me they weren't going to leave.

"Have you seen much of Mr. Byrd since you got him off?"

"I never met the man."

Crimmens said, "Bullshit. He was your client. You don't meet your clients?"

"Levy was my client. Barshop, Barshop paid the tab. That's what lawyers do."

Bastilla said, "So it was Levy who hired you?"

"Yes. Most of my clients are lawyers."

Attorneys can't and don't rely on the word of their clients. Often, their clients don't know the whole and impartial truth, and sometimes their clients lie. Since lawyers are busy lawyering, they employ investigators to uncover the facts.

Bastilla twisted around to see Pike.

"What about you? Did you work on Byrd's behalf?"

"Not my kind of job."

She twisted farther to get a better look.

"How about you take off the shades while we talk?"

"No."

Crimmens said, "You hiding something back there, Pike? How 'bout we look?"

Pike's head swiveled toward Crimmens. Nothing else moved; just his head.

"If I showed you, I'd have to kill you."

I stepped in before it got out of hand.

"Joe didn't help on this one. This thing was Detective Work 101. I must pull thirty cases like this a year."

Crimmens said, "That's sweet. You must take pride in that, helping shitbirds get away with murder."

Crimmens was pissing me off again.

"What are we talking about this for, Bastilla? This thing was settled three years ago."

Bastilla opened her pad and studied the page.

"So you are telling us you have never met Lionel Byrd?"

"I have never met him."

"Are you acquainted with a man named Lonnie Jones?"

"No. Is he your new suspect?"

"During your investigation into the matter of Yvonne Bennett, did you discover evidence linking Mr. Byrd to any other crimes or criminal activities?"

"What kind of question is that? Have you re-arrested him?"

Bastilla scribbled a note. When she looked up, her eyes were ringed with purple cutting down to her mouth. She looked as tired as a person can look without being dead.

"No, Mr. Cole, we can't arrest him. Eight days ago, he was found during the evacuation up in Laurel Canyon. Head shot up through the bottom of his chin. He had been dead about five days."

"I didn't kill him."

Crimmens laughed.

"Wouldn't that be funny, Con? Wouldn't that be too perfect? Man, I would love that."

Bastilla smiled, but not because she thought it was funny.

"He committed suicide. He was living under the name Lonnie Jones. Know why he was using an alias?"

"No idea. Maybe because he didn't like being accused of murders he didn't commit."

Bastilla leaned toward me and crossed her arms on a knee.

"The man's dead now, Cole. Reason we're here, we'd like to examine the reports and work product you have from the Bennett case. Your notes. The people you questioned. Everything in your file."

She waited without blinking, studying me as if she knew what I would say, but was hoping I might not say it. I shook my head.

"I was working on behalf of defense counsel. That material belongs to Alan Levy."

"Levy is being contacted."

Crimmens said, "The fucker's dead, Cole. You got him off. What's it matter now?"

"If Levy says fine, then fine, but I worked for him, Crimmens, not you. There's that little thing about 'expectation of confidentiality.'"

I looked back at Bastilla.

"If the man's dead and you don't think I killed him, why do you care what's in my files about Yvonne Bennett?"

Bastilla sighed, then straightened.

"Because this isn't only about Bennett. Lionel Byrd murdered seven women. We believe he murdered one woman every year for the past seven years. Yvonne Bennett was his fifth victim."

She said it as matter-of-factly as a bank teller cashing a check, but with a softness in her voice that spread seeds of ice in my belly.

"He didn't kill Yvonne Bennett. I proved it."

Bastilla put away her pad. She got up, then hooked her bag on her shoulder, finally ready to go.

"Material linking him to the murder was found in his home. He murdered a sixth woman the summer after his release. His most recent victim was murdered thirty-six days ago, and now he's murdered himself."

Crimmens licked his lips as if he wanted to eat me alive.

"How do you feel now, Mr. Thirty-a-Year?"

I shook my head at Bastilla.

"What does that mean, you found material?"

"Something in your files might help us figure out how he got away with it, Cole. Talk to Levy. If we have to subpoena, we will, but it'll be faster if you guys come across."

I stood with her.

"Waitaminute—what does that mean, you found something? What did you find?"

"A press conference is scheduled for this evening. In the meantime, talk to Levy. The sooner the better."

Bastilla left without waiting, but Crimmens made no move to follow. He stayed on the file cabinet, watching me.

I said, "What?"

"Escondido and Repko."

"Why are you still here, Crimmens?"

"You don't recognize me, do you?"

"Should I?"

"Think about it. You must've read my reports."

Then I realized why he was familiar.

"You were the arresting officer."

Crimmens finally pushed off the cabinet.

"That's right. I'm the guy who arrested Byrd. I'm the guy who tried to stop a killer. You're the shitbird who set him free."

Crimmens glanced at Pike, then went to the door.

"Lupe Escondido and Debra Repko are the women

he killed after you got him off. You should send the families a card."

Crimmens closed the door when he left.

2

ON A moonless night three years before Bastilla and Crimmens came to my office, someone shattered Yvonne Bennett's skull in a Silver Lake parking lot, one block north of Sunset Boulevard. The night was warm, though not hot, with the scent of spider lilies kissing the air. The weapon of choice was a tire iron.

Yvonne Bennett was twenty-eight years old when she died, though everyone I interviewed—including two former roommates and three former boyfriends—believed she was nineteen. As it was for many in Los Angeles, her life was a masquerade. She lied about her age, her past, her work history, and her profession. Of the twenty-three people I interviewed when I tracked her movements on the night of her death, three believed she was a student at UCLA, two believed she was a student at USC, one believed she was a graduate student working toward a doctorate in psychology, and one or more of the rest believed she was a production assistant, a makeup artist, a florist, a clothing designer, a graphic artist, a bartender, a waitress, a sales clerk at Barney's on Wilshire Boulevard, or a sous chef who worked for Wolfgang Puck. Though she had been arrested for prostitution twice, she was not and never had been a streetwalker. She was a bar girl. She picked up men in bars and brokered the cash before leaving the premises. Even with the arrests, she denied being a prostitute, once telling a former roommate that, though she dated men for money, she never took money for sex. This, too, was a lie.

There wasn't much in my files about Yvonne Bennett or Lionel Byrd because I hadn't spent much time on his case, eight days start to finish. Any moron could have solved it. No shots fired, no beatings given or received. The Batman cape stayed home.

I passed the pages to Pike as I read them.

At the time of his arrest, Lionel Byrd was a legitimate suspect in the murder. He had been seen talking to Yvonne Bennett earlier that evening and he had a criminal history with prostitutes—two pops for soliciting and a misdemeanor assault conviction eighteen months earlier when he argued with a prostitute about her services. Byrd was still on probation when Crimmens picked him up.

A twenty-two-year-old coffee-shop barista and aspiring actor named Angel Tomaso was the last person to see Yvonne Bennett alive when she entered the alley behind his coffee shop at eleven-forty P.M. Her body was discovered at twelve-sixteen A.M. These two times created the thirty-six-minute window during which Bennett was murdered, and would prove key to the charges against Byrd being dropped.

Though the evidence against him was largely circumstantial, Lionel Byrd confessed the crime to Crimmens and his partner at the time, a fellow Rampart detective named Nicky Munoz. This sounds more telling than it was. With the assault prior and the witnesses who saw them together, Crimmens convinced Byrd he was cooked on the murder and promised a lesser charge if Byrd confessed. When Levy viewed the confession tape, it was clear Byrd had no knowledge of the crime; Crimmens had fed him the information with leading questions. Byrd later recanted, but by then the damage was done. The confession and its supporting evidence were enough for a murder charge to be brought.

Levy convinced me that Byrd was being given the rush with the jacked-up confession. He also convinced the judge, who threatened to toss the confession. Eight days later I found a time-coded security video placing Byrd in the Two Worlds Lounge in Hollywood at the same time Yvonne Bennett was being murdered sixteen-point-two miles away. Levy, the bartender on duty that night, and I met with the prosecutor in the judge's chambers three days later, where, at the judge's suggestion and in hopes of avoiding a slam-dunk acquittal, the deputy district attorney dropped the charges.

Nothing in my files made me doubt myself.

Nothing there made me feel wrong. They didn't need Sherlock Holmes to put it together.

Pike tamped the pages together.

"How was it you found the tape and not Crimmens and Munoz? They had the same information as you."

"Crimmens had the confession, so he was lazy. We had a list of the places Byrd claimed he was in that night, but he only knew a few of the bars by name. We had to figure out where he was by working off the descriptions."

"Uh-huh."

"All of the bars checked out except the last one. He said he stopped for a nightcap at a place like a tiki bar that had bamboo. Everyone, including me, thought it was in Silver Lake."

"But it wasn't."

"We found a bar like that, but not the one he meant. It was a lesbian bar. It wasn't a tiki place, but it was small and dark with bamboo furniture. This was the only place that came close to his description, but the bartenders denied he was there. That sealed the deal for Crimmens, but here was the tell: Byrd told Crimmens he argued with the bartender because the bartender wouldn't let him run a tab. On the tape, he says, that guy was a prick."

"A guy."

"The bartenders were women. All the other bars had checked out, so him getting it wrong about the bartender bothered me. Byrd had an apartment in Hollywood back then, so I looked for something closer to home. That's where I found it, a little place between Santa Monica and Sunset. They were trying to look like the Alaskan wilderness. They had these fake totem poles behind the bar, not tiki idols. They still had the security tape, and there he was, having his drink. The time code put him in Hollywood during the window when Yvonne Bennett was murdered. The judge agreed. The DA. Everybody. That's why they dropped the charges."

Maybe I was still trying to convince myself, but I didn't see the hole. I didn't see how Lionel Byrd could have killed her, and I didn't see how Bastilla could be so certain that he had.

Pike said, "What about the other murders?"

"I was all over this guy's life for eight days. I had his priors. I had everything. There was nothing to suggest he was a killer or was involved with anyone who was."

Pike put my files aside.

"Only now the police say Byrd did it."

I got up for a bottle of water and looked for the fire Pike had seen, but the fire was out. The firefighters had moved in hard and killed it. That's the best way to stop these things. Kill them before they grow.

I returned to my desk.

"Listen, take off for Ray's without me. I'm going to call Levy."

"I can wait."

I scrolled through my Palm for Levy's number and put in the call. I had not called or spoken with Alan

Levy in almost three years, but his assistant immediately recognized my name.

"Alan's in court, but he told me to find him. He might not be able to talk, but I know it's important. Can you hold while I try?"

"I'll hold."

Pike hadn't moved, so I covered the mouthpiece.

"You don't have to wait. I'm going to be here a while."

Pike still didn't move. Then Levy came on, speaking quickly in a low voice.

"Have you heard about Lionel Byrd?"

"Two detectives just told me Byrd was good for seven murders, including Yvonne Bennett. Is this for real?"

"I got a call this morning from Leslie Pinckert in Major Crimes—did Pinckert talk to you?"

"A detective named Bastilla was here. Crimmens was with her. They told me they have something that puts Byrd with the murders, but wouldn't say what."

"Wait, hang on—"

Muffled voices and court sounds whispered in the background, then he returned.

"Byrd had pictures of the victims in some kind of album. That's all she would tell me. They don't want this thing out of the bag until they've gone public."

"That asshole Crimmens tells me I got two of those women killed, and they're playing it tight? I need more than that, Alan."

"Just settle down."

"They wanted my files."

"I know. Did you give them anything?"

"Not until I spoke with you. I thought there might be a privilege issue."

"Are you in possession of anything that wasn't copied to me?"

"Just a few notes I didn't bother typing up in the formal reports."

"Okay. Get everything together, and we'll make time tomorrow. I want to cooperate with these people, but I have to review the material first."

"Did Byrd have a picture of Bennett? Did Pinckert tell you that much?"

Levy hesitated, and suddenly the sounds of justice behind him were loud.

"Pinckert promised to call this evening when she has more leeway to talk. We'll discuss it tomorrow."

The line went dead.

Pike was still watching me.

"What did he say?"

"He thinks they're keeping it buried until they know how to spin it."

"Hollywood Station covers the canyon. If a body was found up in Laurel, Poitras should know."

Lou Poitras was the detective-lieutenant in charge of the homicide bureau at Hollywood Station. He was also a friend. If a body dead from suspicious circumstances was found up in Laurel Canyon, Lou's detectives would have rolled to the scene before Bastilla and her task force were involved.

I immediately called his office, and got a sergeant named Griggs on the line. I had known Griggs almost as long as Poitras.

"Homicide. Lieutenant Poitras's office."

"It's me. Is he in?"

"Yes, he's in. Some of us work for a living."

"That's right, Griggs. And the rest of us are cops."

"Eff you."

Griggs hung up.

I redialed the number, but this time Poitras answered.

"Are you harassing my sergeant again?"

"Did your people roll on a DB suicide up in Laurel by the name of Lionel Byrd?"

The easy banter in his tone hardened as if I had flipped a switch.

"How did you hear about this?"

"A cop named Connie Bastilla just left my office. She told me something was found with his body that puts Byrd with seven killings."

Poitras hesitated.

"Why would Bastilla tell you about this?"

"Byrd was up for the murder of a woman named Yvonne Bennett. I was on the defense side. I found the evidence that freed him."

Poitras took even longer to answer this time.

"Wow."

"What do they have?"

"I don't know what to tell you."

"Does that mean you won't tell me?"

"It means I don't know what they have. You know Bobby McQue?"

Bobby McQue was a senior detective on Lou's squad.

"Yeah, I know Bobby."

"Bobby had it, but downtown rolled in when they saw we had a possible serial. They cut us out."

"So what did McQue find before you were out? C'mon, Lou, I need to know if this is real, man. Right now, it feels like a nightmare."

Poitras didn't respond.

"Lou?"

Behind me, Pike spoke loud enough for Poitras to hear.

"Tell Poitras to man-up."

"Was that Pike?"

"Yeah. He was here when Bastilla showed up."

Poitras hated Pike. Most L.A. police officers hated Pike. He was once one of them.

Poitras finally sighed.

"Okay, listen. The chief running the task force wants a tour before they go public, so I gotta go up there later. You want, you can meet me up there now. We'll walk you through the scene."

Poitras gave me the address.

"We won't have much time, so get up there right now."

"I understand."

Poitras hung up.

"He's going to let me see Byrd's house."

Pike said, "Poitras won't want me up there."

"I'm just going to see what they have. You don't need to come."

Pike moved for the first time since Crimmens and Bastilla left. Maybe I had stood a little too quickly. Maybe my voice was a little too high. Pike touched my arm.

"Were you right three years ago?"

"Yes."

"Then you're still right. You didn't get those two women killed. Even if the police have something, you didn't kill them."

I tried to give him a confident smile.

"Say hi to Ray. If it's bad, I'll give you a call."

Pike left, but I did not leave with him. Instead, I went out onto the balcony and let the bone-dry heat swallow me. The glare made me squint. The nuclear sun crinkled my skin.

Picture the detective at work in his office, fourth floor, Hollywood, as the Devil's Wind freight-trains down from the desert. Though dry and brutally harsh, the desert wind is clean. It pushes the smog south to the sea and scrubs the sky to a crystalline blue. The air, jittery from the heat, rises in swaying tendrils like kelp from the seabed, making the city shimmer. We are never more beautiful than when we are burning.

Knock, knock, thought you'd like to know, after you cleared that guy he murdered two more women, it should be hitting the news about now, their families should be crying about now.

I locked my office and went to see what they had.

The phone rang again as I went out the door, but I did not return to answer it.

3

Starkey

DETECTIVE-TWO CAROL Starkey spilled the fourth packet of sugar into her coffee. She sipped, but the coffee still tasted sour. Starkey was using the large black Hollywood Homicide mug Charlie Griggs had given her as a welcome-aboard gift three weeks earlier. She liked the mug. A big 187 was stenciled on the side, which was the LAPD code for a homicide, along with the legend *OUR DAY BEGINS WHEN YOUR DAY ENDS*. Starkey added a fifth sugar. Ever since she gave up the booze her body craved enormous amounts of sugar, so she fed the craving. She sipped. It still tasted like crap.

Clare Olney, who was another hard-core coffee hound, looked on with concern.

"You'd better watch it, Carol. You'll give yourself diabetes."

Starkey shrugged.

"Only live once."

Clare filled his own mug, black, without sugar or milk. He was a round man with a shiny bald dome and pudgy fingers. His mug was small, white, and showed the stick-figure image of a father and little girl. The legend on its side read WORLD'S GREATEST DAD in happy pink letters.

"You like working Homicide, Carol? You fitting in okay?"

"Yeah. It's good."

After only three weeks, Starkey wasn't sure if she liked it or not. Starkey had moved around a lot during her career. Before coming to Homicide, she had worked on the Juvenile Section, the Criminal Conspiracy Section, and the Bomb Squad. The Bomb Squad was her love, but, of course, they would not allow her back.

Clare had more coffee, noodling at her over the top of his cup as he worked up to ask. They all asked, sooner or later.

"It's gotta be so different than working the bombs. I can't imagine doing what you used to do."

"It's no big deal, Clare. Riding a patrol car is more dangerous."

Clare gave a phony little laugh. Clare was a nice man, but she could spot the phony laugh a thousand clicks out. They laughed because they were uncomfortable.

"Well, you can say it's no big deal, but I wouldn't have the guts to walk up to a bomb like that, just walk right up and try to de-arm it. I'd run the other way."

When Starkey was a bomb technician, she had walked up to plenty of bombs. She had de-armed over a hundred explosive devices of one kind or another, always in complete control of the situation and the device. That was what she most loved about being a bomb tech. It was just her and the bomb. She had been in complete control of how she approached the device and when it exploded. Only one bomb had been beyond her control.

She said, "You want to ask me something, Clare?"

He immediately looked uncomfortable.

"No, I was just—"

"It's okay. I don't mind talking about it."

She did mind, but she always pretended she didn't.

Clare edged away.

"I wasn't going to—"

"I had a bad one. A frakkin' earthquake, for Christ's sake, imagine that shit? A temblor hit us and the damn thing went off. You can dot every *i*, but there's always that one frakkin' thing."

Starkey smiled. She really did like Clare Olney and the pictures of his kids he kept on his desk.

"It killed me. Zeroed out right there in the trailer park. Dead."

Clare Olney's eyes were frozen little dots as Starkey had more of the coffee. She wished she could spark up a cigarette. Starkey smoked two packs a day, down from a high of four.

"The paramedics got me going again. Close call, huh?"

"Man, Carol, I'm sorry. Wow. What else can you say to something like that but wow?"

"I don't remember it. Just waking up with the paramedics over me, and then the hospital. That's all I remember."

"Wow."

"I wouldn't go back to a radio car. Screw that. Day to day, that's way more dangerous than working a bomb."

"Well, I hope you like it here on Homicide. If I can help you with anything—"

"Thanks, man. That's nice of you."

Starkey smiled benignly, then returned to her desk, glad the business of her bomb was out of the way. She was the New Guy at Hollywood Homicide, and had been the New Guy before. Everyone talked about it behind her back, but it always took a couple of weeks before someone asked. *Are you the bomb tech who got blown up? Did you really get killed on the job? What was it like on the other side?* It was like being dead, motherfucker.

Now Clare would gossip her answers, and maybe they could all move on.

Starkey settled at her desk and went to work reviewing a stack of murder books. This being her first homicide assignment, she had been partnered with a couple of veterans named Linda Brown and Bobby McQue. Brown wasn't much older than Starkey, but she was a detective-three supervisor with nine years on the table. McQue had twenty-eight years on the job, twenty-three working homicide, and was calling it quits when he hit thirty. The pairings were what Poitras called a training rotation.

Brown and McQue had each dropped ten ongoing cases on her desk and told her to learn the books. She had to familiarize herself with the details of each case and was given the responsibility of entering all new reports, case notes, and information as the investigations developed. Starkey had so much reading to do it made her eyes cross, and when she read, she wanted to smoke. She snuck out to the parking lot fifteen or twenty times a day, which had already caught Griggs's eye. *Jesus, Starkey, you smell like an ashtray.*

Eff you, Griggs.

Starkey palmed a cigarette from her bag for her third sprint to the parking lot that day when Lieutenant Poitras came out of his office. Christ, he was big. The sonofabitch was pumped-out from lifting weights like a stack of all-terrain truck tires.

Poitras studied the squad room, then raised his voice.

"Where's Bobby? McQue on deck?"

When no one else answered, Starkey spoke up.

"Court day, Top. He's cooling it downtown."

Poitras stared at her a moment.

"You were with Bobby on the house up in Laurel, right?"

"Yes, sir."

"Pack up. You're coming with me."

Starkey dropped the cigarette back in her purse and followed him out.

4

THE LATE-MORNING sun bounced between sycamores and hundred-foot eucalyptuses as I drove up Laurel Canyon to the top of Lookout Mountain. Even with the heat, young women pushed tricycle strollers up the steep slope, middle-aged men walked listless dogs, and kids practiced half-pipe tricks outside an elementary school. I wondered if any of them knew what had been found up the hill, and how they would react when they heard. The family-friendly, laid-back vibe of Laurel Canyon masked a darker history, spanning Robert Mitchum's lurid "reefer ranch" bust to Charlie Manson creeping through the sixties rock scene to the infamous "Four on the Floor" Wonderland Murders starring John "Johnny Wadd" Holmes. Driving up through the trees and shadows, the scent of wild fennel couldn't hide the smell of the recent fire.

The address Lou gave me led to a narrow street called Anson Lane cut into a break on the ridge. A radio car was parked midway up the street with a blue Crown Victoria behind it. Poitras, a detective I knew named Carol Starkey, and two uniforms were talking in the street. Starkey had only been on the bureau for a few weeks, so I was surprised to see her.

I parked behind the Crown Vic, then walked over to join them.

"Lou. Starkey, you driving now?"

"I shot Griggs for the job."

Poitras shifted with impatience.

"Catch up on your own time. Starkey rolled out with Bobby when the uniforms phoned in the body. They were on it until the task force took over."

"All of a day and a half. Fuckers."

Poitras frowned.

"Can we watch the mouth?"

"Sorry, Top."

Poitras turned toward the house.

"You wanted to see what we have, this is it."

The house was a small Mediterranean with a Spanish tile roof heavy with a mat of dead leaves and pine needles. The lot was narrow, so the living quarters were stacked on top of a single-car garage. The garage door was splintered as if a latch had been pried, probably so the police could gain access. A rickety stair climbed the entry side of the garage to a tiny covered porch. On the far side of the garage, a broken walk disappeared between overgrown cedar branches where it ran alongside the garage. A single knot of crime scene tape was still tied to the garage, left by whoever pulled down the tape.

Poitras squinted up at the house like it was the last place on earth he wanted to go.

"Starkey can lay out the scene for you, but we don't have any of the forensics or case files. Downtown has everything."

"Okay. Whatever you have."

"It's going to be hotter than hell up there. The AC's off."

"I appreciate this, Lou. Thanks. You, too, Starkey."

Poitras stripped off his jacket, and we followed him up.

Stepping into the house was like walking into a furnace. A ratty overstuffed chair had been pushed against a threadbare couch and a coffee table. Swatches of cloth had been cut from the arms and the back of the chair, leaving straw-colored batting bright against stained fabric. The stains were probably blood. Light switches, door jambs and the inside front doorknob were spotted with black smudges from fingerprint kits. More black was smudged on the telephone and coffee table. Starkey immediately took off her jacket, and Poitras rolled up his sleeves.

Starkey said, "Bleh. This smell."

"Tell him what you found."

Starkey glanced at me as if she wasn't sure how to start.

"You knew this guy, huh?"

"I didn't know him. I worked for his lawyer."

42

Just being asked if I knew him seemed to imply we were friends, and left me feeling resentful.

Poitras said, "Describe the scene, for Christ's sake. I want to get out of here."

Starkey moved to the center of the room, indicating an empty spot on the floor.

"The chair was here, not over by the couch. Once the body was out, the SID guys moved things around. He was here in the chair, slumped back, gun in his right hand—"

She held out her right hand with the palm up, showing me.

"—a Taurus .32 revolver."

"The chair was in the middle of the floor?"

"Yeah. Facing the television. A bottle of Seagram's was on the floor by the chair, so he had probably been hitting it. As soon as Bobby saw the guy he said that stiff's been here a week. It was a mess, man."

"How many shots fired?"

Poitras laughed, and moved closer to the door.

"You think he had to reload?"

Starkey said, "One spent, up through the bottom of his chin. Wasn't much blood. A little on the floor here and up on the ceiling—"

She indicated an irregular stain on the floor, then a spot the size of a quarter on the ceiling. It looked like a roach.

Poitras spoke from the doorway. Sweat had beaded on his forehead and was running down his cheeks.

"The coroner investigator said everything about

the body, the gun, and the splatter patterns was consistent with a self-inflicted wound. We haven't seen the final report, but that's what he told them here at the scene."

Starkey nodded along with him, but said nothing. I tried to imagine Lionel Byrd slumped in the chair, but his image was formless and grey. I couldn't remember what Byrd looked like. The only time I had seen him was on a videotape of his confession to the police.

I considered the neighboring houses. From the front door, I saw the roof of the black-and-white and the houses across the way. A woman was standing in a window across the street, looking down at the police car. Safe in her air-conditioning.

"Anyone hear the shot?"

Starkey said, "Remember, the guy had been dead for a week before we found him. No calls were made to 911, and none of these people remembered hearing anything on or around the day of death. Everyone was probably buttoned up from the heat."

Poitras said, "Tell him about the pictures."

Starkey had been watching me, but now she glanced at the floor. She seemed uncomfortable.

"He had an album with Polaroid pictures of his victims. There were seven pages with a different vic on each page. We thought they were fake. You see something like that, you think it's gotta be phony, like that porno stuff with girls pretending to be dead? We didn't know the shit was real until Bobby recognized one of the girls. It was fucking disgusting."

"The mouth."

I said, "Where did you find the album?"

"On the floor by his feet."

Starkey positioned herself as if she was sitting in the chair and touched the top of her left foot.

"Here. We figured it slid off his lap when he went for the gold—"

She suddenly glanced up.

"He only had one foot. The other was screwed up."

Lionel Byrd had lost half of his right foot in a garage accident when he was twenty-four years old. I hadn't remembered it before, but now I recalled Levy telling me about it. The settlement had left Byrd with a modest disability payment that supported him the rest of his life.

Poitras said, "It was Bobby put it together. One of the vics was a prostitute named Chelsea Ann Morrow. Bobby knew her, and after we had Morrow, we faxed the pictures through the other divisions. That's when the IDs started coming. Downtown rolled in that afternoon."

I stared at the floor as if I would suddenly see the album. Maybe that was why Starkey kept looking at the floor. Maybe she could still see it.

"Did he leave a note?"

"Uh-uh."

I glanced at Starkey.

"So all you found were the pictures?"

"We pulled a camera and a couple of film packs. There was a box of ammo for the gun. If the task force guys found anything else, I don't know."

"Pictures don't mean he killed them. Maybe he bought them on eBay. Maybe they were taken by one of the coroner investigators."

Poitras stared for a moment, then shrugged.

"I don't know what to tell you. Whoever took them, the geniuses downtown decided he's good for it."

The scores of black fingerprint smudges seemed to be moving. They were worse than roaches. They looked like swarming spiders.

"Can I see it?"

"What?"

"The album."

"Downtown has it."

"What about crime scene snaps?"

Starkey said, "The task force. They cleaned us out, man. The CI's work and everything from SID went to them. Witness statements from the neighbors. All of it. They hit this place like an invasion."

A car door slammed, drawing the three of us to the porch. A senior command officer and a younger officer had just gotten out of a black-and-white. The senior officer stared up at us. He had a tight grey butch cut, razor-burned skin, and a nasty scowl.

Poitras said, "Shit. He's early."

"Who's that?"

"Marx. The deputy chief in charge of the task force."

Starkey nudged me.

"You were supposed to be gone before he got here."

Great.

Poitras moved to greet him, but Marx didn't want to be greeted. He came up the steps at a quick march, locked onto Poitras like a Sidewinder missile.

"I ordered this scene to be sealed, Lieutenant. I specifically told you that all inquiries would be handled through my office."

"Chief, this is Elvis Cole. Cole is a personal friend of mine, and he's also involved."

Marx didn't offer to shake my hand or acknowledge me in any way.

"I know who he is and how he's involved. He conned the DA into letting this murderer go."

Marx was a tall rectangular man built like a sailing ship, with tight skin stretched over a yardarm skeleton. He peered down at me from the crow's nest like a parrot eyeing a beetle.

I said, "Nice to meet you, too."

Marx turned back to Poitras as if I hadn't spoken.

"I'm not just being an asshole here, Lieutenant. I clamped the lid so nobody could run to the press before the families were notified. Two of those families have still not been reached. Don't you think they've suffered enough?"

Poitras's jaw knotted.

"Everyone here is on the same side, Chief."

Marx eyed me again, then shook his head.

"No, we're not. Now get him out of here, and take me through this goddamned house."

Marx went into the house, leaving Poitras to stare after him.

I said, "Jesus, Lou, I'm sorry."

Poitras lowered his voice.

"The real chief's out of town. Marx figures if he can close this thing before the chief gets back, he'll get the face time. I'm sorry, man."

Starkey touched my arm.

"C'mon."

Poitras followed Marx back into the house while Starkey walked me down. The two uniforms and Marx's driver were talking together, but we kept going until we were alone. Starkey fished a cigarette from her jacket as soon as we stopped.

"That guy's an asshole. It's been like this all week."

"Is Marx really going on TV tonight?"

"That's what I hear. They wrapped up their work last night."

"A week to cover seven murders?"

"This thing was huge, man. They had people on it around the clock."

She lit the cigarette and blew a geyser of smoke straight overhead. I liked Starkey. She was funny and smart, and had helped me out of two very bad jams.

"When are you going to quit those things?"

"When they kill me. When are you going to start?"

You see? Funny. We smiled at each other, but her smile grew awkward, and faded.

"Poitras told me about the Bennett thing. That must be weird, considering."

"Was her picture in the book?"

Starkey blew more of the smoke.

"Yeah."

I looked up at the house. Someone moved in the shadows, but I couldn't tell if it was Poitras or Marx.

Starkey said, "Are you okay?"

When I glanced back, her eyes were concerned.

"I'm fine."

"It was me, I'd be, I dunno, upset."

"He couldn't have killed her. I proved it."

Starkey blew another cloud of smoke, then waved her cigarette at the surrounding houses.

"Well, he didn't have any friends here in the neighborhood, I can tell you that. Most of these people didn't know him except to see him, and the ones who knew him stayed clear. He was a total asshat."

"I thought the task force cut you out."

"They used us here with the door-to-door. Lady at that house, he told her she had a muscular ass. Just like that. Woman at that house, she runs into him getting his mail and he tells her she could pick up some extra cash if she dropped around one afternoon."

That was Lionel Byrd.

"Starkey, you're right. Byrd was a professional asshat, but he didn't kill Yvonne Bennett. I don't believe it."

Starkey frowned, but the smile flickered again.

"Man, you are stubborn."

"And cute. Don't forget cute."

I could have told her I was also sick to my stomach, but I let it go with cute.

She drew another serious hit on the cigarette, then flicked it into a withered century plant. Here we were in fire season with red-flag alerts, but Starkey did things like that. She pulled me farther away from the uniforms and lowered her voice.

"Okay, listen, I know some things about this Poitras doesn't know. I'm going to tell you, but you can't tell anyone."

"You think I'm going to run home and put it on my blog?"

"Guy I worked with at CCS is on with the task force. He spent all week analyzing the stuff we pulled out of the house. You won't like this, but he told me Byrd's good for the killings. He says it's solid."

"How does he know that?"

"I don't know, moron. We're friends. I took his word for it."

Starkey nudged me farther from the uniforms again and lowered her voice even more.

"What I'm saying, Cole, is I can have him explain it to you. You want me to set it up?"

It was like being thrown a life preserver in a raging storm, but I glanced up at the house. Poitras was standing in the door. They were about to come out.

"I don't want you to get in trouble."

"Hey, fuck Marx. The real chief gets back, he'll

probably ream the guy a new asshole. You want in with my guy or not?"

"That would be great, Carol. Really."

The woman across the street was still in her window, watching us as I left.

5

STARKEY SET me up with a Criminal Conspiracy Section detective named Marcus Lindo, who
was one of many detectives brought in from the divisions to assist with the task force. She cautioned that
his knowledge was limited, but told me he would help
me the best he could. When I called him, it was clear
from the start that Lindo didn't want to see me. He
told me to meet him at a place called Hop Louie in
Chinatown, but warned he would not acknowledge
me in any way if other police officers were present. It
was as if we were passing Cold War secrets.

Lindo showed up at ten minutes after three with a
royal blue three-ring binder tucked under his arm. He
was younger than I expected, with espresso skin, nervous eyes, and glasses. He walked directly to me and
did not introduce himself.

"Let's take a booth."

Lindo put the binder on the table and his hands on
the binder.

"Before we get started, let's get something straight. I can't have this getting back to me. I owe Starkey plenty, but if you tell anyone we sat down like this, I will call you a liar to your face and then it's on her. Are you good with this?"

"I'm good. Whatever you say."

Lindo was scared, and I didn't blame him. A deputy chief could make or break his career.

"My understanding is you want to see the death album. What is it you want to know?"

"Three years ago I proved Lionel Byrd did not kill Yvonne Bennett. Now you guys are saying he did."

"That's right. He killed her."

"How?"

"I don't know how, not the way you mean. We broke the casework down into teams. My team worked on the album and the residence. The vic teams worked the ins and outs on the vics. I know the book. The book is how we know he's good for it."

"Having pictures doesn't prove he killed these women. Pictures could have been taken by anyone at the scene."

"Not pictures like these—"

Lindo opened the binder, then turned it so I could see. The first page was a digital image of the album's cover showing a hazy beach at sunset and curving palms. The cover was embossed with gold script lettering: *My Happy Memories*. It was the type of album you could buy at any drugstore, with stiff plastiboard pages sandwiched between clear plastic cover sheets that adhered to the plastiboard. You could peel the cover sheet up, put your pictures on the page, then press the cover sheet back into place to hold the pictures. Just seeing the cover creeped me out. *My Happy Memories.*

"There were twelve pages in all, but the last five were blank. We recovered fiber and hair samples trapped under the cover sheets, then lasered everything and put it in the glue for prints—"

Lindo checked off the elements with his fingers.

"Front cover, back cover, inside front cover, inside back cover, the seven pages with the pictures plus the five blanks, the twenty-four plastic cover sheets, plus all seven Polaroids. All of the discernible prints or print fragments matched one individual—Lionel Byrd. The fibers came from Byrd's couch. They're running DNA on the hair now, but it's going to match. The criminalist says it is eyeball-identical with Byrd's arm hair."

"Who's the criminalist?"

"John Chen."

"Chen's good. I know him."

Lindo turned the page. The next scan showed a single Polaroid of a thin young woman with short black hair and hollow cheeks. She was on her right side on what appeared to be a tile floor in a darkened room or enclosure. The wall behind her was burned by the glare from the camera's flash. Her left cheek was split as if she had been struck, and a red trace of blood had run down her face to drip from the end of her nose.

Three overlapping drops were spotting the floor. A cord or wire was wrapped so deeply into her neck it disappeared into her skin. Someone had labeled the bottom of the scan with the victim's name, age, date of death, and original case number.

Lindo touched the image.

"This was the first victim—Sondra Frostokovich. See the cut here under her eye? He coldcocked her first to stun her. That was a unifying element of his M.O. He stunned them so they couldn't fight back."

"Was she raped?"

"None of them were raped, so far as I know. Again, I didn't work the individual cases, but this guy didn't play with them—there wasn't any rape, torture, mutilation, or any of that. You can see that much in the pictures. Now check this out—"

Lindo touched the page by her nose.

"See the blood drops below her nose? Three drops, two overlapping. We compared this picture with the original shots taken by the coroner investigator. The crime scene pix show a puddle about the size of her head. Likely your boy was in front of her for the strike that cut her cheek, then strangled her from behind. The blood started to drip as soon as she was down. Three or four drops like this, she couldn't have been down more than twenty seconds before he snapped the picture."

"He wasn't my boy."

"Point is, we have time-specific indicators in pretty much every picture that marks them at or near the time of death. This is his second victim, Janice Evans-field—"

The second picture was of an African-American woman with Rasta hair whose neck had been slashed so many times it was shredded. Lindo pointed out a blurry red string floating across her face.

"See that? We didn't know what it was until we enhanced it."

"What is it?"

"That's blood squirting from the carotid artery at the base of her neck. See how it arcs? She wasn't dead yet, Cole. She was dying. This exposure was taken at the exact moment her heart beat. That kinda rules out some cop later at the scene, doesn't it?"

I looked away, feeling numb and distant, as if the pictures and I weren't really in the booth, so I could pretend I wasn't seeing them.

Lindo showed me each of the remaining victims, and then a photograph of a clunky black device with knobs and sensors like you'd see in a dated science fiction movie.

"Okay, the second way we put him with the murders is by the camera. These cameras, they push the picture out through a little slot when you snap the exposure. The rollers leave discrete impressions on the edges of the picture—"

It was easier to look at the picture of the camera.

"Like the rifling in a gun barrel marks a bullet?"

"Yeah. This is a discontinued model. All seven pictures were taken with this camera, which we recovered in Byrd's house. The only prints on the camera belong to Lionel Byrd. Ditto the film packs we found in the camera."

He showed me a picture of two film packs, one labeled with the letter *A*, the other with *B*.

"Partials belonging to a different individual were found on the unopened film, but we believe they belong to the cashier or sales clerk where he bought the film. The lot numbers gave a point of sale in Hollywood, not far from Laurel Canyon. You see how it's adding up?"

Lindo went through his facts with the mechanical precision of a carpenter driving nails.

"Byrd bought the film. Byrd put the film in the camera. Byrd, using the camera, took seven photographs that could only have been taken by someone present at the time of the murders. Byrd was at one time charged in the murder of one of the women whose death shot—a photograph taken within moments of her death—has now been found in his possession. Having taken the pictures, Byrd then placed them with his own hands in this sick fucking book. Byrd then picked up a gun with his own hands, as evidenced by fingerprints found on the gun, cartridge casings, and ammunition box recovered in his home, and blew out his own fucking brains. What we have here is called a chain of reason, Cole. I know you were hoping we wouldn't have squat, but there it is, and it is good."

I suddenly wanted to see Yvonne Bennett again, and

flipped to the fifth picture. Yvonne Bennett stared up at me with mannequin eyes. Brain matter and pink shards of bone were visible, along with a bright ball that had apparently been placed in the wound. I didn't remember seeing the ball in the wound when Levy showed me the coroner's picture.

"What's this round thing?"

"It's a bubble. The M.E. says air was probably forced into an artery when he beat her, then floated out when she died. It made a blood bubble."

I wanted to look away, but didn't. I stared at the bubble. It had not been present in the coroner's picture. At some point between when the two pictures were taken, it had popped. I took a deep breath and finally looked away.

"Did you read the murder book on Yvonne Bennett?"

"Told you, we had teams for each vic. I worked the album."

"We had a hard time frame in which she was killed. Byrd was in Hollywood when this woman was killed. How could he be two places at once?"

Lindo leaned back. He seemed tired and irritated, like I was too slow to keep up.

"Here's the short version—he wasn't because he didn't have to be."

"This wasn't something I made up, Lindo. Crimmens and his partner had the same window. There wasn't enough time for Byrd to kill her in Silver Lake, then get to Hollywood."

Lindo closed the book. He wasn't going to stay much longer.

"Cole, think about it. You got a hard edge on one side of your window when the body was discovered. The other side, you have this dude who was the last person to see her alive, what was his name, Thompson?"

"Tomaso."

"I'm not saying Tomaso lied, but shit happens. People get confused. If Tomaso was off on the time, your window was wrong."

"It wasn't just my window. Crimmens talked to him, too."

"We know that, man. Marx put Crimmens on the task force to cover that evening. Crimmens thinks it flies. If Tomaso was off by even twenty minutes, Byrd had time to kill her and then get to your bar."

"Did Crimmens talk to Tomaso about this?"

"What's the boy going to say—he was sure? I don't know if they talked to him or not, but either way it wouldn't matter. Physical evidence trumps eyewitness testimony every time, and we have the evidence. That's it, Cole. I have to go."

"Hang on. I still have a question."

He glanced at the door as if the entire sixth floor of Parker Center might walk in, but he stayed in the booth.

"What?"

"What about the suicide?"

"I don't know anything about it. I worked on the book."

"Did someone tie Byrd with the times and locations where these women were killed?"

"Other people handled the timelines. All I know is the book."

"Jesus Christ, didn't you people even talk about this? When Bastilla and Crimmens came to see me, they wouldn't even tell me these pictures exist."

Lindo's eyebrows lurched nervously and he pulled the binder close.

"They wouldn't?"

"They wouldn't tell me anything, and now I meet you, and you know the book, but you don't know a whole hell of a lot about anything else."

"Maybe I don't need to know, Cole."

He tucked the binder under his arm. He was fine as long as we were lost in the science, but now he was frightened again.

"You better not tell anyone about this, Cole. This is just between us."

"I'm good with it, man. Don't worry about it."

He started to say something else, but stood and walked away without looking back.

I stayed in the dark booth, still seeing the pictures. I closed my eyes to shut them out, but the pictures came to life. The blood spurted from Janice Evansfield's throat with each beat of her heart, the stream growing weaker as her heart slowly died. The red pool expanded around Sondra Frostokovich as blood dripped from her nose, the metronome drops logging the time of her death. The bubble of blood swelled in

Yvonne Bennett's wound until it burst. Seeing the images felt like being trapped in a gallery with nightmares spiked to the wall, but I could not believe it. I told myself not to believe it.

I imagined Lionel Byrd in the chair with the album. In my mental movie, he turns the pages one by one, reliving each murder. The gun is on the chair beside his leg. If he has the gun, then he has planned his own death. He will take the gun and the album to the chair. He will reminisce about his work. Maybe he will even regret these things. Then, when he's had enough, he will join his victims in death. I wondered if he thought about how he would shoot himself. Up through the bottom of the mouth or in the temple? Up through the mouth feels creepy. You might miss the kill shot, but blow off your mouth. Then you might wake up in the hospital, alive, charged with the murders, mouthless.

I would have gone for the temple. I thought Lionel Byrd would have gone for the temple, too.

6

ANGEL TOMASO had been alone when he saw Yvonne Bennett disappear into the alley. There had been no way to double-check his version of events, but he had seemed like a good kid with a steady job, and was well liked by his co-workers. Crimmens had believed his story was solid, too. The time window was the one thing we all agreed on, but now the police didn't seem to feel it was important. Maybe they had talked to him, and maybe he had changed his story. I decided to ask Bastilla.

I worked my way back across the city, climbed the stairs to my office, and let myself in. The message light was blinking and the counter showed four new messages. I opened a bottle of water, dropped into place at my desk, and played back the messages.

The first message was straightforward and direct. An anonymous male voice told me to fuck myself. Great. The incoming ID log registered his number as private. The second message was a hang-up, but the third was from the pest control service that sprays my house for spiders and ants. They had found a termite infestation under my deck. Could today get any better? The fourth message was similar to the first, but left by a different male caller.

"We're going to *kill* you."

He screamed "*kill*" as loud as he could.

This voice was younger than the earlier voice and shaking with rage. One threat would have been easy to write off as a crank, but this made three. Maybe something was going around.

I deleted the messages, then found Bastilla's card on the edge of my desk and called her.

"Bastilla."

"This is Elvis Cole. I have a question for you."

"When can I have your files?"

"Take it easy, Bastilla. That isn't why I'm calling."

"We don't have anything else to talk about."

"I didn't call to argue. I'm here in my office to get the papers together. I'm seeing Levy about it tomorrow morning. He doesn't think there will be a problem."

She hesitated, then sounded mollified.

"All right. What?"

"Did Angel Tomaso change his story?"

"Tomaso."

Like she had so much on her plate she couldn't remember.

"Tomaso was the last person to see Yvonne Bennett alive, or don't you know that? He was Crimmens's witness."

"Right. We couldn't find him."

"Tomaso was a major element in establishing the time frame. How can you ignore him?"

"We didn't ignore him. We just couldn't find him. That happens. Either way, the evidence we have is overwhelming."

"One more thing—"

"Cole, you're not a participant in this."

"Was Byrd a suspect in any of the seven cases?"

"Only yours."

Mine. I now owned Yvonne Bennett.

"Besides Bennett."

"That's how good this guy was, Cole—there were no suspects in any of the cases except Bennett. That was the only time he fucked up. Now if you want to know anything else, you can read about it in the paper tomorrow."

Bastilla hung up.

Bitch.

I decided to make a copy of the Lionel Byrd file. I would keep the original, but bring the copy to Levy. If he gave me the okay, I would give the copy to Bastilla.

I reread the pages and the notes as I fed them through the machine until I came to the witness list. The list showed a work number for Tomaso at the Braziliana Coffee Shop and a cell number. It had been three years, but I decided to give them a try. The cell number brought me to a bright young woman named Carly, who told me the number had been hers for almost a year. When I asked if she knew Tomaso, she told me she didn't, but offered that I was the second call she'd received from people trying to find him. The police had called, too.

I said, "When was that, Carly?"

"A couple days ago. No, wait—three days."

"Uh-huh. You remember who called?"

"Ah, a detective, he said. Timmons?"

"Crimmens?"

"That's it."

At least Crimmens had done his due diligence.

I tried the coffee shop next and heard exactly the same thing. Crimmens had called for Tomaso, but the current manager had never met Angel, had no idea how to reach him, and was pretty sure Tomaso had left the job more than two years ago because that was how long she had worked there. I hung up and went back to copying the file.

Angel Tomaso had not been my witness. Crimmens had located and interviewed him two days after Yvonne Bennett's murder, but I didn't begin working on the case until almost ten weeks later. The prosecution had been required to share their witness list with Levy under the rules of discovery, along with all the necessary contact information for those witnesses. I came to these pages as I copied the file, and found a handwritten note I had made with a different name and number for Tomaso.

When Crimmens first identified Tomaso as a witness, Tomaso was living with his girlfriend in Silver Lake. By the time I contacted him at the coffee shop ten weeks later, Tomaso had split with his girlfriend and was bunking in Los Feliz with a friend of his named Jack Eisley. Though Tomaso's work and cell phone numbers were good at the time, I had interviewed him at Eisley's apartment and still had Eisley's address and number. I finished copying the file, separated the original from the copy, then brought Eisley's number to my desk.

Three years after the fact, the odds were slim, but I called Eisley's number. His phone rang five times, then was answered by a recording.

"This is Jack. Leave it after the beep."

"Mr. Eisley, this is Elvis Cole. You might remember me from three years ago when I came to see Angel Tomaso. I'm trying to locate Angel, but I don't have a current number. Could you give me a call back, please?"

I left my cell and office numbers.

Progress.

Maybe.

Doing something left me feeling better about things, though not a whole lot. I was heading for the door with Levy's copy of the file when the phone rang. Maybe it was the lateness of the hour, but the ringing seemed unnaturally loud.

I returned to the desk.

The phone rang again.

I hesitated, then felt stupid for waiting.

"Elvis Cole Detective Agency."

Silence.

"Hello?"

All I heard was breathing.

"Hello?"

The caller hung up.

I waited for the phone to ring again, but the silence remained. I went home to watch the news.

7

THE SUN was lowering as I traced the winding streets off Mulholland Drive toward home. I live in a house held fast to the steep slopes overlooking Los Angeles. It is a small house on the lip of a canyon I share with coyotes and hawks, skunks and black-tailed deer, and opossums and rattlesnakes. More rural than not, coming home has always felt like leaving the city, even though some things cannot be left behind.

My house did not come with a yard the way flat-land houses have yards. It came with a deck that hangs over the canyon and a nameless cat who bites. I like the deck and the cat a lot, and the way the lowering sun will paint the ridges and ravines in a palette of purple and brass. The termites, I can do without.

When I rounded the final curve toward home, Carol Starkey's Taurus was at my front door, but Starkey wasn't behind the wheel. I let myself in through the kitchen, then on into the living room, where sliding glass doors open onto my deck. Starkey was outside, smoking, the hot wind pushing her hair. She raised her hand when she saw me. Starkey never just dropped around.

I opened the sliders and stepped out. "What are you doing here?"

"You say that like I'm stalking you. I wanted to see how it went with Lindo."

She snapped her cigarette over the rail. The wind caught it, and carried it out into the canyon.

"We're in the hills, Starkey. This is a tinderbox up here."

I studied the slope long enough to make sure we weren't going to be engulfed by an inferno. She was watching me when I looked up.

"What?"

"So how did it go?"

"The leading theory seems to be I misread the time frame when Bennett was murdered. Not only me, but the original investigating detectives."

"Uh-huh. That possible?"

"It's always possible, but these guys don't think it's important enough to double-check the key witness. They decided it doesn't matter."

"Maybe it doesn't. What Lindo told me sounds pretty good."

"That doesn't excuse the loose ends. These guys are in such a hurry to close the case they're not even waiting for all the forensics to come back."

We lapsed into silence for a moment, then Starkey cleared her throat.

"Listen, Marx might be a jackass, but Lindo's good. A lot of the people working on this thing are good. Either way, that old man had the book. He was all over that book. You can't forget that."

She was right. Either way, Lionel Byrd had an album of photographs that could only have been taken by a person or persons at the scene when the murders were committed. A book and pictures Byrd and only Byrd had touched.

"Starkey, let me ask you something. What do you make of the pictures?"

"As in, what do I think the pictures mean or why do I think he took them?"

"Both, I guess. What kind of person takes pictures like this?"

She leaned on the rail, staring out at the canyon. Starkey wasn't a trained psychologist, but she had spent a large part of her time at CCS profiling bomb cranks. The people who built improvised explosive devices tended to be serial offenders. Understanding their compulsions had helped her build cases.

She said, "Most of these guys, they'll take hair or a piece of jewelry or maybe some clothes as a way of reliving the rush. But pictures are a deeper commitment."

"What do you mean?"

"These women were murdered in semi-public places. He didn't take them into the desert or some soundproof basement somewhere. They were killed in parking lots or near busy streets or in parks where someone could happen by. Grabbing an earring or a handful of hair is easy—you grab it and run—but he had to stick around to take the pictures. He chose high-risk locations to make his kills, then increased the risk by staying to take a picture when someone might see the flash."

"Maybe he was just stupid."

Starkey laughed.

"I think he got off on the complexity. He was tempting fate by taking the pictures, and each time he got away with it he probably felt omnipotent, the same way bomb cranks feel strong through their bombs. The rush isn't so much the actual killing—it's the getting away with it."

"Okay."

"Did Lindo talk to you about the composition?"

I shook my head. Lindo hadn't mentioned the composition, and I hadn't thought about it. The pictures had all looked pretty much the same to me.

"A picture isn't a part of the experience like a more traditional trophy—it's a composition outside of the experience. The photographer chooses the angle. He chooses what will be in the picture, and what won't. If the picture is a world, then the photographer is the god of that world. This dude got off by being God. He needed to take the pictures because he needed to be God."

I couldn't see Lionel Byrd feeling like a god, but maybe that was the point. I tried to imagine him stalking these women with the clunky, out-of-date camera, but I couldn't picture him with the camera, either.

"I don't know, Starkey. That doesn't sound like Byrd."

Starkey shrugged, then looked at the canyon again.

"I'm just sayin', is all. I'm not trying to convince you."

"I know. I didn't take it that way.

"Whatever this jackhole did or however he was involved, you need to understand you aren't responsible for his crimes. You played it straight up and did your job. Don't eat yourself up about it."

I met Carol Starkey when Lou Poitras brought her to my house because a boy named Ben Chenier was missing. Starkey helped find him, and the friendship we developed during the search grew. A few months later, a man named Frederick Reinnike shot me, and Starkey visited me regularly at the hospital. We had been building a history, and the friendship that grew with it made me smile.

"I ever thank you for coming to the hospital all those times?"

She flushed.

"I was just trying to score with Pike."

"Well, thanks anyway."

She kept her eyes on the canyon.

"Hear much from the lawyer?"

The lawyer. Now I turned toward the canyon, too. Once upon a time I shared my life with a lawyer from Louisiana named Lucy Chenier. Ben was her son. Lucy and Ben had moved to L.A., but after what happened to Ben they returned to Louisiana and now we lived apart. I wondered what Lucy would think of Lionel Byrd, and was glad she didn't know.

I said, "Not so much. They're getting on with their lives."

"How's the boy?"

"He's good. Growing. He sends me these letters."

Starkey suddenly pushed from the rail.

"How about we go somewhere? Let's hit the Dresden for a few drinks."

"You don't drink."

"I can watch. I'll watch you drink while you watch me smoke. How about it?"

"Maybe another time. I want to catch the news about Byrd."

She stepped back again and raised her hands.

"Okay. I got it."

We stood like that for a moment before she smiled.

"I gotta get outta here anyway. Hot date and all."

"Sure."

"Listen—"

Her face softened, then she lifted my hand, turned it palm up, and touched the hard line of tissue that ran across four fingers and most of the palm, cut when I was fighting to save Ben Chenier's life.

"You think you have scars, mister?"

She touched the side of my chest where Reinnike put me in the hospital with a 12-gauge shotgun. Number-four buckshot and two surgeries later.

Starkey smiled.

"You oughta see my fuckin' scars, Cole. I got you beat all to hell."

The bomb that killed her in a trailer park.

She dropped my hand.

"Don't watch the news, man. Just forget it."

"Sure."

"You're not going to forget it."

"No."

"Maybe that's why I love you."

She punched me in the chest and walked out of my house.

That Starkey is something.

I put on the TV to get ready for the news, then took out a pork chop to thaw. Service for one. I drank a beer standing in the kitchen, offered myself another, then returned to the television when the news hour rolled around. Earnest news-jock Jerry Ward looked Los Angeles in the eye and intoned in his best understated delivery: *Murders solved by bizarre discovery in Laurel Canyon*.

Then Jerry arched his eyebrows.

When Jerry arches his eyebrows, you know you're in for something bizarre.

I had plenty of time to grab another beer. The lead story was a visit by the president, who had arrived in town to survey the recent fire damage. The second story reported on rebuilding efforts and the decreasing chance of more fires in the coming days. News of the fires segued nicely to the bizarre discovery of Lionel

Byrd. I was probably on my third beer by then. Or fourth.

Jerry gave the story almost three minutes, intercut with a clip of Marx at his press conference. During the clip, Marx held up a clear plastic evidence bag containing what appeared to be the actual album, and described the "portraits of death" as "trophies taken by a deranged mind." The only victims mentioned by name were the most recent victim, a twenty-six-year-old Pasadena native named Debra Repko, and Yvonne Bennett. My stomach tightened when I heard her name.

The Bennett mention was a simple statement that Byrd had been charged at the time of her murder, but the charges were dropped when conflicting evidence surfaced that apparently cleared Mr. Byrd. Neither I nor Alan Levy was mentioned. I guess I should have been thankful.

Marx looked pretty good with his full-dress uniform and his finger in the air, proclaiming the city safer, as if he had personally rescued another victim instead of finding a rotting corpse. He declared he was personally offended by Byrd's release when he had been brought before the altar of justice in the Bennett case, and promised to do everything in his power to ensure such outrages never happened again.

I said, "Wow. Altar of justice."

Marx was flanked by a city councilman named Nobel Wilts, who congratulated Marx on the fine police work. The woman I had seen across the street from Byrd's house was interviewed in a ten-second clip, saying she would sleep easier tonight; and the mother of Chelsea Ann Morrow, the third victim, was interviewed at her Compton home. I wondered how the cameras had gotten to the mother and the neighbor so quickly, since the press conference had happened within the past hour or so. Marx or Wilts had probably tipped the media so they could set up for the prime-time coverage.

When the story changed to a toy recall, I brought the remains of my beer out to the deck.

The winds blow fiercest at sundown in a last furious rush to the sea, and now the trees filling the canyon below me whipped and shivered. Grey eucalyptus; scrub oak and walnuts; olive trees that looked like dusky green beach balls. Their branches rattled like antlers, and their brittle leaves fluttered like rice paper. I listened and drank. Maybe Marx and his task force were right about Tomaso. Tomaso had seemed like a bright, conscientious kid who wanted to help, but maybe he had tried too hard to be helpful. Change his answer by half an hour, and everything changed. Make a mistake by thirty minutes, and suddenly Lionel Byrd had the time to kill Yvonne Bennett, drive back to Hollywood, and stop for a fast one before heading home. Nothing like a double shot of Jack after crushing a woman's skull.

I was still listening to the trees when the phone rang, and a quiet female voice came from two thousand miles away.

"Is this the World's Greatest Detective?"

I immediately felt better. I felt warm, and at peace.

"It was. How're you doing?"

Lucy said, "Was?"

"Long story."

"I think I know part of it. Joe called."

"Pike called you?"

"He said you could use an ear."

"Did Joe really call?"

"Tell me about Lionel Byrd."

The canyon grew dark as I told her. As the outside darkness deepened, the houses dotting the banks and ridges of the canyon glowed with flickering lights.

When I finished, she said, "So what do you think?"

"It's just the thought of it, I guess. Sometimes you can't duck the blame even when you do everything straight up and by the book."

"Do you believe Byrd killed those seven people?"

"Looks that way, but I don't know. The facts appear to be on their side."

"It might look that way, but do you believe it?"

I hesitated, thinking back through everything Lindo and Starkey had told me, and also everything I had learned three years ago on my own.

"No. Maybe I should, but I don't. I know Byrd. Not the way someone who knows him would know him, but I put everything I had into reconstructing his life on the night Yvonne Bennett was murdered. That night, I owned him. I had him by the places he went, the people he met, what he said to them, and how he said it. I knew how loud he talked, how little he tipped, where he sat, and how long he stayed before moving on. An A-list predator would have blended into the background, but Byrd was loud, crude, obvious, and drunk. I knew him on that night better than anyone, and I do not believe he killed Yvonne Bennett. Maybe he knew the murderer, I guess that's possible, but he did not kill Yvonne Bennett. I do not believe it. I can't."

"Listen to me. Are you listening?"

"Yes."

"Even if the worst is true, what happened here is not your fault. You will feel bad, and you will mourn because something so ugly happened, but you have always acted with a good heart. If this terrible thing is true, do you know what you will do?"

I nodded, but didn't answer.

"You will man up and ranger on. I will personally fly out on the L-jet, and hold you. Do you hear me?"

The L-jet was our personal joke. If Lucy had a private jet, it would be the L-jet.

I said, "You're holding me now."

"I'm not finished. Have you been drinking?"

"Yes."

"Listen to me."

"I miss you."

"Shut up and listen. I want you to listen to me."

"I'm listening."

"Say something funny."

"Lucy, c'mon—"

78

She raised her voice.

"Say something funny!"

"Something funny."

"Not your best effort, but it's a start. Now hang up."

"Why?"

"Just hang up. I'll call right back."

She hung up. I held the phone, wondering what she was doing. A few seconds later it rang. I answered.

"Luce?"

She shouted.

"Answer like you mean it!"

She hung up again. I waited again. The phone finally rang, so I answered the way she wanted.

"Elvis Cole Detective Agency. We find more for less. Check our prices."

Her voice came back as gentle as a kiss.

"That's my World's Greatest."

"I love you, Luce."

"As a friend."

"Sure. Friends."

"I love you, too."

"We could be friends with benefits."

"You never give up."

"Part of the benefit package."

"I'd better get going. Call me."

"Call you what?"

She hesitated, and I knew she was smiling. I could feel her smile from two thousand miles away, but then my own smile faded.

I said, "Do you think I'm kidding myself?"

"I think you want to be convinced. One way or the other, you'll have to convince yourself."

I stared at the black canyon below, and the lights showing warm on the ridges.

"If Byrd didn't kill them, then someone else did."

"I know."

She was silent for a while, then her voice was soft and caring.

"You told me the facts were on their side. If you don't like their facts, find your own facts. That's what you do, World's Greatest. No one does it better."

She hung up before I could answer.

I held the phone for a while, then called Pike. His machine picked up with a beep. Pike doesn't have an outgoing message. You just get the beep.

I said, "You're a good friend, Joe. Thanks."

Part Two
UP IN THE CANYON

Part Two
UP IN THE CANYON

8

THE WIND died during the night, leaving the canyon behind my house still and bright the next morning. I brought in the paper, then went into the kitchen, where the cat who shared the house was waiting. He's large and black, with delicate fur and more scars than an Ultimate Fighter after a bad run. He loves me, he worships Joe Pike, and he pretty much hates everyone else. All the fighting has had an effect.

I said, "How's life in Cat Land?"

When your girlfriend lives two thousand miles away, you talk to your cat.

He was sitting by his dish where he waits for breakfast, only this time he brought his own. The hindquarters of a tree rat were on the floor by his feet.

The cat blinked at me. Proud. Like I should fall to and dig in.

He said, "Mmrh."

"Good job, m'man. Yum."

I cleaned it up with paper towels, then gave him a

can of tuna. He growled when I threw away the legs, but the tuna helped him get over it.

I made a cup of instant coffee, then put on a pot of real coffee to brew while I read the newspaper's coverage of Lionel Byrd: *Killer Leaves Bloody Album of Death.*

The *Times* had done a good job with so little time. The story was tight and direct, describing how uniformed officers had discovered Byrd dead by his own hand while evacuating Laurel Canyon during the recent fires. The "death album" and the pictures within it were described in tasteful detail. A photograph of Marx and Councilman Wilts appeared on page six, along with a sidebar article identifying the seven victims and showing the locations of their murders. Yvonne Bennett's description left me feeling sad. She had draped herself in lies like summer scarves to convince people she was other than she was, but now a cold five-word phrase summed up her life: *twenty-eight-year-old prostitute.*

Only a single paragraph mentioned that Byrd had been charged with her murder, focusing more on his history of violence toward prostitutes than why the charges had been dropped. As with the newscast the night before, neither Levy nor I was mentioned. After the way Marx carried on when we met, I had expected him to publicly condemn us, but he had not.

I finished the story, but hadn't learned much more than I already knew. Marx had spoken much about the album and Byrd's criminal history, but presented no additional evidence linking Byrd to the victims or the crime scenes. No comment was made about DNA, witnesses before or after the fact, how Byrd selected and stalked his victims, or how he avoided detection.

I clipped out the article and map, then used the names and dates to search online for articles published at the times of the original murders. There wasn't much to find. Only four of the seven murders had made the local papers, producing a total of nine published pieces spread over the seven years. I made notes as I read.

Sondra Frostokovich, the first victim, had been given six column inches in a single article. Described as an office manager in the city administration, her body was found in a downtown office building empty for renovation. She had been strangled only four blocks from the city administration building where she worked. The story ended with a pro forma plea that anyone with knowledge of the crime contact a Central Bureau Homicide detective named Thomas Marx. I wondered if it was the same Marx. Had to be. I wondered if he even remembered.

Janice M'Kele Evansfield was the second victim, whose arcing blood showed that she was still alive when the picture in Lindo's book was taken. Her body had been discovered at the edge of the Brentwood Country Club in one of the richest parts of L.A., eleven months and sixteen days after the Frostokovich killing. A follow-up article two weeks later reported there were no suspects in the case and requested the public's help.

Unlike Frostokovich and Evansfield, the third, fourth, and fifth victims were prostitutes. Chelsea Ann Morrow, Marsha Trinh, and Yvonne Bennett had not been covered by the local papers, but the sixth victim, a homeless woman named Lupe Escondido, made the front page because of the horrific nature of her murder. On a cooling night in October, she had been doused with gasoline while sleeping behind the Studio City Park and burned to death. In the picture Lindo showed me, she had been engulfed by yellow flames. I hadn't even been able to tell she was human.

I read about Escondido, then went to the kitchen because I needed a break from the deaths. The cat purred when I looked at him. He was by the garbage bin where I dumped his rat. I opened the bin, fished out the legs, and put them in his dish.

I said, "You earned them."

The final two articles were about the most recent victim, Debra Repko.

Like the first victim, Repko was white, educated, and professional. She had recently earned an MA in political science from USC, after which she was hired by a downtown political consulting firm called Leverage Associates. Sometime between eleven P.M. and two A.M. thirty-six days before Lionel Byrd's body was discovered, she was struck from behind and suffocated by having a plastic garbage bag held over her head. This event occurred behind a strip mall two blocks from her apartment on the outskirts of Hancock Park, just south of Melrose Avenue. She was survived by her parents and three brothers, all of whom were heart-broken by the news of her death.

I pushed the articles aside, got a bottle of water, and went out onto my deck. The wind had died sometime during the night, and now two red-tailed hawks floated overhead. They had been down with the wind, but now they were up. They appeared to be hunting, but maybe they just enjoyed being in the sky. Maybe, for them, there was no difference.

Thirty yards away, my neighbors were out on their own deck, reading the morning paper. They waved when they saw me and I waved back. I wondered if they were reading about Byrd.

I drank some of the water, then stretched through the traditional twelve sun salutes from the hatha yoga. My neighbor Grace shouted across the hillside.

"Do it naked!"

Her husband laughed.

The yoga flowed into a tae kwon do kata. I kicked and punched with focus from one side of the deck to the other, running one kata into the next, not the classic Korean forms, but combinations I had created: a little wing chun, a little krav maga, a little shen chuan. I moved through all three planes of space, working with greater intensity until sweat splattered the boards like rain and the pictures of dead people had faded. When I finished, Grace jumped to her feet and applauded.

I shouted, "Your turn. Naked."

She lifted her T-shirt, flashing her breasts. Her husband laughed again.

These neighbors are something.

I drank the rest of the water, then went back inside as the phone rang. It was Alan Levy's assistant.

"Mr. Cole?"

"Did Alan see the news about Lionel Byrd?"

"Yes, sir. He'd like you to bring by your file at ten if that time works for you."

I told him the time worked fine, then returned to my notes. I combined the information I learned from Lindo and the *Times* with the facts I found online, then organized it into a chart:

```
1—Frostokovich—wht—10/2—strngld—dwntn—(Marx!)
2—Evansfield—blk—9/28—stab—Brtwd—jog—(?)
3—Morrow—blk—10/7—blntfc—Hywd—pros—(?)
4—Trinh—asn—9/23—stab—Slvrlk—pros—(?)
5—Bennett—wht—10/3—blntfc—Slvrlk—pros—(Crimmens)
6—Escondido—lat—10/9—fire—StCty—hmls—(?)
7—Repko—wht—7/26—suff—HanPk—conslt.—(?)
```

When you study these things you look for patterns, but patterns were in short supply.

The victims were of diverse ethnic and economic backgrounds, and none had been raped, bitten, chewed, or sexually abused. Two of the murders occurred in Silver Lake, but the others were scattered throughout the city. The only common elements seemed to be that all of the victims were women and six of the seven murders had occurred in the fall.

The most recent murder was different. Where the

first six victims had all been murdered in the fall, Debra Repko had died in the early summer, almost three months ahead of the others.

I was wondering why when I had a notion about the dates and went back to my computer. You hear about killers being triggered by astrological events or the zodiac, so I googled an astronomy almanac and entered the dates.

I didn't learn anything about astrology, but the first six murders had all taken place within two days either way of the new moon—the darkest nights of the month. Repko had been murdered when the moon was nearing its three-quarter phase. After six consecutive murders in darkness, Debra Repko had been killed when the night sky was brilliantly lit.

I checked the time. It was after nine, but I dug out Bastilla's card and called. She was clipped and abrupt when she answered.

"Bastilla."

"It's Elvis Cole. You have a minute?"

"Can I pick up the files?"

"I'm seeing Levy at ten. Christ, Bastilla, can't you ride a different horse?"

"I have a lot to do, Cole. What do you want?"

"How did you guys explain the differences in the Repko murder?"

Bastilla didn't speak for a moment. I heard noises in her background, but couldn't tell if she was at her office or in her car.

"What are you talking about?"

"Debra Repko was murdered three months out of sync with the others."

"Thank you. We know."

"She was killed on a night with a three-quarter moon. The first six were killed under a new moon. That's a major change in method."

"Believe it or not, we know our business here. If you expect me to review our investigation with you, you're out of your mind."

"Your asshole partner Crimmens telling me I got two women killed makes it my business, too."

"Good-bye, Cole. We're done."

The line went dead in my ear, but I grinned hard at the phone.

"Bastilla, I'm just getting started."

I showered, dressed, then packed up the copy of my files and went to see Alan Levy.

Finding my own evidence.

9

PICTURE THE detective swinging into action. I picked up the freeway at the bottom of the Cahuenga Pass and called John Chen as I headed downtown. Chen was a senior criminalist with LAPD's Scientific Investigation Division, and one of the greediest people I knew. He was also a total paranoid.

Chen answered so softly I could barely hear him.

"I can't talk. They're watching me."

You see?

"I'm calling about Lionel Byrd. You have a minute?"

Lindo mentioned Chen had worked on the case.

"What's in this for me?"

The greed.

"I'm not convinced Byrd killed Yvonne Bennett. I have questions about the most recent victim, too. She doesn't match up with the others."

"You're talking about Repko?"

"That's right."

Chen lowered his voice even more.

"It's weird you're asking about her."

"Why weird? Is she different from the others?"

"Not so much, but the way they're handling her is different. Shit—Harriet's coming. I gotta go."

Harriet was his boss.

"Call me, John. Repko and Byrd. I need your work, the CI, the medical examiner—whatever you can get. I'm heading downtown now."

"This is going to cost you."

Twenty minutes later I pulled into the parking garage beneath Barshop, Barshop & Alter, and brought the copy of my file upstairs to a lobby rich with travertine, cobalt glass, and African teak. Low-life criminals like Lionel Byrd could never hope to hire them, much less afford their fee, but Levy saw Byrd's trumped-up confession as a ticket to argue before the California Supreme Court. After twenty years of practicing criminal law, Levy boasted a ninety-eight-percent acquittal rate and seven arguments before the California Supreme Court. Six of the seven were decided in Levy's favor and resulted in precedent-setting case law. It was for this opportunity that Levy agreed to represent Lionel Byrd pro bono—for free. Levy's firm even threw in my fee.

Levy's assistant was waiting when the elevator opened.

"Mr. Cole? I'm Jacob. If you'll come with me, please."

Alan was on the phone when we reached his office,

seated behind a desk that probably cost a hundred thousand dollars. He raised a finger, indicating he would be with me in a minute, then made a brushing gesture, the brush telling Jacob to leave.

Levy was a large man in his late forties with a wide head, bulging eyes, and poorly fitting clothes. He carried himself as if he was embarrassed by his appearance, but juries probably related to the sloppy clothes and awkward manner. I figured he was faking it. The first thing you noticed when you stepped into his office were the pictures of his family. Framed photographs of his wife and two little girls smiled down from the walls.

When Levy finished the call, he offered his hand as he gestured at the files.

"Is that everything?"

"Yeah. I kept a copy for myself."

"That's fine. I just want to be sure we're on firm legal ground before we hand them over. Here, let's sit."

He took the files and motioned me to a soft leather club chair on the other side of his office. He dropped onto the opposite chair, leaning forward like he was about to fly off a diving board.

I said, "You see the news?"

"I did. I also met with a representative of the DA's office and Chief Marx this morning. Would you like coffee? Jacob could get you a coffee."

"I'm fine. What are we going to do about this, Alan?"

The bulging eyes blinked.

"About what? I'm going to let them examine the files. I don't see any reason not to cooperate."

"Not the files. Byrd. He didn't kill Yvonne Bennett."

A line appeared between his eyebrows and he shook his head.

"There's nothing to do, Elvis. Pinckert and Marx explained their investigation to me this morning. If I had this information three years ago, I would not have taken his case."

I expected Levy to be angry, but he wasn't. Alan Levy was never reversed. Levy was the guy who got the *other* guy reversed. Instead, he looked sad.

"Alan, we proved he could not have killed Yvonne Bennett. We *proved* it."

Levy studied me for a moment, then spread his hands.

"I make up stories. That's my job, Elvis. Making up stories within the defined parameters of an established structure. That's what I do."

Talking to a genius is hard work.

"I don't know what you're talking about."

"The law. I start with a list—names, dates, events, whatever—information on a page, facts without a narrative structure. My job is to frame those facts with a narrative, you see? A story. The opposing counsel, they have exactly the same facts, and they have to make up a story, too. The facts are the same, but the stories are always different. Same facts, two different stories, and whoever tells the best story convinces the jury. I am very good with my stories, Elvis. I can take a list of facts, any facts at all, and create the most wonderful stories. I do that better than almost anyone."

I was growing impatient. He was giving a lecture in narrative theory, and I was the retard who couldn't keep up.

"What does this have to do with Lionel Byrd?"

"I'm not saying I couldn't prove it again. I'm telling you I wouldn't take the case. Chief Marx and Ms. Pinckert were very open with me this morning. I wasn't always polite, but they were patient. They convinced me."

"They convinced you Byrd was good for the killings."

"Yes."

"Because he had these pictures."

"They were thorough in their presentation. Tell you the truth, I was impressed."

"I've seen scans of the album. I know how they broke it down and what they found with the camera and the film packs. Having this album doesn't mean he killed them."

Levy raised his eyebrows.

"I'm not the only one who's had a meeting."

"All the album means is Byrd and the person who took the pictures were somehow connected."

"I made the same point. These people aren't stupid, Elvis. They investigated the possibility of a second killer or some sort of an association, but found nothing to support that idea—no likely suspects were identified through his call register, nothing was found in his residence or vehicle, and no forensics belonging to anyone else was found on the album or pictures."

"They couldn't find Angel Tomaso, either. They're right about this only if they ignore what Tomaso said in a sworn statement, and that's what they're doing. They're assuming he made a mistake."

"Maybe he did."

"You thought he was right at the time."

"If Tomaso was telling me the same thing today, I would *still* believe him, but I would discount his statement. A person can tell the truth as he knows it, but be mistaken in what he knows. That happens all the time."

I expected Levy to come out swinging for having been cast in a role that potentially made him look like the villain in Marx's Circus of Justice, but, instead, we were arguing.

"So what you're saying is, three years ago when we proved this guy couldn't have killed Yvonne Bennett, we were wrong."

An embarrassed smile flickered at the corners of his mouth as if he couldn't bring himself to admit it.

"No, we were right. We were right with the information we had at that time. There's a difference."

"Did they go over the other six victims with you?"

He nodded.

"Okay. Do you remember Lionel Byrd?"

Now he frowned, wondering where I was going.

"Of course I remember him."

"I've only spent a few hours with this, Alan, but here's what I found: None of these women were raped, bitten, or sexually abused. No contact means no DNA. The kill-zones were spread all over the city and the murder weapon changed with each killing. Six of the seven were murdered at the new moon—when there's no moon at all."

"I know what it means."

"All of this makes it more difficult for the police to connect the crimes, which implies forethought and planning. Think about it, Alan—anyone can be a short-term spree killer, but it took an organized mind to hunt humans for seven years and get away with it. We're talking about a top-of-the-food-chain predator. Byrd wasn't up to it. He doesn't fit the profile."

Levy smiled as if he was proud of me.

"I like it. Same facts, different story. You've created a story you can live with."

"This isn't a story."

"It's too complex. See, that's the problem. He had the pictures and the camera. He didn't take hair or jewelry—he took the pictures. A simple story is always best. The truth lies in simplicity."

"You think they're right or they just have the best story?"

"The right story is always the best story."

Levy frowned at the pictures of his wife and children.

They wore white in almost all of the pictures. I hadn't noticed their clothes before. Behind him, downtown Los Angeles spread to the east, swept clean by the hot desert winds.

"I understand you're upset, Elvis. I am, too. I fought for Mr. Byrd three years ago, and won, but this time it's not my game."

"You fought because you thought you would get another State Supreme Court argument out of it."

"Well, yes, but nevertheless. Last time we were right, but this time they're right. The facts change, the story changes. It has to."

I stood, and went to the door.

"Tell you what, Alan, after I talk to Tomaso, maybe the story will change again."

He gave me the same frown he had been giving the pictures.

"Well, do what you want, but you're only going to end up embarrassing yourself. You'll look like a sore loser."

Alan Levy, with his ninety-eight-percent acquittal rate and seven appearances before the California Supreme Court, worried about being a sore loser.

"Alan, did you make a deal with Marx to keep your mouth shut?"

"What are you talking about?"

"Marx and Wilts were screaming the charges against Byrd should never have been dropped, but they never brought up your name."

Levy's face darkened.

"Don't forget to have your parking validated on the way out."

John Chen called as I was leaving the building. He was even more paranoid than before.

10

CHEN TOLD me to meet him under the Fourth Street Bridge. It was a desolate, industrial part of Los Angeles, where the river was framed by concrete and warehouses, and was mostly known for the cardboard encampments under the bridge. Twenty minutes later I was watching the homeless people when Chen pulled up in an SID wagon. Chen was tall and skinny, and watching him get out of the wagon was like watching a question mark unfold. He studied the surrounding buildings as if he were checking for spies, then hurried to my car.

I said, "There are maybe ten thousand places easier to meet than here."

"And ten thousand places we could be seen. I'm on my way out to a hatchet murder in El Monte."

He shoved a manila envelope into my lap, but suddenly pulled it back, his oversize glasses making him look like a suspicious parrot.

"Did you tell anyone you were calling me?"

"Of course not. Did someone say something?"

"Ten minutes after we talked, Harriet pulled me into the hall. She warned me not to talk to you."

"She used my name? Me, specifically?"

"Not you specifically, but who else would she be talking about? It's been like that all week. Everything top secret and way off the weird meter."

He looked around again, and I caught myself looking, too.

I said, "How is Repko being handled differently?"

"I worked her case six weeks ago when she was first murdered—before this stuff with Byrd came up."

"Okay."

"Then we get the book, right? There isn't going to be anything new—I did the full workup and analysis when she was murdered. But last week Harriet tells me they want me to pull more samples from her clothes."

"You had to exhume her?"

Chen looked annoyed.

"No, man, her old clothes. Her furniture. They found this girl dead in an alley, and now they wanted me to go to her house. I'm, like, why would something from Lionel Byrd turn up where she lived? Harriet says, just go vac the goddamned clothes."

"So?"

"This girl was murdered almost two months ago. New people are living in her apartment. Her parents cleaned out the place and brought her effects home with them. It's a forensic nightmare, dude, but there I am with these poor people, the mother crying, her fucking brothers looking like they want to kick my ass, vaccing her clothes."

"You find anything to connect her to Byrd?"

"I don't know. You know what a blind test is?"

"No."

"They gave us samples to compare with the samples I vacced from her clothes, but the comparison samples didn't come with a name—only a number. Blind. We asked why we were running blind tests, Harriet told us don't ask. She said if we told anyone we were cooking blinds, she would have our asses in the can. I don't know if we got any hits or not. Everything went to Harriet, and Harriet made the comparisons."

Like Marx ordering Poitras to seal Byrd's home.

"What were you testing?"

"Hair, fiber, the usual stuff."

"What did the homicide cops say?"

Chen made a derisive snort.

"They wouldn't discuss the case with us, either. We gave our reports to Harriet, and Harriet did whatever she did with them. I guess she passed them up to the task force. Those task force guys wouldn't even talk about what they were doing with the divisional dicks, and those guys are *pissed*."

Chen was describing a major departure from protocol. Detectives worked closely with criminalists as their cases evolved, and task force detectives almost always worked with divisional detectives because the divisional dicks had relationships with witnesses and the victims.

I thought about what he was saying and what it might mean.

"Did Byrd kill these people?"

Chen looked surprised.

"Well, yeah. Nothing we found suggests or supports anything else. Here, check it out—"

He finally handed me the envelope. Chen had copied the SID work product on Repko and Byrd along with the CI's crime scene descriptions and the medical examiner's autopsy protocols.

I skimmed the reports about Debra Repko first. Her condition as described was in keeping with everything I had been told or read on the Internet, and only served to underline how little I knew about the victim. Blood tests showed a .02 alcohol level, which indicated she had consumed at least one but not more than two drinks in the hours preceding her death. This suggested a social drink or glass of wine with dinner, but I had no way of knowing. Unlike the police, I knew absolutely nothing about Debra Repko and her life, which made my guesses meaningless.

I moved on to the reports about Lionel Byrd. Everything confirmed what I had already been told by Starkey and Lindo until I read the list of items documented when Byrd's body was recovered. A single tablet identified as oxycodone was found beneath his chair.

"Was he taking oxys?"

"He had three in his system along with the booze.

He wasn't incapacitated, if that's what you're thinking. He was just numb."

"He have a scrip?"

"Street buy. The tab we found was a Mexican import. The M.E. figures he used because of the foot. That foot was a mess."

"So he was in a lot of pain with the foot?"

"Yeah."

"Bad enough to keep him from driving?"

He would have to leave his house for street drugs or someone would have to deliver them.

"I'm just telling you what the M.E. said. I didn't examine his foot."

I got lost in the pages. Most of them were just numbers and charts, so I stopped looking at them.

"Did you find anything that directly connects Byrd to Repko?"

"No."

"Any of the other victims?"

"Uh-uh, but I don't know what the blind samples were. I don't know if they got any hits on those or not."

The two of us stared at each other until Chen's pager buzzed. He frowned when he glanced at it.

"Crap. I gotta get going. They're looking for me."

Chen opened the door but hesitated before he got out.

"You know what I think? They closed the case, but the case isn't really closed."

"You think?"

"What else, bro? You think this girl had Lionel Byrd over for dinner?"

Chen hurried back to his car, and I watched him drive away.

II

I WANTED to read Chen's reports more carefully, and opted to read them at Philippe, a cafeteria-
style sandwich shop nearby in Chinatown. I could
have read them under the bridge or anywhere else, but
even world-class detectives get hungry. Philippe
claims they invented the French dip sandwich in 1908,
and maybe they did, but either way they have been
serving the same killer sandwiches ever since. The
double-dip turkey is my fare of choice.

I never got to the reports. I had just mounted a
stool at one of the long family-style tables when
Jack Eisley returned my call about Angel Tomaso.
Eisley remembered me, though we had only met
the one time I interviewed Tomaso at Eisley's apartment.

He said, "I saw the thing on the news and thought,
hey, that's Angel's dude. Talk about blast from the
past. And then you call."

Philippe was so noisy with the lunch-hour crush, I

took the phone and the sandwich outside. The double-dip *jus* ran down my arm.

"I need to speak with him. It's pretty important."

"About this?"

"Yeah."

"Angel moved back to Texas. He got really down on the whole acting thing and went back to Austin. Had to crash with his aunt. I'm, like, dude, are you *sure*?"

Eisley wanted to chat.

"Great. You have a number in Austin?"

"I called last night after the news, but his aunt said he came back to L.A. a few months ago. It's the actor thing, man. If you're an actor, you're an *actor*, you know? It was only a matter of time."

"Even better. So what's his number here in L.A.?"

"She wouldn't give it to me. She said she'd pass on my message, but she doesn't give out numbers without permission. This was only last night. I'll probably hear from him today."

If she passed on the request.

If Angel called.

If Eisley phoned back with the number.

"Jack, have the police contacted you about Angel?"

"No, uh-uh. Why would they do that?"

"Listen, I know his aunt is supposed to give him your message, but you mind letting me have her number? I'd like to talk to her."

Unlike Angel's aunt, Eisley didn't mind giving out information. I scratched out her number while turkey *jus* stained my pad, then drove to my office to make the call. With any luck, I would find Angel Tomaso before the end of the day and crack the case by sundown.

When I reached my building, I left my car in the parking garage and walked up the four flights to my floor.

I liked the building and my office, and had been there for many years. The office next to mine was occupied by an attractive woman who sold wholesale beauty supplies and sunned herself on the adjoining balcony. Across the hall was an insurance agent I rarely saw, though the two women who worked for him showed up every day like clockwork.

Everything about the building was normal until I reached my office and saw the doorjamb was split near the knob. Jambs do not split by themselves.

I leaned close to the door, but heard nothing.

I stepped across the hall and looked at my door from a different angle. A woman's voice came from the insurance office, but it sounded normal. No one was screaming for help. No one was talking about the terrible noise she had heard from the private eye's office across the hall.

I went back to my door, listened again, then pushed the door open.

Papers, files, and office supplies were scattered over the floor like trash blown by the wind. The couch was slashed along its length. My desk chair and the director's chairs were upended, and the glass in both French doors had been kicked out, leaving jagged teeth in the frame. My computer, answering machine, and Mickey Mouse phone were part of the debris. Mickey's left ear was broken. Everything that was on my desk the night before had been swept to the floor.

I started at the mess until I heard tocking. The Pinocchio clock was still on the wall, smiling its oblivious smile. His eyes tocked side to side, sightless, but reassuring.

"I wish you could talk."

I went behind my desk to right my chair, but the chair was wet and smelled of urine. I left it in place. The file I had on Lionel Byrd was scattered on the floor with everything else. I gathered it together, then went down to the car for my camera and took pictures for the insurance. After the pictures, I called Lou Poitras, who told me he would send a radio car. I had to use my cell, what with Mickey being broken.

While I waited for the police, I called Joe Pike.

He said, "You think it ties in with the calls you were getting yesterday?"

"The timing's too perfect for anything else."

"Something with Byrd?"

"I don't know, but I'm not sure that was the point. The file is still here, and the way it was dumped with everything else it's likely they didn't read it. They slashed the couch and kicked out the glass in the French doors. It looks more like vandalism. Somebody pissed on my chair."

"Maybe they want the vandalism to cover the search."

"Maybe. I'll go through everything, see if anything's missing."

"You want me to come over?"

"There's nothing to do. The police are on the way."

"Maybe I should sit on your house. Make sure nobody pisses on your couch."

"That might be a good idea."

I called my insurance agent, then the building manager to let him know about the break-in and arrange for the doors to be fixed. We ended up shouting at each other. After the shouting, I went across the hall to ask my neighbors if they had seen or heard anything. None of them had, but everyone wanted to see the damage, so I let them. Two patrol officers arrived while they were looking, questioned me, then set about writing up the complaint. While the officers surveyed the damage, one of the women from the insurance office told us she had worked until almost eight-thirty the night before, so whoever did this had come after she had gone.

The senior officer, a sergeant-supervisor named Bristo, said, "You work late like that, ma'am, make sure you lock your door."

She patted a little handbag.

"Don't think I sit up here alone."

Bristo said nothing. Everyone packs.

When the police and the women from across the hall were gone, I took a soap dispenser and paper towels from the bathroom at the end of the hall. I cleaned the urine off my chair, piled the debris on the couch so I could move without stepping on things, then went back to work. You let something like a vandalized office screw your day, pretty soon you're calling in sick for a pimple.

Three minutes later I was speaking with Angel Tomaso's aunt, Mrs. Candy Lopez. I explained my relationship with her nephew, and told her it was urgent I speak with him.

She said, "Give me your name and number. I will tell him you called."

"It would be faster if I call him directly."

"It might be faster, but I'm not going to give you his number. I don't know you. For all I know you're a nut."

I didn't know what to say to that.

She said, "And please note the idiot who called last night has given my number to you without my permission, and here you are—a person completely unknown to me—invading my privacy. He gives my number to strangers, he might as well write it on a bathroom wall."

"I'm sorry, Mrs. Lopez. I wouldn't interrupt your day if it wasn't important. Angel was a witness in a criminal investigation three years ago, and now some conflicting evidence has surfaced."

"I understand. I will tell him all this when we speak."

"Did you tell him that Jack Eisley called?"

"I left a message on his machine. You call him, that machine is all you get. I am sure he is busy *rehearsing*."

She pronounced "rehearsing" with a snooty theatrical accent.

"So Angel is back here in Los Angeles?"

"He is. And, by the way, Angel is no longer Angel. He is now *Andy*."

She pronounced Andy without a trace of her Spanish accent, as if it were the most boring name in the world.

"Excuse me?"

"Angel Tomaso was too ethnic, he says. He is now Andy Thom. As if Hollywood has been waiting for the one and only *Andy Thom*!"

Angel probably hadn't gotten much artistic support back home.

I said, "Please call him right away. He'll remember my name. Tell him I need to speak with him as soon as possible."

"I'll tell him you're Steven Spielberg. You'll hear from him more quickly that way."

I put down the phone, thinking about Angel's new name and the likelihood of hearing back from him in the foreseeable future. I decided it wasn't likely.

I checked the L.A. area codes for an Andy Thom, found nothing, then called a casting agent I knew named Patricia Kyle. Pat Kyle had worked for every major studio and network in town, along with most of the commercial and video producers. She was currently successful, prosperous, and happy, which was much different from the day she hired me to help with an abusive ex-husband who thought it within his rights to shatter her windshield and terrorize her at work. I convinced him otherwise, and Pat Kyle has thought well of me ever since. If Angel Tomaso aka Andy Thom was serious about being an actor, three months was plenty of time to enroll in acting classes, pound the pavement for auditions, and send headshots to casting agents.

Pat Kyle said, "Never heard of him."

"His real name is Angel Tomaso. Out of Austin."

"Latin?"

"Yeah. Does it matter?"

"Only in how you search. Actors are faces and a face is what you look like. Some of the smaller agencies specialize in ethnic actors. Do you know if he's SAG or AFTRA?"

"Don't know."

"Ever had a paid acting job?"

"The way his aunt was talking, I doubt it. First time he was out here didn't work out. That's why he went back to Austin. He's only been back for three months."

Pat told me she would ask around, then we hung up and I settled back in my broken office to read over Chen's reports. I thought about the Mexican oxycodones. If Byrd was in so much pain he couldn't walk or drive, he probably needed a steady supply. If he couldn't walk or drive, someone might have delivered, and maybe that same someone might know how he came by the pictures. I decided to ask his neighbors.

At one-fourteen that afternoon I packed up the file

on Byrd, locked the office as best I could, and went down to my car. When I pulled out of my building, a black Toyota truck with tinted glass fell in behind and followed me.

12

THE BLACK Toyota turned toward Laurel Canyon with me, but so did half a dozen other cars. No one shot at me or behaved in an overly aggressive manner, so I told myself I was being paranoid. Your office gets trashed, it's easy to imagine you're being followed.

But two blocks later I slid through a yellow. The driver of the Toyota busted the red to keep up, then jammed on his brakes as soon as he was clear of the light. So much for my imagination. Two men appeared to be in the cab, but I couldn't be sure with the heavily tinted glass.

I took an abrupt right turn without using my blinker, and the Toyota turned with me. When he came around the corner, I saw a sticker on his front bumper. It was a promotional sticker for a chick band called Tattooed Beach Sluts.

I turned again and pulled to the curb, but the Toyota didn't follow. When it still hadn't appeared five minutes later, I continued on into Laurel Canyon. If I didn't watch myself, I would become the new Chen.

Broken branches and leaves littered the streets in the canyon and were piled against parked cars and curbs like drifting snow. The big cedars and eucalyptuses hung motionless for the first time in days, drooping now as if resting from their fight with the wind. The smell of their sap was strong.

When I reached Byrd's house, the police and the crime scene tape were gone, but a news crew and a short-bed moving van were at the bottom of the steps. The news crew was up on the porch, interviewing an older man with dyed-black hair and liverish skin. A white Eldorado was parked behind the van. The Eldo probably belonged to the interviewee, who likely owned the house and had been Byrd's landlord. While they talked, two Latin guys lugged pieces of furniture down to the truck.

I was waiting for the reporter to finish when I saw the woman in the vine-covered house across the street. She was back at her window, watching the interview, so I decided to start with her.

I climbed her steps, but before I reached the top, she opened the window.

"Go away. I've had enough of this."

"I'm with Easter Seals. Don't you want to help dying children?"

She slammed the window.

I continued to her door, then leaned on the bell until she answered. She had seemed older from across the street, with her grey hair up and frizzy.

"I'm not really from Easter Seals. I just said that."

"I know you're not, and I know you know I know. You're with the police. I saw you here yesterday, and you saw me."

Her name was Tina Isbecki. I introduced myself, letting her think what she thought. Operators like me are trained to go with the flow. This is called "lying."

I glanced across at the interview.

"Who's that?"

"Sharla Lee. She's on the news."

"Not the reporter. The man she's interviewing."

"That's Mr. Gladstone. He owns the house."

The police had released the house, and now Mr. Gladstone was dumping the furniture. He would have to clean the house, paint it, and hope he could find a tenant who wouldn't mind living where a multiple-murderer blew out his own brains.

I turned back to Tina Isbecki.

"Saw you on TV last night, saying now you could sleep easy. You looked very natural."

The Detective, buttering up the hostile subject.

She scowled.

"That isn't at all what I said. I told'm now I could sleep because all the goddamned cops were out of the neighborhood. They made it look like I meant Mr. Byrd."

"Did you know him very well?"

"I tried to avoid him. He was crude and offensive. The first time we met, he asked if I enjoyed anal sex.

Just like that. Who would say something like that?"

Welcome to Lionel Byrd.

"Was he close to anyone here in the neighborhood?"

"I doubt it. A lot of these people are renters and boarders, and most are just kids. They come and they go."

Which was pretty much what Starkey had told me.

"You must have been asked these things a hundred times."

"A thousand. Let me answer your other questions to save us both time—"

She ticked off her answers, bending each finger back so far I thought it might snap.

"No, I never saw anything suspicious. No, he never threatened me. No, I did not know he had been arrested, and I did not hear the gunshot. And yes, I am surprised he killed all those women, but this is Laurel Canyon."

She crossed her arms with a smugness indicating she had answered every question I could possibly ask.

I said, "Did he have many visitors?"

"I never saw anyone."

"Do you know how he got his drugs?"

The smugness vanished.

"A quantity of nonprescribed oxycodone was found in his home. Do you know what that is?"

"Well, of course I know, but I barely knew the man. There's no reason I would know he was a drug addict."

"I understand. But we're wondering where he got the pills."

"He didn't get them from me."

Defensive.

"On the day of the evacuation, it was you who told the officers he was housebound?"

"That's right. I was concerned. He hadn't been driving, what with his foot. He couldn't press the brake."

"When was the last time you saw him driving?"

"Believe it or not, I have more to do than watch my neighbors."

"This isn't a test. I'm trying to get an idea how difficult it was for him to get around."

"Well, I don't know. A few weeks, I guess. I know his foot had been getting worse. Some days he couldn't even come for the mail, and it would pile up."

I couldn't think of anything else to ask, so I thanked her and went down to the street. Gladstone was still being interviewed, so I knocked on the neighboring doors. No one was home at most of the houses, and the few people who were either had never met Byrd or had seen him only in passing. Only one person I interviewed had exchanged words with him, and she described him as crude, vulgar, and offensive, just like Tina Isbecki. Nobody had witnessed anyone visiting his house.

By the time I finished knocking on doors, the news crew was leaving. I squeezed around the movers' truck and climbed the steps just as Gladstone emerged from the house.

Gladstone was locking the front door, and scowled when he saw me approaching.

"Cut me some slack, all right? I didn't know the sonofabitch was a maniac."

"I'm not a reporter. I'm investigating the case."

I showed him the ID, but he had been looking at IDs all week. He waved me off.

"I got nothing to say. The man paid his rent and never made trouble. Now I got a house with brains on the ceiling and people like you wasting my time. I gotta get this place cleaned out by the end of the day."

He ducked past me and hurried after his movers.

I returned to my car, but didn't leave. The moving crew locked their truck, then rumbled away with Gladstone behind them. When they were gone, I got out of my car and pushed past low-hanging cedar boughs onto the walkway alongside the garage. A black plastic garbage can blocked the walk, but a flight of stairs led up to a door.

The can was filled with towels, bedding, old clothes, and plastic grocery bags bulging with discarded food and kitchen supplies. Gladstone had tossed things that would spoil—apples and oranges, a cantaloupe, hamburger patties and chicken, and all the usual things that accumulate in a refrigerator. I was probably the fifth or sixth person to go through these things, so I didn't expect to find anything useful.

I squeezed past the garbage can, climbed to the door, let myself in, and walked through the house. Not much was left.

A few small pieces of furniture remained in the living room, but the couch, the television, and the suicide chair were missing. The bathroom was even worse. Nothing remained on or around the vanity, in the medicine cabinet, on in the cabinet under the sink. So much for checking prescriptions. The bedroom and bedroom closet had been emptied. The bed, Byrd's clothes, and everything else was gone. All that remained was a single cardboard box filled with shoes, belts, and personal possessions like old cigarette lighters, pens, and a broken watch. I went through it, but found nothing. A note would have been nice: *For free home delivery, call Friendly Neighborhood Dope Dealer.*

I walked through the house again, searching for a telephone. I found three phone jacks, but the phones were gone. The police would have taken them to check their memory chips.

I ended up back in the kitchen, finding a jack above the counter beside a small corkboard. Business cards and take-out menus were pinned to the board. Alan Levy's card was pinned at the top for easy reference. It looked greasy and dark, as if it had been there a while. The rest of the board was cluttered with discount coupons and flyers.

Even with everything Gladstone had discarded, the kitchen counters were crowded with cartons and cans and other food waiting to be tossed. It was a lot of food for someone who hadn't been able to leave his house, and much of it looked pretty fresh.

I went back downstairs to the garbage, and dumped the fruit and other things out of the grocery bags. They were the thin plastic bags that people keep to line their wastebaskets. Most people get home from the market, they take out their groceries but leave the receipt in the bag.

Byrd had kept plenty of the bags, and Gladstone had used them when he cleaned out the house. I dumped fourteen bags and found five receipts. The receipts were all from the Laurel Market at the bottom of the canyon, and all showed the date of purchase. Lionel Byrd's body was discovered eight days ago, and the M.E. determined his death had occurred five days earlier. I did the math. The date of the most recent receipt was two days before Lionel Byrd died. If he was in too much pain to drive, I wondered how he had gone shopping.

I put the bags and the trash back into the can, then headed down to find out. Tina Isbecki watched me go. I waved. She waved back. We were getting to be friends.

13

THE RURAL vibe of Laurel Canyon set the sixties stage for crossover folk-rockers like David Crosby, Graham Nash, and Joni Mitchell to write about peaceful easy feelings, cocaine cowboys, and very nice houses with two cats in the yard. The high, tight trails wrapped through the ridges were only a few blocks from Sunset Boulevard, but, separated from the city by steep canyon walls, felt as if they were miles in the country. That rural sensibility was preserved and sustained by a small encampment of shops, markets, and restaurants at the base of the canyon.

I pulled into the tiny parking lot, then ambled into the market. You get a peaceful easy feeling, amblin' is how you walk.

The market was larger than it looked from the outside, with a high ceiling and narrow aisles jammed with goods, supplies, and candy. A pretty young woman was seated behind the register. An older man wearing a Lakers cap was behind a nearby deli counter, mixing a large bowl of tuna salad.

I took out a picture of Lionel Byrd I had clipped from the paper and showed it to the woman.

"Could you tell me if you recognize this man? His name was Lionel Byrd. He was a regular customer here."

She blinked at the picture with wide, curious eyes.

"Are you a policeman?"

"Nope. Elvis Cole. I'm a private investigator."

She smiled, the smile making her even prettier.

"Is that really your name?"

"What, Cole?"

"No, silly, Elvis. I'm Cass, like Mama Cass Elliot. She used to live right up the hill. A dude comes here, his name is Jagger, and a dude named Morris who says he was named after Jim Morrison, but that's kinda sketchy."

The sixties live.

Cass called over her shoulder.

"Phil, can you come see this, please?"

Phil put down the bowl of tuna and came up behind her, wiping his hands on a towel. Cass showed him the picture.

"Was this guy a customer?"

Phil considered the image.

"He's the one they found in the fire. You didn't see the news?"

Cass didn't know what we were talking about.

Phil said, "Yeah, he used to get the curry chicken. It

126

was always the same. The curry chicken on a sesame roll. He had a bad foot."

Phil was a score. They might have shot the bull while Phil made Byrd's sandwich, and Phil might remember something useful.

"That's right. He was here about two weeks ago, just before he died. Do you remember what you talked about?"

Phil handed back the picture, shaking his head.

"Sorry, bro. He hasn't been in for a couple of months, something like that. It's been a while."

"He was here exactly fifteen days ago, and two days before that. I found these at his house."

I showed him the two most recent receipts. Phil squinted at them as if they were an incomprehensible mystery, then shook his head.

"I don't know what to tell you. We get busy, I wouldn't have seen him if he didn't buy a sandwich."

The tingle faded, but Cass brightened and spoke up.

"We might have delivered. Let's see if Charles remembers."

Phil was still squinting at the receipts.

"There's no delivery charge, see? We didn't deliver. There would be a charge if we delivered."

Cass said, "Oh, don't be a gob."

She went to the end of the counter and shouted for someone named Charles. A stock clerk in a green apron ambled out from between the aisles. It wasn't just me.

Phil took the picture, and showed him.

"You deliver for this guy? The name was Byrd."

Phil glanced at me again.

"Where'd he live?"

"Anson Lane. Off Lookout, up past the school."

Charles took his turn with the picture, then shook his finger as if the finger was helping him fish up the thought.

"The dude with the foot."

"That's the one."

"Yeah, man, I saw it in the paper. That stuff was crazy."

"You delivered groceries to him two weeks ago?"

"Nope, I never delivered to him. I know him from the register, but he hasn't been down in a while. Ivy came for his things."

Cass laughed.

"Oh, *that* chick!"

I said, "A girl named Ivy picked up his groceries?"

"He'd phone the order, and she'd pick it up. He had to stop driving."

Cass was making a big loopy grin.

"Charles was so totally into that chick."

Charles flushed.

"Stop it, dude. Discretion."

"Who's Ivy?"

Cass touched the midpoint of her left forearm.

"She had a broken heart here on her arm. The wreckage of Charles's love."

"*Dude!*"

Cass was pleased with Charles's mortification and crossed her arms smugly.

"She lived up there in the big redwood house. A total hippie throwback to the commune age."

Charles shot a sulky glance at Cass.

"It's not a commune. Dude rents out his rooms, is all. Ivy crashed there for a few weeks."

Cass mouthed her words with exaggerated volume.

"Not long enough to drop her shorts."

Phil laughed and went back to his tuna.

The big redwood house was next door to Tina Isbecki. I had been there less than an hour ago and spoken with a bald man named Lloyd and a woman named Jan who identified herself as a screenwriter. Neither had known anything about Lionel Byrd, and no one named Ivy was present.

"I was just up there talking to Lloyd. Ivy doesn't live with them anymore?"

"Uh-uh. She went home."

Great. The only person I'd found who had any contact with Byrd had ridden the tornado back to Oz.

"Because of what happened?"

"She left before the fires. She only had the room while her real place was being repaired. They found mold in her bathroom."

Charles suddenly looked alarmed.

"Hey, he didn't kill her, did he? Is she dead?"

"No, it's nothing like that, but I'd like to speak with her. You know how to reach her?"

Cass made swoony eyes.

"Ooohhh, yeeaaahhh."

Then she mouthed, "Stalker."

Charles couldn't give me Ivy Casik's phone or address, but he knew how to find her apartment. Ivy's car had died in the parking lot, and Charles had given her a lift to pick up cash for the repair. He had brought her to an apartment in Hollywood.

I copied the directions, thanked them for the help, then went out to my car.

When I reached the parking lot, a stocky kid in a Foo Fighters T-shirt and black wraparounds was peering at the interior. You drive a '66 Corvette, you get that. He saw me coming, and stepped away.

"Nice ride. Want to sell it?"

"No, thanks."

"Too bad. I could rock a car like this."

He lit a cigarette, then drifted away to a blue Mustang. He stared at my car as he smoked. Vehicle envy.

I headed back to Sunset, then followed Charles's directions east into Hollywood. Things were looking up. I had a real, live lead who might even be able to provide something useful. Of course, the odds she knew anything useful were probably along the lines of getting brained by a meteor, but you take your hope where you find it.

I was feeling so good, I almost didn't see the black Toyota pickup pull into traffic behind me. It was the same Toyota with the Tattooed Beach Sluts sticker. A few seconds later, the Foo Fighters' blue Mustang appeared a few cars behind.

Ivy Casik's address would have led me into the low foothills near the Hollywood Bowl, but I drove south through West Hollywood in a loose circle around the Farmers Market, watching my rearview mirror.

The Mustang tightened up on the truck, then the truck turned off. A few blocks later, the truck was waiting at a cross street ahead of me. As I drove past, the truck turned in behind, and the Mustang disappeared. We went on like that, leapfrogging through the city, with one or the other of them always behind me but never for very long. They were using radios or cell phones to coordinate their moves.

When I was certain they were following me, I took my pistol from under the seat, put it beside my leg, then called Pike. He was still watching my house.

Pike said, "You get a tag?"

"Mud on their plates. Nice trick, seeing as how we haven't had rain in five months."

"You think they're police?"

The Foo Fighter seemed pretty young for an officer, but a lot of guys in their early twenties looked younger.

"Could be. Bastilla was pissed off when I told her I was looking for Tomaso. Maybe they're the same guys who searched my office."

Pike grunted.

"An officer wouldn't piss on your chair."

"Crimmens phonied a confession in a capital crime. He would piss on a chair if he thought he could cover the search by making it look like vandalism."

"Okay."

"I'm on my way to see a woman named Ivy Casik up by the Bowl. When you're on them, I'll lose them, then you can follow them home."

"I'm all over it."

"Thought you might be."

I turned north toward the hills and maintained an easy, meandering pace, watching them drift in and out of the mirror. Sometimes I didn't see them for blocks at a time, then one or the other would reappear.

I slipped into a shoulder harness, then covered it with a light cotton jacket. The day was too hot for the jacket, but the jacket covered the gun.

Sixteen minutes later, Pike called.

"I'm on the Mustang."

"Good hunting."

I closed the phone and picked up speed.

14

I TURNED up Hillcrest into an older residential area with winding streets, high curbs, and plenty of sturdy palms. When I climbed into the curves, the truck and the Mustang were easy to lose. They would probably circle for a while, blaming each other for losing me, but then they would head for home, unaware Pike was with them. After I finished with Ivy Casik, I would join him, but they wouldn't know that, either. Then we would talk.

I parked beneath a jacaranda tree across from Ivy's building, then headed for her apartment. Ivy lived in Apartment 4, which was the bottom unit at the back of the courtyard. I rang the bell twice and knocked, but she wasn't home. Perfect.

Ivy wasn't much of a lead, but she was the only lead I had, so I returned to my car. Twenty-two minutes later, a dusty Ford Neon appeared and parked on the opposite curb. A tall young woman with serious eyes and straight hair climbed out. She had the broad shoulders and defined legs of an athlete and was wearing running shorts, a thin T, and blue Saucony running shoes, as if she had been for a run. The little heart on her forearm stood out like a strawberry.

I followed her into the courtyard, hurrying to catch up.

"Ivy Casik!"

She jumped sideways as if I had shouted "Boo," and seemed about to run.

"Sorry. I didn't mean to startle you."

She glanced at the other apartments as if she might start calling for help.

"You scared the hell out of me."

"Sorry."

I held out a card.

"Elvis Cole. I'd like to ask you about Lionel Byrd, the man you knew as Lonnie Jones."

She backed away, still searching the apartments for help.

"Who are you?"

"I'm a private investigator. Just look at my card."

"Anyone can get a card."

I spread my arms.

"I could show you my gun."

She hesitated, but seemed to grow calmer. I put away the card and held out my license.

"Licensed by the State of California, see? I'm sorry I scared you."

"You're a policeman?"

"Private, but the police will want to talk to you. I would have called before I came, but I didn't have your number."

She studied the license as if it was difficult to read.

"You *are* Ivy Casik, aren't you?"

She glanced up, but seemed to be getting used to me.

"Why are you here?"

"About Lionel Byrd, the man you knew as Lonnie Jones."

"Yes?"

I couldn't tell from her answer if she recognized his name or not.

"The people at Laurel Market told me you knew him. A clerk named Charles. Did you read the newspaper this morning?"

"Charles."

"Yes. Do you have any idea what I'm talking about? You knew the man as Lonnie Jones?"

She seemed to think about it, then hooked her hair behind her ear.

"I'm sorry. This is all so weird. That guy in the paper, he was really Lonnie?"

"I understand. Kinda creeps you out, doesn't it?"

"Yeah. You want to come in? It's easier than standing out here."

Her apartment was small and clean, with only a single couch and coffee table in the living room, and a small circular table near the kitchenette. The furniture was new, and had the efficient lines of furnishings that had probably come with the apartment. The kitchenette was immaculate. So were the floors and the table. The only thing out of place was a newspaper, open to the story about Byrd.

Ivy offered me a bottle of water, took one for herself, then perched on the edge of the couch. I pulled one of the dining chairs closer to sit with her.

I said, "Has anyone talked to you about this?"

"You mean the police?"

"They questioned your former neighbors last week. They pretty much spent all this past week up on Anson, interviewing people."

"I had no idea. I saw the paper, and I thought, ohmigod, that's Lonnie, but the picture was so bad. I was like, is this a joke?"

"It isn't a joke."

"This is surreal."

"How well did you know him?"

"I picked up groceries for him a couple of times. It's not like we hung out."

Her voice took on a defensive whine, as if I had accused her of being a serial-killer sympathizer.

"It's okay, Ivy. You didn't know."

"Here he was with the cane, and he asked for some help. He didn't say anything obnoxious. I was going to the market anyway. What was I supposed to say, no? He was just an old man."

She flipped her head. When she moved, her hair

swayed like a curtain in the breeze.

I said, "Did he ask you to pick up drugs?"

"Uh-uh. I just stopped at the market a few times. They don't have a pharmacy."

"Not prescription drugs. He was using oxycodone manufactured in Mexico. He would have gotten them illegally."

She sat taller, and her lips tightened into a bud. It was a rough way to ask, but I wanted to see her reaction.

"I didn't buy drugs for him."

"Okay. I had to ask."

"Do you think I'm a dealer?"

"You might not have known what you were buying. He might have asked you to pick up a package, and you didn't know what was in the package."

"Only the market."

"If he couldn't drive, someone had to get them for him. I'm not saying it was you."

"Well, it sounds like you are. I was just trying to be a nice person, and now you're accusing me of being a dope connection. I really resent this."

"I'm not accusing you. I know it sounded like that, but I'm not."

"Whatever. Am I going to have to do this again with the police?"

"Probably, but they're not nearly as much fun as me."

Her mouth tightened again, which is almost always

a sign I'm wearing out my welcome.

My cell phone vibrated, so I excused myself and checked the call. It was Pike. I told her I had to take it, and opened the phone.

Pike said, "You with the girl?"

"That's right. Where'd they go?"

"Nowhere. The Pony parked as soon as you lost them. We're on Franklin at the bottom of Hillcrest."

"What about his helper?"

"The truck left. Four or five streets feed down from these hills, so the truck probably set up at a different location."

"Okay."

"If the Pony leaves, you want me to follow?"

"Absolutely."

I closed the phone.

"Sorry. We're almost finished."

"Whatever."

"Did he ever do or say anything that made you fearful?"

"I wouldn't have gone to the market for him if I was scared of him."

"Okay. Did he ever ask if he could take your picture?"

She gave an exaggerated shiver. She knew I was talking about the album.

"Yuck. No. I would've told him to fuck off."

"All right. One last thing. Did he say or do anything that made you think—or makes you think now, in retrospect—that he was suicidal?"

She grew distant for a moment, then went to the newspaper. She touched it, but did not pick it up.

"Not like, I'm going to blow my brains out, but he was depressed. He was really scared of the police. He thought they were out to get him."

"He did?"

"The police framed him for murder. He talked about it a lot."

I took a slow breath.

"He told you about Yvonne Bennett?"

"How the police tried to frame him. He hated the police. He said they were always trying to get him. I mean, here's this gimpy little man going on with a major persecution complex, and it sounded so made up."

"He didn't make it up."

"Are they really writing a book about him?"

I shook my head, not understanding, and Ivy Casik went on.

"Someone came to see him about how the police framed him. The guy told him it could be a book and a movie, and all this stuff, and Lonnie was bragging how he was going to be rich, and it all sounded so absurd."

My mouth felt dry, but wetting my lips didn't help.

"Who was this person?"

"I don't know. A reporter, he said. This reporter was doing a story about how the police fucked him over."

Ivy Casik was an attractive young woman. It was

easy to imagine Byrd making up stories about books and movies to impress her.

"Did you see this person?"

"It was just something Lonnie told me, like the dude brought this little tape recorder and asked lots of questions."

"A dude who came to the house?"

"Yeah. Do you think he was lying?"

"I don't know."

"I thought he made it up until I saw the paper. They really did charge him with murder. They really did drop the charges. Those things were true."

"Yes," I said. "Those things were true."

A new player had entered the crime scene. An unnamed person who might have approached Lionel Byrd to discuss the subject of murder, and who might or might not even exist. If someone had been looking for Lionel Byrd, I wondered how they had found him. Everyone on Anson Lane thought Lionel Byrd was Lonnie Jones.

I wondered how I could find out if Lionel Byrd's story about the reporter was true. The police should have gone through Byrd's phone records and back-checked the numbers, so Bastilla probably already knew, but she probably wouldn't tell me. Maybe the guy in the Mustang would know.

After Ivy Casik let me out, I called Pike, filled him in, and asked about the Mustang.

"What's our boy doing?"

"Still hasn't moved."

"Any sign of the truck?"

"Nope."

"I'm on the way."

I had only gone three blocks when the black Toyota pulled out of a side street in front of me. I wasn't sure it was the same truck, but the Toyota bucked high on its springs and powered away. He had probably been searching the area while the Mustang waited below, and was as surprised to see me as I was to see him.

Cops with a busted surveillance would have stopped to badge me, but the Toyota ran. I thought he would run for the flats and the freeways and his buddy in the Mustang, but he skidded onto a cross street instead, climbing higher in the hills. He probably felt he had a better chance of losing me the higher we went, but I pushed after hard, closing the gap.

The curves grew tighter the higher we climbed, looping and crossing like snakes. I wanted to call Pike, but the driving was fast, and my hands were filled with the shifter and wheel. I didn't think he knew where he was going or where the streets went; he just drove it, trying to leave me behind. We busted through stop signs, circled the same streets, turned downhill hard and then it was over. He had turned into a cul-de-sac. He was trapped.

The driver's window was down, and the driver was watching me. His eyes were large and bright from the chase, but waiting to see what I would do.

He was big, with beefy forearms and heavy shoulders, but a wispy mustache and zits on his chin made him look even younger than the Foo Fighter. He couldn't have been more than seventeen or eighteen. He was a kid.

I had once seen three grown men shot to death by an eleven-year-old with an AK-47. I took out my pistol, but did not raise it. He was no more than ten yards away.

"Get out of the truck. Keep your hands where I can see them."

His door opened. He raised his hands, then slid out. He looked even younger once he was out, like a baby-faced high-school lineman. I thought he might run because kids always run, but he didn't.

I said, "Close it."

He pushed the door closed.

I got out of my car, holding the gun down along my leg because I still didn't know what he might try or what I might have to do when he tried it.

"On your knees. Fingers laced on your head."

He did what I told him. Here we were in a small cul-de-sac in a residential neighborhood where someone might step out for the mail or come home from school. I holstered the gun, snapped the safety strap, then stepped away from my car.

"What in hell are you doing?"

A voice behind me said, "This."

Something hard slammed into the back of my neck and dropped me into the street. That's when I realized

142

the kid had not been trying to get away. I had not trapped the black Toyota in the cul-de-sac. He had trapped me.

15

THE NEW man was a muscular young guy with high and tight hair, bleached-grey eyes, and the brutal tan of a man who lived in the sun. He had the back of my shirt, dragging and spinning me to keep me off-balance, and punching down hard as I tried to roll away.

The man who hit me knew what he was doing. He moved fast to stay behind me, controlling me from behind as he punched me in the head. I didn't reach for my gun, and I didn't try to get up. You have a gun in a situation like this, you have to protect it; if the other guy gets it he will shoot you to death. And if you try to get up, you can't defend yourself, so I fought from the ground. Picture the detective as a crab on its back.

The kid from the truck shouted something I couldn't understand, then he was kicking me, but he wasn't as good as his friend. He stood over me like a light pole without bothering to move. I hooked a round kick through his ankles, and swept his feet from under him. The kid landed on top of us as the blue Mustang flashed into view.

When the kid fell, I dragged him closer, trying to roll him onto the first guy. The first guy clawed me backwards, but the kid bucked up and broke us apart. I turned to get the first guy in front of me, but he drove into me with his head down like a linebacker. The Foo Fighter was running toward us to join in the fight.

I went over backwards again, but this time I tied up the first guy and pulled him in close. He should have kept driving through me, but he jerked backwards, trying to get away. He was pulling back so hard that when I let go he popped up like a target. I hit him in the throat and the mouth, then hooked the kid high on the cheek with an elbow. The first guy was getting up when the Foo Fighter slammed into his back like a battering ram. The first guy went down face-first, but the Foo kept going. Pike powered him through the first guy and along a graceful arc into the side of my car. His collarbone snapped.

Then Pike had his .357 and I had my gun, and all of it stopped.

Pike said, "Guess these guys aren't cops."

I sucked air, trying to catch my breath. My head throbbed. So did my shoulder, my back, and my right knee. The Foo Fighter held his shoulder, gritting his teeth like it burned. The kid was on his knees, his eye bloody and swelling. The first guy rose to a knee, watching Pike as if he wanted to go for more. The first guy was the oldest.

Pike said, "You okay?"

"Uh-huh."

"Look winded."

"Uh."

"I got it."

Pike moved on them the way he'd done a hundred times when he was a police officer, pushing them down as he gave the commands.

"Belly. Fingers laced behind your heads."

They assumed the position. We patted down the Foo Fighter and the kid, but when I touched the oldest guy he shoved my hand.

"Don't fuckin' touch me, piece of shit."

"You trash my office?"

"Fuck you."

I planted a knee on the back of his neck and touched him anyway. None of them had weapons. I took their wallets, and matched the pictures on their DLs to their faces. The kid was Gordon Repko. He was eighteen years old. The Foo Fighter was Dennis Repko, who was twenty. The oldest was Michael Repko, age twenty-four. All three showed the same home address in Pasadena, California. Michael Repko was also carrying a military ID card, identifying him as a sergeant in the United States Army Reserve. That explained the high and tight cut and fierce desert eyes. They had frightened John Chen when he went to their house, and now they had frightened me.

I gimped to my car and leaned on the fender. I felt tired in a way that had nothing to do with fighting for my life in a cul-de-sac in the Hollywood Hills.

"Debra Repko was their sister."

Pike lowered his gun, but didn't put it away.

Dennis Repko said, "You got her killed, you fuck. It's your fuckin' fault."

Pike said, "Mm."

I looked from brother to brother and felt even more drained by the hate and fear in their faces. The Pasadena address was a nice one. These three kids had probably never wanted for anything, had a solid family, and attended good schools. Three angry white boys, wanting to dump their grief on the person they blamed.

"You trashed my office and followed me to get some payback. That what it is?"

Michael Repko said, "So what are you going to do, shoot us? Fuck you. I'll fight you right here. Man to man."

Pike said, "You just did. You're on your ass."

I went back to Michael, and squatted to look at him.

"I might have shot you. I might have shot your brothers, and I could still have you arrested. This was stupid."

Gordon said, "She was our *sister*."

Gordon, the youngest, was crying.

I took a breath and went back to my car. The first death threat had come even before Bastilla and Crimmens came to my office and hours before Marx went on the news. Since my involvement with Lionel Byrd hadn't been mentioned in the news or by the press, I had a pretty good idea how these guys learned my name.

"The police told you I worked for Byrd?"

Dennis said, "They could've put him in prison, but you and some ass-licking shyster got him off."

"Who told you that, Crimmens?"

Michael said, "Was that you or wasn't it? I'd like to kick that lawyer's ass, too."

Levy.

Pike tucked the gun under his sweatshirt.

"What do you want to do?"

I went to Gordon, then Dennis. Gordon's eye was swelling. Dennis had trouble moving his arm.

Dennis said, "Get away from me, bitch."

I looked back at Michael.

"Gordon won't need stitches, but he should get some ice. Dennis needs a doctor."

Michael said, "Fuck you. No one gives a shit what you say."

I tossed back their wallets.

"I'm sorry you lost her. I'm sorry she's dead, and for what you and your parents are going through, but I don't believe Lionel Byrd killed your sister."

They came to their feet, Dennis bent to the side because of the collarbone. Gordon touched his eye, and seemed confused by the blood on his fingers. Dennis and Gordon watched their older brother, taking their cues from him.

Michael said, "That's bullshit. The police said he did it."

"Marx rushed the investigation so he could make a splash on TV. A lot of things got lost in the rush."

"That's bullshit."

"Is it?"

I told them how Debra's murder was off the timeline, how the others had all been murdered on moonless nights. I told them how Byrd was so gimped up in recent weeks with his bad foot he could barely walk, and had been flying on oxycodone the night he died. I told them how Marx shut down the case even before all the forensics were run, and that no one had yet spoken with the most important witness in Yvonne Bennett's murder—Angel Tomaso. I told them about everything except the blind tests. They would talk about the things I was saying, and they might even tell the police. I didn't want the wrong people to know I knew about the blinds.

When I finished, Gordon, the youngest, sneered.

"What makes you so much smarter than the police?"

"Maybe I'm just lucky."

Dennis said, "The cops didn't tell us any of this."

"Okay, maybe I'm smarter."

Michael frowned.

"Maybe you're just trying to duck the blame."

"Byrd didn't die after the first murder or the fourth or the sixth. He died after Debra's murder, so maybe something about her or her murder triggered everything else."

Michael glanced at his brothers, then wet his lips.

"Like what?"

"I don't know, but I'm the only one looking, and I need your help."

Dennis shook his head.

"You want us to help you?"

"The only way I can figure this out is to start with your sister. If I knew more about Debra, I might be able to figure out why her murder was different."

Gordon said, "Like what?"

"The autopsy report shows she had a drink on the night she was murdered. Did she meet a friend after work?"

The three of them stared at me.

"If so, where did they meet? Was the friend a man or a woman, or was Debra alone?"

Dennis glanced at Michael, then shook his head again, but now he was thinking.

"We don't know."

"I don't know either, and I need your help to find out these things."

Now Dennis and Gordon were both staring at Michael.

"Mikie, I think we should."

I shrugged, saying the next move was his.

"Here we are, Michael. You can accept what the police say, case closed, done deal, or you can follow it through to find out whether or not I'm trying to duck the blame."

Michael glanced at his brothers. Dennis nodded, trying to encourage him. Gordon's good eye was hopeful.

"Our folks have been through a lot."

"Do they think I'm responsible, too?"

Michael nodded.

"Then it will be hard."

"We gotta talk."

I gave him the card with my home and cell numbers. He stared at it.

"You'd give me your home number?"

"I believe what I told you. Decide if you want to help and let me know, but either way I'm going to do it."

Michael hesitated, maybe thinking of offering his hand to close the deal, but didn't. We were finished.

Michael went to the Mustang with Dennis and got in behind the wheel. Gordon climbed back into the truck. They drove away, leaving us in the quiet cul-de-sac.

Pike sighed deeply.

"Her brothers."

I said, "Yes."

16

MY PANTS were torn at both knees, my shirt was ripped and missing two buttons, and my hands and right forearm were scraped, dirty, and seeping. I should have gone home or picked up some ice or maybe even gone to the Emergency Room, but I drove to the Best Buy in Hollywood. I bought a computer and a cordless phone for my office to replace the broken things. I would have bought a new chair, but a chair wouldn't fit in my car. The skin in front of my right ear and above my right eyebrow was tender and swelling, and the back of my head was worse. The register clerk stared as she rang me up.

She said, "You're bleeding."

"Tripped in the parking lot."

"I gotta call the manager if you wanna file a claim."

"That's all right. I'm tough."

I pressed my handkerchief on my forearm to cover the blood.

After the Best Buy, I stopped at a True Value hardware store for two gallons of latex interior paint, a roller, and a package of disposable plastic drop cloths. The color was named Eggshell. The total for everything including the Best Buy came to $1,868.52. Anyone else would get jumped by criminals, rogue cops, or lunatics, but I got pounded by three angry brothers mourning the death of their sister.

When I got home, I filled two plastic bags with ice, stretched out on the couch, then called an old-school newsman named Eddie Ditko. Eddie had worked for every newspaper in Southern California, and most of them more than once. He knew the newspaper business inside and out.

I said, "If a reporter was working on a particular story, and I knew the subject but not the name of the reporter, could I find out who the reporter is?"

"What paper?"

"Don't know. All I know is the story."

"Jesus Christ, what story?"

Patience wasn't one of Eddie's strengths.

"Lionel Byrd."

"You got no shot. Every paper in town is working on Byrd."

Eddie broke into a deep, shuddering cough. Eddie has smoked three packs a day for almost sixty years. I think he was born smoking. He made a gakking sound, then spit.

"You okay?"

"It's these allergies."

Smoker's denial.

"The reporter in question was working on Byrd before everyone else. He was supposedly doing a story on how Byrd had been prosecuted on the Yvonne Bennett murder with a bad confession. He told Byrd there might be a book or a movie in it."

"You don't know where the guy works?"

"No."

"The *L.A. Times* has something like eight hundred fifty writers, and that's just the *Times*. Toss in the *Daily News*, the *L.A. Weekly*, *La Opinión*, and all these little papers, you see what we're talking about?"

"Don't writers get assigned these things? Wouldn't his editor know?"

"Just because the guy was working the story doesn't mean it was assigned. That's called sniffing out the news. You do your research, then pitch your piece to your editor if you think it has heat. Some of these feature writers and columnists, they don't even pitch."

"So you're saying there's no way to ask around. Even though this could lead to a blowout story."

Eddie was silent. I heard his lighter flick. I heard him inhale. Sniffing out the news.

"What kind of blowout story?"

"Maybe the reporter was a reporter, but maybe he wasn't. Maybe this individual had a play with what happened to Lionel Byrd or with the murders."

"I'm listening."

"What if I told you even though this case has been

publicly closed, the police are continuing to run DNA comparisons against a certain blind sample?"

"These tests are ongoing?"

"These tests are ongoing."

Eddie inhaled again.

"Lemme see what I can find out."

I threw away the ice, then searched for Bastilla's card. Her task force would have identified all the calls going into or out of Byrd's number, especially on the days leading up to his death. A legitimate writer or reporter would have identified himself, and Bastilla would know the full story. I didn't trust she would give me the truth, but I wanted to see her reaction.

"Bastilla, it's Cole—"

"Hey, man, thanks for getting those files to us. Levy messengered them over."

"No problem. Now how about one for me—were any journalists, reporters, or news agencies on the calls to or from Byrd's house?"

Bastilla hesitated.

"Why would you ask something like that?"

"A woman named Ivy Casik used to pick up groceries for him. Byrd told her a reporter was writing a book about how he was railroaded for the Bennett murder. She told me this person visited him on at least two occasions prior to his death."

Bastilla hesitated even longer.

"Who's Ivy Casik?"

"She used to rent a room up on Anson across the street. She helped him out when he couldn't drive.

You might want to talk to her."

"How do you spell her name?"

I spelled it and gave her Ivy Casik's address.

"One more, Bastilla—"

"It's late and I want to get out of here. The case is closed, man. We're finished. That's it."

"Is it? Were any of Byrd's calls to a drug connection or someone who might have supplied him with the oxys?"

"How do you know about that?"

"Were there?"

"Good night, Cole. Really."

"Guess your task force disbanded too soon."

"Fuck off."

I took a shower, then cleaned the scrapes with hydrogen peroxide. I felt a little better after I put on fresh clothes but was still at loose ends, wondering why blind samples were being compared to the forensics Chen had been ordered to collect weeks after Debra's murder. The results would have been in the news if their tests put Lionel Byrd with Debra, so Byrd still wasn't a match.

Michael Repko called at twenty minutes after eight. He sounded subdued, and spoke in a low voice as if he didn't want to be overheard.

"You want to talk about Debra, I guess it's okay."

"Is it okay or not, Michael? Guesses don't help."

"It's not so easy over here. Everyone blames you."

"I understand that, Michael. So where are we going with this?"

He gave me their address and told me to come over at ten the next morning.

"All right. I'll see you at ten."

"Something better come of this or we're gonna take up where we left off."

Then he hung up.

Tough to the end.

I sat on the couch feeling angry and bad. I grew so angry I called Bastilla again, but this time she didn't answer.

When her message beeped, I said, "It's Cole again. Tell your pal Crimmens the next time I see him I'm going to kick his ass."

I hung up, but felt even worse.

I took two Tylenol and two Aleve, then drove down to my office. I carried the paint and the new things upstairs. It was after hours and late, and I was the only person on my floor. The building manager had moved quickly. A new door had been installed, which was good, but they had set a new deadbolt and lock. Picking the lock took almost fifteen minutes, but I worked steadily and carefully, and soon the lock opened.

I set up the new phone and the computer and put the old stuff into a cardboard box, then put the box in the hall. I pulled the couch and the file cabinets and the little fridge away from the walls, covered them with the plastic drop cloths, then put Pinocchio where he would be safe. I had the walls painted in less than an hour, opening both French doors to help the paint dry. The walls would need a second coat, but I could wait for the weekend.

I took up the drop cloths, pushed the furniture back into place, then swept and vacuumed. I made my office as neat as I could, then sat at my desk with the Mickey Mouse phone. The base was broken and split. Mickey's left ear had been knocked off and his arm was cracked. Buying a new phone would have been easier, but Mickey and I had been together a long time.

Fixing the Mouse took longer than painting the office. I superglued the base together, then reattached Mickey to the base. Several small pieces were missing, but he didn't look so bad. The ear came last. I spread the glue, then set the ear and held it until the bond was tight. Mickey looked pretty good when I finished, but the cracks were now part of him. I would always see them.

Part Three
WHAT THEY NEVER TELL YOU

17

MY BODY felt brittle the next morning, but my face was as tender as an heirloom tomato. Stretching and a hot shower helped with the stiffness, but they didn't do much for my face. I tried to eat, but was too anxious about meeting the Repkos.

I reread the materials I had about Debra. Though I did not have the police report, the CI report Chen gave me listed the original investigating detectives as Robert Darcy and David Maddux. I wondered if they had been included on the task force and returned when Chen was sent to collect the second set of samples.

Though the medical examiner's protocol showed a minimal blood alcohol level, no mention was made of Debra Repko's activities that night or in the days preceding her death. These were things I wanted to know. As I reread the newspaper accounts, I was struck again by the similarities between Repko and the first victim, Sondra Frostokovich. Both were white, educated, and had worked downtown in a capacity related to city government. This might be relevant, but I had no way to know.

I reread the reports until I realized I was stalling. I did not want to face the Repkos, but then nothing was left except for the drive to Pasadena. I gathered my things and left.

The Repko family shared a lovely ranch-style home in an upper-middle-class neighborhood east of the Rose Bowl. I left my car on the street, walked up a long, used-brick drive, and rang their bell. It was a difficult walk to make, going to see a family who believed I was responsible for their daughter's death. I was queasy and tried breathing deep, but the breathing didn't help. Maybe I would puke on their floor.

Michael answered as if he had been waiting. His eyes widened when he saw me, and the two of us studied each other. An angry red mark creased his right cheek and his upper lip was thick and mottled.

He said, "You're pretty dinged up."

"You, too."

The smell of lilacs was strong. Their home felt like a funeral parlor, which, I guess, it was. Michael lowered his voice as he let me in.

"Go easy with my mom."

"I'm not going to kneecap anyone."

Michael led me into a spacious living room where Dennis and Gordon were waiting with their parents. Gordon's eye was purple and Dennis's left arm hung in a sling. Family photographs were dotted around the room, but an enormous photo of Debra hung above the fireplace. More pictures of Debra crowded the mantel and hearth, along with stuffed animals and yearbooks and keepsakes. Her family had created a shrine.

Michael's head drooped when we faced his parents. He no longer looked like the hardened troop who had tried to beat me to death with his brothers.

Michael said, "This is him."

Him.

Mrs. Repko, propped in a wing chair as if she were made of marble, stared at me with open loathing. She was in her late fifties, with the stocky, large-bone build of her sons. Mr. Repko was ten years older than his wife; a thin man with the rheumy eyes of someone who had been drinking too much every night without regretting it the next morning. He had a high forehead and glasses, and looked nothing like his sons. Debra had gotten his looks. He frowned at the marks on my face, and glanced at his sons as if he wanted to say something, but didn't.

I said, "Thank you for seeing me. I know this is difficult."

"Michael tells us you believe the police have it wrong."

"I have some questions, is all. I'll try to make this quick."

"Get to it then. Let's try to make this as pleasant as possible."

I took out my notepad. Hiding behind a 3x5 pad was an easy way to avoid the condemnation in their eyes.

"I need some background information about Debra, but I also want to know what the police did and what they asked you about."

Mrs. Repko crossed her arms.

"It sounds like he's trying to blame the police for something."

Mr. Repko glanced at his wife, then studied me as if he thought I was setting him up.

"The police have been good to us. They've been very kind. We won't say anything bad about them."

"I'm asking so I'll know how the police framed their investigation. If I know what they did, it will save time by suggesting a direction. You see?"

Michael said, "Mom. C'mon."

Gordon said, "Can we just do this, please?"

Mr. Repko adjusted his pants. He still wasn't comfortable, but he had let his sons talk him into seeing me and now he was stuck.

"All right, then. What?"

I glanced at the pad again. The three hundred Spartans would not have approved.

"I understand the police sent a criminalist to your home last week."

"That's right. He looked through Debra's things."

"Did they tell you what they were looking for?"

"The criminalist didn't say much. He was a very odd man."

"Not the criminalist. The police. Was that Darcy and Maddux?"

Michael said, "Darcy and Maddux are gone. These

were new cops—Bastilla and Munson. A detective named Crimmens was here, but he left. We haven't seen Darcy and Maddux in a while."

Munson was new. I scratched his name onto the pad.

Mr. Repko nodded along with his son.

"Detectives Bastilla and Munson are on this special task force they have. We don't know what happened to Darcy and Maddux."

"Uh-huh. And what did Bastilla and Munson tell you they were looking for?"

"Some kind of samples. That's all they said, really, that they needed to collect samples from Debra's things. They asked if we'd had them laundered or whatnot, but other than that they didn't get into specifics."

"Uh-huh. And did they ask you questions about anything or anyone in particular?"

Mrs. Repko squinted and grew even more strained, like a violin string tightened to the breaking point.

She said, "They told us about her murderer with those sick, twisted pictures. They wanted to warn us because it was going to be on TV. They wouldn't show us the pictures, but they warned us. I asked to see her. I wanted to see the picture he took, but they wouldn't let me—"

Her eyes reddened and blinked. Gordon touched her arm and whispered, "Mom."

She blinked harder, but Gordon's touch settled her. I wanted to ask more about Bastilla and Munson, but changed the subject to Darcy and Maddux.

Mr. Repko explained that Darcy and Maddox had come to Pasadena on the morning Debra's body was found. At that time, the detectives believed Debra resided in Pasadena because her parents' address was still on her driver's license. When they were told Debra had taken an apartment, Darcy and Maddux asked to see it, so Dennis and Mr. Repko drove into the city to let the detectives into her apartment. Michael and Gordon had stayed with their mother.

I said, "I'd like to talk to her neighbors about visitors she might have had, or if men had come around. That type of thing. I'm sure the police did the same, but I want to hear it for myself."

Mr. Repko nodded.

"All right."

"Was she seeing anyone?"

Dennis said, "Not since Berkeley. She dated a few guys at grad school, but they were more like friends, not boyfriend-girlfriend."

"How about the men at work? Did she mention anyone she might have liked at work?"

Mrs. Repko had relaxed when her husband was doing the talking, but now she visibly tensed again.

"Once she went to work she didn't have time to date. They work them like slaves at that place."

"Leverage Associates?"

Michael nodded.

"Yeah. Debra worked hard, but she loved it. She was a politics wonk. It was her dream job."

Mrs. Repko pulled her arms into her sides.

"It was an awful job, the hours she worked."

Gordon said, "Mom, she loved it."

"I don't care."

I cleared my throat to bring their focus back to me.

"Did she see someone on the night it happened?"

Mrs. Repko said, "We have no idea. She worked that night. All she did was work."

"The medical examiner's report indicates she had a drink earlier that evening."

Mrs. Repko leaned forward, her face softening for the first time since I entered the room.

"It did?"

"Yes, ma'am. A drink or a glass of wine. The level was very low."

Mrs. Repko blinked. The blinking grew faster, and her eyes turned red.

"Well, I just don't know. How could we know? When she was here, we knew, but not after. I never saw why she had to have that apartment, working right downtown like she did. If she hadn't taken that damned place none of this would have happened."

Gordon spoke softly.

"She was twenty-six years old, Mom."

"Oh, you shut up. Just ... please."

She squinched her eyes and waved her hand as if trying to brush away something that could not be brushed. It was easy to see her making that same move a hundred times a day in a terrible endless loop. Her daughter's death came down to the apartment, to growing up and moving away because if she had stayed home her parents could have protected her.

Mr. Repko suddenly blurted out Debra's apartment address and the name of the manager, a man named Toler Agazzi, but Mrs. Repko's pain filled the room and everyone in it like radiant heat. The sons all stared at the floor. Mr. Repko couldn't look at his wife. I stared at Debra's portrait. The picture had probably been taken when she was a senior in high school. She was an attractive girl with clean features and smart eyes.

I cleared my throat and shifted. I wanted Mrs. Repko to see me looking at her daughter. I wanted her to know that her daughter was real to me. When I knew she was staring at me, I looked at her.

"What about her girlfriends, Mrs. Repko? I'll bet Debra had a lot of close friends. She probably has friends she's been friends with all the way back to grade school."

Mrs. Repko glanced at the picture, then me. She wet her lips, then we were both looking at the picture. Here they were, the Repkos, upscale and educated, as close as you could come to a Norman Rockwell family portrait except that one of them had been murdered. Scratch Debra from the painting. Draw Xs over her eyes.

Her mother said, "Yes. Yes, she did. The sweetest girls."

"Could you give me their names and numbers? I might like to talk to them."

"All right. Of course I could."

And this time Mrs. Repko didn't tense in that horrible way when she answered.

I said, "When it first happened, did Darcy and Maddux take anything from her apartment?"

Mr. Repko adjusted his pants again, thinking, then nodded.

"They took her computer and her phone, I think, and a few other things."

"They took her hard line or a cell?"

"Well, the cell was in her purse, so they already had it. She wasn't robbed, you know; everything was still in her purse, even her money. But she had a cordless in the apartment. They gave me a receipt. I have it, if you want."

"That would help. Also, if you have Debra's phone bills I'd like to see them."

"We have them. I kept everything in a file."

Mr. Repko left to get the file, so I turned back to Mrs. Repko.

"Did the police return the items they took from her apartment?"

Mrs. Repko nodded.

"Detective Maddux brought back some things."

"He bring back her phone, too?"

Mrs. Repko suddenly stood, with her sons straightening as if she might suddenly tip over.

"Here, I'll show you," she said. "You probably want to see, so let me show you. I want you to see what you've done."

Michael glanced at Gordon, then lowered his voice again.

"Go get Dad."

18

MRS. REPKO didn't wait for her sons or her husband. She pulled me through the house to a girly room with frills and collages Debra had probably made during high school. I went in with her, but Michael and Dennis stopped at the door.

The room was immaculate; the bed tightly made, the pillows fluffed, the desk neat and waiting to be used. The room was small, but neatly decorated with a teenage girl's furniture and bright curtains. The only items that seemed out of place were a large cardboard box against the wall and an overstuffed chair covered with a zebra fabric.

Mrs. Repko went to the chair.

"Most of the furniture at her apartment was rented, so it went back to the company. But she bought this chair, god knows why, this ugly thing, so we kept it."

Mrs. Repko ran her hand over the fabric, then gripped it hard, digging her fingers in as if she was hanging on for her life. She heaved once as her eyes filled, and Michael and Dennis almost knocked me over as they went to her. They took her arms as she shuddered, and gently led her from the room, Michael's soft voice in her ear.

"C'mon, Mama. You have to make that list for Mr. Cole. Let's make his list."

Mr. Repko appeared with an envelope as they helped her away. He said something after them I didn't hear, then gave me the envelope.

"The last month, like you wanted. Got the cell in here and the one from the apartment. This is what I gave the police. The receipt they gave me when they took her things is in here, too."

He had made copies of the bills for the police. He had gone through the numbers, noting those he recognized and which were personal or job related, and then he had called each number to ask who it was and how they knew his daughter. He had made handwritten notes in the margins. The police had asked him to do this, and I would have asked the same. The receipt showed that the police had taken—

(1) Apple laptop computer
(1) Panasonic 5.8 GHz cordless phone
(1) Samsung cell phone
(1) red leather address book
(1) blue checkbook
(assorted) papers

The papers would have been bank statements,

phone bills, and any notes or scribbles they found. The receipt was signed *Det. R. Darcy.*

I gestured at the desk and the boxes.

"These are the things Darcy and Maddux returned?"

"Some of it, yes. They returned whatever they took, those items there on the receipt. Most of these things we packed up ourselves."

"How about Bastilla and Munson? Did they take anything?"

Mr. Repko thought for a moment.

"No. The criminalist was back here, but the detectives mostly stayed out in the front with us. The boys were back here, keeping an eye on things."

"This is when Bastilla and Munson were telling you about Byrd."

"That's right."

"So it was an informational visit. They didn't ask any questions."

"A few, I guess. They wanted to know the same things you and the other detectives asked about. I think they were making conversation until the criminalist finished."

"That's probably it."

The box held a few assorted paperbacks and magazines, and some pots and pans Debra had probably bought for when she wanted to cook. Her computer was back on her desk here at home just where it had been before she moved out, and her cell phone was in the little change dish where she had probably always kept it. Mrs. Repko had hung Debra's clothes and returned her toiletries and makeup to her bathroom. They had put everything back in its place as if she had never left. It was so sad I wanted to cry.

I searched the box and desk, then went to the closet and studied the clothes. She hadn't been wearing any of these things when she was murdered. Everything in the closet had been safely back at her apartment, so it made no sense to search for fibers unless Bastilla and Munson believed someone else was involved.

I said, "Lots of clothes. It must have taken the criminalist a long time."

"He was back here for a long time."

"You were talking with the detectives all that time?"

"That's right. It was very emotional for us."

"I'm sure. I'm curious, Mr. Repko—did Bastilla and Munson ask about anything, other than informing you about Byrd?"

"You mean about Debra?"

"Yes, sir. About Debra. All that time you were talking, I'm sure they had questions."

He thought some more.

"Men. Boyfriends. That kind of thing. They asked about her job."

"At Leverage?"

"Who she liked, who her friends were, if she mentioned anyone. That kind of thing. I don't think we were very much help. I didn't see what it had to do with this man, Byrd."

"So they were interested in Leverage?"

"I guess you could say that, but like I said, I think they were making conversation—"

Then he frowned as a thought occurred to him.

"Well, there was the one thing, but I don't know if this is what you mean—"

"What's that?"

"Detective Bastilla wanted the guest registry from the burial service. They wanted to make a copy of it."

"Was she suggesting Byrd might have come to Debra's burial?"

"It seems unlikely, don't you think, considering?"

I didn't tell him I thought the idea of Lionel Byrd attending her funeral was absurd.

"That's an interesting notion, Mr. Repko. Could I see it?"

"They haven't returned it yet. When she returns it, would you still like to see it?"

"Yes, sir. That would be good."

He walked me back to the living room. The brothers looked up as if they thought I was going to announce the big breakthrough, but all I could do was tell them I would call with any developments. Mrs. Repko was not with them, but Michael handed me a short list of names and numbers. When Mr. Repko showed me to the door, Michael started to follow, but Mr. Repko stopped him.

"I'll walk Mr. Cole to the door. I'd like a word with him alone."

Michael met my eyes, and I followed his father out.

When we reached the entry, Mr. Repko hesitated before he opened the door.

He said, "I really don't know what to say to you."

"There's nothing to say."

He stared at the floor, then straightened as if it took an enormous effort. He studied my face. His boys had marked me up pretty good.

"Michael told me what happened. I guess you could have had them arrested. I imagine you can still sue us."

"I don't know what you're talking about."

He looked away again, as if the weight of maintaining the contact added to his burden and he had to drop it before continuing.

"Those first few weeks, all I thought about was what I would do when the police found him. All those terrible fantasies you have, shooting him at his trial, hiring a mobster to kill him if they sent him to prison."

"Yes, sir."

"Then, when they didn't, I was so scared he would get away with it, and then they did, but now—"

He trailed off, and I could see the weight of his pain crushing him—his face sagged, his shoulders slumped, his back bent. It was awful to see, but I had seen worse and would see worse again.

"I'm sorry for what the boys did, Mr. Cole. I would not have allowed it. Please let me pay for any damages."

"I'd better get going, Mr. Repko."

I left him without looking at him or saying anything more. I walked down his lovely drive and into the lovely street, and stood by my car, wondering why Connie Bastilla would want the funeral registry. Murderers often attended their victims' funerals, and sometimes left flowers or cards. It was possible Bastilla checked the registry for Byrd's name as a pro forma part of her investigation, like dotting an *i* or crossing a *t*, but it was also possible she was checking for a different signature—someone whose DNA was currently an unidentified blind sample in anonymous tests.

I was still thinking about it when a grey Crown Victoria eased up the street and took forever to reach me. It idled to a stop, and two men in sunglasses stared at me. The passenger and the driver were both in their early thirties with short dark hair and ties but no jackets. They wore short-sleeved shirts and the flat, empty faces that came with having to wear bad clothes while riding around in a bad car. The passenger's window rolled down.

I said, "You're either cops or the Men in Black. Which is it?"

The passenger held up his badge, then tipped it toward the backseat.

"I'm Darcy. He's Maddux. Let's talk about Debra Repko."

I didn't want to get in their car.

"So talk. I can hear you."

Darcy glanced in his side-view like someone might

be behind him. Maddux leaned across his partner to see me.

"You're Cole, right? The dude who got off Lionel Byrd?"

"Tell you what, Maddux—how about you kiss my ass?"

"We don't think Byrd killed her. Now get in, and let's talk about it."

I got in, and we talked.

19

MADDUX PULLED into the shade of an enormous elm, but left the engine running with the AC on high. Darcy was the larger of the two, with fleshy hands and the slow moves of a man who thought things through. Maddux was different. He flicked and fluttered like a man wound tight by a grudge. Once we were parked, they hooked their elbows over the top of the front seat, propping themselves sideways. Darcy faced me, but Maddux glanced everywhere as if he was worried someone might see us.

Darcy said, "Nice set of lumps there, bro. Those brothers are something, aren't they?"

"It's an acne flare-up."

"Sure. Mrs. Repko called us this morning. She wanted us to do something about you."

"So this is you, doing something?"

Maddux stopped squirming long enough to glare at me.

"This is us sticking our necks out. One day we're

ordered to give up our work, a week later, Marx and his asshats clear seven cases."

"Maybe the asshats are better than you."

"And maybe they pulled Byrd out their ass."

Darcy and Maddux were watching me. We were under an elm tree in Pasadena, and they shouldn't have been here and they shouldn't have been talking to me. They were probably detective-twos, but they probably hadn't been on the bureau for more than six or eight years. They might be guys on their way up or they might be guys who had already topped out, or maybe they were working for Marx. If they weren't, they were hanging out over the edge just by talking with me.

I said, "You have a problem with what the task force is saying, you should take it up with them."

"We tried. They told us to eat it."

Darcy smiled at his partner.

"Actually, they told us the case was no longer our concern. We didn't like that. Then they refused to return our case files. We liked that even less."

"So this is what we call an off-the-record conversation?"

"Something like that. Either way, we don't think they should have closed the case."

Their curious cop gaze rested on me, content to wait beneath the elm for the world to turn and the seasons to change and the sun to cool.

I said, "What if I told you the case isn't closed? What if I said the task force was here pulling fibers off the girl's clothes at the same time Marx went public about Byrd?"

Darcy's eyes narrowed to tiny slits.

"I'd tell you to keep talking. I'd say if we like what you're doing, we might be willing to help."

I walked them through Bennett first, then sketched out Byrd and what I knew of the other murders and how Debra Repko was different. I told them about Ivy Casik and the reporter who might or might not be a reporter. Darcy and Maddux knew almost nothing about Byrd or the previous five murders, but they had worked on Debra Repko's case for almost five weeks before it was taken, and were willing to tell me about it.

Debra Repko had spent the day performing her duties at Leverage Associates, then accompanied five other Leverage employees to an evening political event where she assisted with media interviews. Once the interviews ended, Debra and her supervisor, a woman named Casey Stokes, walked to their cars together. Casey Stokes was the last person known to have seen Debra Repko alive.

Darcy and Maddux caught the case the following morning, and thought they lucked into a game-winning break right away.

Darcy said, "One of the shop owners where her body was found called, saying he had a security video of the murder. We thought we had the killing on disk."

"Waitaminute—you have something on tape?"

"DVD. It was digital."

Maddux waved his hand like he was chasing away a fly.

"It was nothing. The guy rigged up a do-it-yourself surveillance kit because kids were tagging the building, only the cheap fuck set it up wrong. All he got were shadows."

"Could you see any part of the incident?"

"Not even. SID dicked around with it for a couple of weeks, but said the digital information just didn't exist, so Darcy here gave it to his brother-in-law."

"My brother-in-law works for a CGI house in Hollywood. You know what that is?"

"Sure."

Computer-generated images were a mainstay of Hollywood special effects.

"He offered to take a look, but it was a long shot. By that time, we had other lines—"

Maddux interrupted.

"The manager at her apartment house looked pretty good, a dude named Agazzi. I'm all over this guy. I still think he's good for it, and he could have gone into her apartment any time he wanted. If Bastilla and Munson were out here looking for fibers, they might have been looking for him."

Darcy shook his head.

"Maddux and I don't agree. He likes Agazzi, but one of Repko's neighbors at the apartment, a woman named Sheila Evers, told us Repko was seeing a married man."

Maddux shook his head.

"*If* there's a boyfriend. Personally, I think the broad made up that stuff. We couldn't find anyone who confirmed a boyfriend."

I showed them the names Mrs. Repko had given me.

"You check with her friends?"

Darcy glanced at the names, then passed it to Maddux.

"Yeah. They didn't know anything. Said Debra never mentioned a boyfriend or lover or seeing a married guy, but here's this good-looking young woman, it's easy to think we're talking about someone she met at work."

It was reasonable, especially considering the amount of time Mrs. Repko complained her daughter had worked. If Debra was always working, then her only opportunity to meet men was through work.

I said, "Mr. Repko told me Bastilla and Munson were asking about Leverage. They made out they were just making conversation, but they were asking about the people Debra worked with."

Darcy and Maddux traded another glance.

Darcy said, "When we talked to Leverage about Debra's evening, they were cooperative. Then the boyfriend angle presented itself. When we told them we wanted to interview the male clients she worked with, they hit the brakes."

"They wouldn't tell you who she worked with?"

"They didn't have a problem letting us talk to the male employees at Leverage, but they dug in hard when it came to naming their clients. We pushed, and we were told to lay off."

"Their clients are politicians, Cole. We got a call saying the brass would review the matter and get back to us."

"The brass. Parker Center?"

"It came through Parker, but who knows where it started? Couple of weeks later, Leverage got back to us, but they basically chose who we could talk to."

"You think Leverage is hiding something?"

Maddux smirked automatically, but Darcy was more considered.

"I don't know, Cole. Maybe they just didn't want their clients linked to a murder investigation. I get that. But most people are murdered by people they know. A wife gets murdered, the first person you look at is the husband. Doesn't matter if he's the greatest guy in the world, you look at him because that's how it works. You clear the people who were the closest to the vic first, then work your way out. We weren't allowed to clear Leverage."

Maddux said, "Agazzi was close. He lived right down the hall."

Darcy sighed, tired of hearing about Agazzi. He had probably been sighing like that for as long as they were partners.

"We know she left the dinner event alone, but we don't know if she stopped on her way home. It's possible she picked up someone, but I'm thinking this guy was waiting for her."

"Because they went for a walk."

"That's right. If she asked some dude back to her place, they're going inside. So I'm thinking she got home and found someone waiting. Then one or the other of them says let's take a walk. Probably the male because he already has it in his head to kill her and wants to lead her in the right direction. There was no reason for them to walk south that time of night. Maddux and I made the walk, man. All the action is north on Melrose. I think she knew the guy, she was comfortable with him, and he led her into the kill zone."

The corner of Maddux's mouth curled.

"You see this woman going for a stroll with a creep like Lionel Byrd?"

I smiled.

"No, Maddux. I don't."

"Which means if Byrd did the deed, he stalked her or the whole thing was a chance encounter. If you buy either one, you have to buy she went for a walk that night by herself, in the bad direction with no open shops and nothing but darkness, in heels. In heels, for Chrissake. That's bullshit."

Darcy stared at his partner as if he was thinking it through for the thousandth time, then finally shrugged.

"That's where we were when they pulled the plug, Cole. We believe she knew the killer. I believe she was seeing someone on the sly. If we were still on it, we'd be all over Leverage. Especially now with what you've told us."

The three of us sat in their car under the elm in

silence. I thought through everything and tried to put their information in some kind of usable order.

"What happened with the video?"

"Don't know. Some task force douche picked it up before my brother-in-law could get to it."

"Why'd they pick it up?"

Darcy shrugged.

"Don't know."

"What did they do with it?"

"Don't know. We asked, but they wouldn't tell us."

Maddux said, "They wouldn't tell us anything, Cole."

Darcy checked the time, then nudged his partner's arm.

"That's it. Let's take him back."

Maddux dropped the car into gear and pulled a slow U-turn. We headed back toward the Repkos'.

Darcy still had his elbow hooked over the seat, staring at nothing. I could see the passing houses and trees crawl across his sunglasses like a film strip. It was a nice film. It looked like the American dream.

I said, "Why'd you guys bring me in?"

Maddux glanced in the rearview. Darcy came out of his film.

"The Repkos deserve to know what happened to their daughter."

"Meaning you've taken the case as far as you can."

"Man says we're off, we're off. You, on the other hand, can do whatever you want."

Maddux glanced again.

"I just wanna fuck that prick Marx."

Darcy unhooked his arm.

"That, too."

They dropped me outside the Repkos' home, then melted through a tunnel of dappled shade.

20

DARCY AND Maddux had been cut out of the loop. Poitras, Bobby McQue, and Starkey had been cut, and Chen and the criminalists had been forced to work in the dark. People who should have been collaborators with Marx and his task force had been treated as if they couldn't be trusted. I wondered what Marx didn't trust them with.

I sat in my car outside the Repko house, thinking about the video and why Marx pulled it before Darcy's brother-in-law finished trying to recover whatever was recorded. LAPD had a long history of using local special-effects houses to examine and enhance film and video. If you had state-of-the-art specialists available, it made sense to use them. Marx pulling the DVD bothered me because SID was good, and if they said the DVD was junk, then it was probably junk, which was why Marx's play didn't make sense. If the DVD was useless, there was nothing to lose by letting a cutting-edge CGI house see what it could do and everything to gain.

I paged through my notes until I found Lindo's number, then gave him a call. He didn't seem as nervous as when we spoke before. Maybe because he was back to investigating bomb-kook conspiracies.

He said, "What's up, Cole?"

"Do you know what happened to the security video of Debra Repko's murder?"

The surprise in his voice was clear.

"There was a video?"

"One of the shopkeepers where Repko was murdered turned in a recording. How could you not know about this?"

Lindo was silent for a moment.

"Waitaminute—maybe I heard something. It was blank or something was wrong with it?"

"That's the one. A CGI house was working on it when you guys took over."

"Didn't SID say it was no good?"

"The case dicks took a shot with a CGI house. Marx pulled it before the CGI people finished. I'm trying to find out what he did with it."

"No idea, man. Like I told you, my team worked on the book. Wasn't in the book, I don't know about it."

"Who worked on Repko?"

"That was Bastilla and Munson. Yeah, I'm pretty sure Munson was on it."

Munson again.

"Who's Munson?"

"One of the Homicide Special guys, up there with Bastilla. He and Marx go back. I think they used to work together."

"Can you ask them what happened with the disk?"

"Uh-uh, man, no way. I'm not going there. They were the inner circle."

"Just tell them you were wondering about it. No big deal."

"Cole, you don't get this at all. Those people were the people who gave us our orders, and one of our orders was to mind our own business. I ask about this DVD, they'll wonder why. We weren't even allowed to ask about each other's work when we were working together."

"I thought Marx gave the orders."

"Our work went up to the senior supervising detectives, and they brought it to Marx. That's why we called them the inner circle. You had to go through them to get to Marx."

"So each team only saw its own part of the case, but the guys up top put it together."

"It was the only way to keep so much parallel work coordinated. Look at how much we accomplished in just a week."

"Was Crimmens part of that crew?"

"Nah. He was an add-on like me. We had a ton of people in here, man. I heard it was thirty-two people, though I couldn't say. I never met most of them."

I kept thinking about the DVD. It was a piece of

physical evidence. Like every other piece of evidence, it would have been numbered, documented, and preserved in a chain of custody. Even if it was only a useless piece of plastic, its location and uselessness would be a matter of written record.

"Okay. Forget asking. How about you take a peek in their evidence file and tell me what it says?"

"No way. I can't."

"Thirty seconds and you're gone. Just tell me what Marx did with it."

"I physically cannot. They keep the files in an evidence room. It's locked. We could only sign out material specific to our assignment. Since I didn't work on Repko, I don't have access to that material. One of the commanders would have to sign off."

"Don't you find that extreme, Lindo?"

"I find it anal and corporate, but nobody asked me. Use your head. If this disk mattered a damn, we would have seen the video on the six o'clock news."

"It doesn't make sense they would pull it before the CGI house finished their work."

"Maybe that's *why* they pulled it, Cole. How long did that place have it and still hadn't finished? Marx or whoever probably had the FBI do an overnighter. That's what I would have done."

I didn't like it, but Lindo was making sense. The LAPD couldn't make demands on a civilian firm unless they were paying for a service, and Darcy hadn't been paying—he had leaned on his brother-in-law for a favor.

I put down the phone, then tried to decide on a game plan. The next obvious step was to pick up where Darcy and Maddux left off at Leverage, only the people at Leverage had no reason to be cooperative. If they sandbagged two LAPD detectives, they probably wouldn't even bother to return my calls.

I was still thinking about it when I noticed Michael Repko. He was standing in the front window of his house, watching me. He stood as if he had been there a while.

I called him, and watched him fish his cell from his pocket to answer. I could have walked the fifty feet up his drive, but I didn't want to face his mother again.

He said, "Was that Darcy and Maddux?"

"Yeah. Your mother called them."

"Shit, man. I didn't know."

"They told me some things I want to check out, but I'm going to need your help."

"Okay."

"I need to talk to Casey Stokes about your sister, but she's not going to talk to me if I just show up."

"Uh-huh. Sure, I understand."

"I want your father to tell her I'm working for your family. He should keep it vague. All he has to say is he and your mother have some unresolved questions. Will he do that, Michael?"

Michael raised a hand to his head. It was a gesture indicating his anxiety, and he glanced at something or someone deeper inside the house before turning back.

"I could call her. She was really nice at the funeral."

"Not you, Michael. It has to be your father. When she gets this request, she has to feel the weight of Debra's family behind it. Debra's family will be asking the questions, not me. That's the only way she will talk to me."

"I don't know. I could ask."

"He needs to do this, Michael. If I'm working for Debra's family, then I'm representing Debra. If not, they won't talk to me."

Michael stared at me with his hand on his head.

"I guess you are kinda working for us."

"Yes. I'm working for Debra."

"You aren't what I expected."

"Have him call."

"I'm sorry my mom called those guys. I didn't set you up, man."

"Tell your mother something. She was right about Darcy and Maddux. They're good guys. They did a good job for your sister."

"Do they think Byrd killed Debbie?"

It was the first time I had heard her called Debbie.

"Have your father call Casey Stokes. I'm driving there now, so let me know after he speaks with her."

"I'll try."

"One more thing. Were you and your sister close?"

"Well, sure, I guess. What do you mean by 'close'?"

"If she was seeing someone, would she have told you?"

Michael stared at me for another moment, and finally lowered his hand.

"My sister didn't share."

He was still in the window as I drove away.

21

LEVERAGE ASSOCIATES occupied two floors of an older glass building in the downtown business district, not far from City Hall. They were less than fifteen minutes from the Repkos' home in Pasadena. Michael Repko called back twenty minutes later as I circled the building.

"My dad talked to her. You're all set up."

"Okay. That's great."

"He kept it vague like you said. He told her you were working for us. He wasn't so thrilled about that, but he told her."

"This will make things easier, Michael. I'll keep you advised."

I pulled up in front of the building as I closed the phone, parked at a meter, then took the elevator up to the seventeenth floor. It was a nice floor in a nice building with tasteful, conservative decor. Steel letters fixed to the wall read LEVERAGE ASSOCIATES. I identified myself to the receptionist, told her Casey Stokes was expecting me, and took a seat to wait.

I didn't sit long. An attractive African-American woman in a grey business suit came down the hall. She offered her hand with a quick, professional smile and an expression of condolence.

"Mr. Cole, Casey Stokes. I was Debra's supervisor."

"Thank you for seeing me. The Repkos appreciate it."

"I was surprised when Mr. Repko said there were questions. I thought the case was closed."

I tried to look noncommittal.

"Something like this happens, families always have concerns. I hope you understand."

"Oh, of course. Here, we can speak in my office."

She ushered me along a hall decorated with black-and-white photographs of people and places from the city's past—the Angels Flight funicular climbing Bunker Hill, Chavez Ravine when it was goat farms and barrio housing, and William Mulholland opening the aqueduct to bring water down from the Owens Valley. Along with the historic scenes were photographs of past state and local politicians of both political parties. I didn't recognize most of them, but a few had gained national prominence and two had been elected to national office. A Who's Who of California's power elite.

Ms. Stokes was saying, "Do you know what we do here, Mr. Cole?"

"You run political campaigns."

She gave a benevolent smile, as if she was the teacher and I was slow.

"A campaign is a point-in-time event. A political career is an ongoing effort. We manage political careers."

"Ah. The wizards behind the curtain."

"Only if we're successful. We develop election strategies, but we also advise on public relations and help our clients refine or perfect their political identity."

"If I decide to be governor, you'll be my first call."

She laughed. She had a lovely laugh, and a charming, genuine manner.

A faint buzz cut through her laugh, and she took a PDA from her pocket. She glanced at the screen without breaking stride.

"Sorry—a meeting was changed. This business, everything rolls from one crisis to the next."

"I understand."

She thumbed out a reply, then slipped the PDA back into her pocket as we passed a glass-walled conference room before entering her office. Several people were in the conference room shaking hands and smiling. Beyond her office were cubicles with men and women talking on phones or texting. Most appeared to be Debra's age. One might have been Debra's replacement.

Casey Stokes offered me a seat, then went behind her desk. She laced her fingers and maintained the professional smile.

"Now, how can I help?"

"We have a few questions about some things that were brought up during the investigation."

We. The family and the ghost of Debra Repko were now in Casey Stokes's office. She seemed genuinely pained.

"When I remember that evening and what happened only a few hours later—it was awful."

"Yes, ma'am. It was. I understand you were the last person to see her."

"That's right. We attended a dinner honoring Councilman Wilts at the Bonaventure. The councilman is one of our clients."

"So you spent the entire time together?"

"More or less. Debra's job was to make sure each reporter had their five minutes with the councilman before the dinner began. Debra and I. Actually, five of us from Leverage attended, but we all had different responsibilities. Debra and I had our own segment of the evening to handle, so we were together."

"She was your assistant?"

"Debra was what we call a first-year. All our first-years work as floaters to experience the different aspects of what we do. I had Debra join me that night so she could gain experience with the media. Once the interviews were over, our job was finished. We walked out to our cars together."

"Did Debra tell you her plans for the evening?"

"No, nothing like that."

"Maybe mention she was going to meet friends or wanted to stop for a drink?"

Ms. Stokes studied me, then cocked her head.

"What does this have to do with a chance encounter with a maniac?"

"It has to do with her personal life."

Something that might have been sadness flickered in her eyes.

"Now I understand. That rumor about her seeing a married man."

"It's eating at her parents. Especially her mother."

Casey Stokes sighed, and something in her sigh made me feel bad for having said it.

"Mr. Cole, I don't know what to tell you. If Debra was seeing someone, married or otherwise, she never mentioned it to me or anyone else here at Leverage. My understanding is that this rumor started with someone at Debra's apartment building."

"Yes, ma'am, that's where it started."

"Then perhaps you should be asking that person. Debra and I only spoke about politics. She was excited by politics. She wanted to work on a national level. She might have. She was serious about her career."

Her phone rang as she finished. She glanced at her watch, then excused herself to take the call. While she was on the phone, I looked at the people in the conference room. Two men in conservative business suits were making a PowerPoint presentation to the five people who were now seated at the table. The man at the head of the table was a balding guy with a large stomach and white shirt rolled to his elbows. Everyone else was twenty years younger.

While the suits made their presentation, a young man seated beside the older man was texting on his PDA. Nobody seemed to mind. He nudged the older man, then showed him the PDA. The older man took out a PDA of his own and fired off a message. The two guys with the PowerPoint looked as if they didn't know whether to keep going or not.

Stokes put down her phone and checked her watch again.

"I'm sorry I couldn't be more help, but perhaps you'll have better luck with Debra's neighbors. Please tell her parents that, personally, I think this rumor was—and is—absurd."

She stood to show me out, but I didn't stand with her. When I didn't get up, she sat.

"I'm sorry. I don't know what more I can say."

"I'm speaking with you and not Debra's neighbors because of something we learned from the police. I feel awkward about bringing it up, but her family is in a great deal of pain. We need to clear the air."

She waited without saying anything, so I went on.

"The Repkos recently learned that when the rumor first surfaced about Debra being involved with a married man, you folks here at Leverage refused to cooperate. In fact, the detectives felt you were sandbagging them."

Her mouth drew into a knot as she tapped a perfectly manicured nail on her desk.

"That's not precisely true."

"Seems like it should be either true or not true,

Ms. Stokes. Without the 'precisely.'"

She tapped the nail again.

"You have to understand. As a first-year, Debra attended meetings with most of our clients. The police wanted to talk to these people. I understood that. We all understood. But our clients are people who live their lives in the public eye, and here were these officers wanting to question them about a young woman most of them probably didn't remember. Just being questioned could be used against them by their enemies."

"It was a murder investigation. Questions have to be asked."

Ms. Stokes shifted uncomfortably.

"And those questions were asked. You can assure the Repkos we cooperated."

"Stonewalling the investigation for two weeks doesn't sound like cooperation."

"No one here stonewalled. We simply went over the heads of the original detectives and consulted with the command structure. They understood our concerns."

I stared at her.

"The command structure where?"

"The police. We reviewed our concerns with Deputy Chief Marx. He made what could have been—and was—an uncomfortable situation much more tolerable."

"You mean the task force?"

"No, no. This was during the original investigation.

Chief Marx personally ensured that a thorough investigation was conducted, and had our full cooperation. He even interviewed some of the clients himself."

I stared at her so hard she frowned.

"Mr. Cole?"

"Chief Marx oversaw the investigation?"

"That's right. The chief is one of our clients."

I tried to smile. I tried to look as if this was the best news the family could hear.

"Well. That changes things."

Casey Stokes looked relieved.

"I'm so sorry for this confusion."

"Of course. The family will be glad to hear it."

"Please. Tell the Repkos to call me. If they have any questions at all, they can call me."

I nodded. I smiled.

"So. The chief is going into politics?"

"He's considering it. We believe he can be positioned to fill Councilman Wilts's seat when the councilman retires next year. The councilman is quite a fan of Chief Marx."

I smiled even wider.

"How could he be anything else?"

"So please assure Mr. and Mrs. Repko the police had our full cooperation. We simply worked at a level where discretion could be guaranteed."

Her PDA buzzed again. She glanced at the message, then stood.

"I really do have to go now, Mr. Cole. It's been awful for all of us, but I know it's been worse for the Repkos.

Please tell them we would never have done anything to hamper the investigation, and we didn't."

"I'll tell them, Ms. Stokes. Thank you."

Her PDA buzzed once more, and now she touched a button to make it stop. Everyone at Leverage seemed to have them.

"Does everyone here carry one of those things?"

"It's how we stay in touch. One of the perks, but also one of the pains. We carry them twenty-four/ seven."

"Did Debra have one?"

Across the hall, the meeting in the conference room was breaking up. The young guy who had shown his PDA to the older guy was still texting.

Ms. Stokes said, "She did. All of our associates and principals have them. Leverage provides them."

"You saw her with it that night?"

She gave a halfhearted shrug.

"Of course. We used them to coordinate the interviews."

Her PDA buzzed again, but this time she didn't look at it. She touched my arm to herd me toward the door.

"One more thing about this rumor, and I hope her family will find some solace in this. I can't definitively say Debra wasn't involved with someone, but she never hinted at such a thing, or acted the way young women act when they're infatuated. She never mentioned anything like that to me or the other first-years. I know because I asked them, and so did Chief Marx."

Casey Stokes walked me out, but did not say good-bye. I didn't say good-bye, either. I was too busy thinking about Marx.

22

WHEN I reached my car, I shuffled through the papers Mr. Repko had given me. Among them was the receipt Darcy and Maddux provided when they returned the items they had taken to examine. A cell phone and a laptop were on the list, but not a PDA, and I didn't recall seeing it at the Repkos' home.

I found Darcy's card, called him, and asked if they recovered a PDA with Debra's body.

He said, "Sure. It was still in her purse. We gave it back to the family."

"Not her cell phone. She also had a PDA."

"Like a BlackBerry?"

"Yeah. Did you find one?"

"Hang on—"

He spoke to someone in the background, then came back.

"No, nothing like that. We had her cell. Maddux says it was a Samsung."

"I just left Casey Stokes. Leverage gives out PDAs to their associates. Debra used hers that night at the dinner."

"All we had was the Samsung. We ran the call log on the cell and the hard line in her apartment. If we had the PDA, we would've run that, too. Maybe her family has it."

"They would have it only if you gave it to them. It should have been on her body, in her car, or in her apartment."

"I don't know what to tell you. I know you're thinking the killer nabbed it, but how can we know that or prove it? She might have lost the damn thing."

"Hang on, Darcy. Think about this. If Leverage provided the PDA, they probably take care of the bills."

"I know where you're going, but there isn't anything I can do. If this case was mine I'd subpoena their call records and hit up the provider for her email and text messages. But this isn't my case. It's Marx's case, and he closed it."

"Did you know Marx is a client at Leverage?"

Darcy was silent.

"Darcy?"

"You're kidding."

"When Leverage was freezing you guys out, they were talking with Marx behind the scenes. He walked them through the investigation to keep their clients out of the headlines."

"That sonofabitch."

"Uh-huh."

"That's why the pressure came down for us to back off. Nice of him to tell us."

"Marx's name never came up?"

"Not until now. Maddux is going to shit."

I called Michael Repko next. Michael remembered that his sister had a PDA, but didn't know where it was. He agreed to ask his parents and brothers. I was still talking to him when my phone beeped with a call from Pat Kyle. I finished with Michael, then switched over to Pat.

She said, "Am I the best or what?"

"I've been saying that for years, and not just to annoy your husband."

"A little annoyance is good for him. You have something to write with?"

"I do. You find Tomaso?"

"He's with a commercial agency called Figg-Harris. Figg tried to reach him to see if it would be okay to give out his contact info, but the kid hasn't returned his calls. I had to pressure him."

"I get it. Give me the stats."

"Okay. This is his cell."

She read off an 818 phone number and an address in North Hollywood. I thanked her, then called Angel's number, but didn't have any better luck than his agent. Angel's phone rang five times before a message picked up.

"Hey, this is Andy, the next big thing. Leave the 411 and I'll get back. Peace."

Andy. The next big thing.

I left my 411, but didn't wait for the next big thing to get back to me. I headed north toward the valley.

The breathtaking clarity we enjoyed during the Santa Anas had vanished when the winds died. The air, now sleeping, was heavy with haze. A misty shawl blurred the Hollywood Sign and the skyscrapers lining the Wilshire Corridor appeared to be in a fog.

It was almost one o'clock when I dropped off the freeway at Universal to hit Henry's Tacos for lunch. Four tacos later, I turned onto a neat residential street wedged in the flats between Toluca Lake and Studio City. The main house was a small Craftsman with a large porch and a For Sale sign in the front yard. A narrow drive ran past the main house to a converted garage in the rear.

I parked on the street and walked down the drive.

The guesthouse had once been the garage. The double-wide garage door had been replaced by French doors with sun curtains pulled across the doors for privacy. A patio table and chairs sat on the driveway outside the doors, shielded from the sun by an overhead trellis matted with crimson bougainvillea. I rapped on the glass.

"Angel? It's Elvis Cole."

Angel didn't answer.

I rapped again, then stepped off the patio into the yard. Two windows and a door were cut into the side of the guesthouse, and had probably been there before the garage was converted. The backyard was hidden from the neighbors by a chain-link fence overgrown with trumpet vines and more bougainvillea. Violet trumpets drooped from the vines and fought with the bougainvillea for attention.

The side door was locked, and more curtains covered the windows. I returned to the French doors, knocked again, then decided to talk to his landlords. If nothing else, I could ask them to let Angel know I had come by.

I went back along the drive, climbed onto the front porch, and rang the bell. No one answered at the main house, either. I cupped my face to the window, and was able to see the living room, dining room, and part of a hall. The furnishings were gone. The owners or tenants had already moved. Maybe Tomaso had moved out with them and hadn't bothered to tell his agent, but the odds of that were small. Struggling actors would live in their agents' pants if they could.

I went back to the guesthouse to leave a note, but after I wrote it I decided to call Angel again. He might be around the corner, but he could have gone to Vegas with friends and might not be back for weeks.

When his cell phone rang I heard it inside his house. I lowered my phone and listened. The ringing went on for five rings, and then the ringing stopped. Angel's message was playing in my phone.

I said, "Angel?"

Nothing.

I put away my phone, then knocked again. After I knocked I tried the handles. The first set of French doors was locked, but the second set opened when I pulled the lever.

The guesthouse was set up like a studio apartment with a cheap dining table, a TV, and a pull-out couch. A cell phone, wallet, and keys were on the table. Books on acting and directing were stacked on the floor, and unframed posters of modern crime films like *The Big Lebowski* and *Gone Baby Gone* were tacked to the wall. The furnishings were spare, but Angel had filled his apartment with the stuff of an aspiring actor, only now he would never see it again.

Angel Tomaso was facedown on the couch with the side of his head so dark with crusted blood it was black in the bad light. He was wearing a T-shirt and shorts. His bare arms and legs were purple where the blood had settled. Someone had written on the wall in uneven red letters. The message read: *I LOVED U.*

I listened, but knew Angel was alone. The tiny apartment was still, with only a single fly circling the body. In the time I stood in the door, more flies joined the first.

I stepped inside and went to his body. The couch beneath his head was rich with dark blood, and the ceiling above the body showed a thin splatter trail from the rise of the weapon. The side of his head behind his right ear had been struck with something heavy more than one time. Whatever had been used to kill him was no longer present.

The message appeared to have been written in blood, but when I examined it more closely I realized it had been written in lipstick.

The windows and doors showed no sign of forced

entry. His apartment appeared in order, and did not look as if it had been searched. I was careful not to leave fingerprints or disturb the scene. His wallet contained sixty-two dollars, a Visa card, and a Master-Card. A letter from his aunt was unopened on the kitchenette counter. I felt sad when I saw it, thinking he should have opened it when he had the chance.

I studied the body and the blood patterns for a while, then stepped outside to call the police. I sat at the little table beneath the bougainvillea and breathed the good air that didn't smell like the air inside with the body. I should have closed the French doors, but didn't. He had been alone long enough. I thought about Angel's aunt, and knew it would be hard on her and the rest of his family in Austin. It was always hard that way.

I was still sitting there when two uniformed officers came through the picket gate, walked up the drive, and saw me. Then they saw Angel's body through the open doors and told me to raise my hands.

23

"TAKE IT easy. I was just calling you guys."

The older officer said, "I've heard that a thousand times."

Their names were Giardi and Silbermann, Giardi being a senior P-III training officer. Silbermann was a first-year boot, still on probation, and was big on shouting instructions. Giardi told him to settle down. Both of them eyed my face, but neither asked about the bruises.

I identified myself, told them I was armed and why I was present. They didn't handcuff or arrest me, but they checked my ID, took my pistol, and the three of us went to the French doors without entering.

Silbermann said, "Yikes."

"His name was Angel Tomaso, also known as Andy Thom. He was a witness in a murder case three years ago."

Giardi said, "You shouldn't talk without a lawyer."

"I'm not admitting to anything, Giardi, I'm just

telling you. I've been trying to find him. Connie Bastilla down at Robbery-Homicide knows about it."

"She knows about him being dead?"

"She knows I've been trying to find him. As of last week, she was trying to find him, too."

Silbermann checked out my face again.

"You get in a fight with him before you killed him?"

Giardi told him to stop. He called in the situation, then walked me out to the radio car to wait for the roll-outs. Silbermann stayed at the guesthouse, guarding the scene in case anyone shot their way past me and Giardi.

I said, "How did you guys know to come here?"

"Anonymous male caller reported a DB. Was that you?"

"Not me. Like I said, I was about to call when you guys arrived."

"Save it for the detectives. They're on the way."

Two more radio cars arrived, one with a sergeant-supervisor who ordered the street blocked off, and then the detectives arrived. One of the detectives was Crimmens.

Giardi met them on the drive, then pointed my way. Crimmens never took his eyes off me as Giardi gave his report. When Giardi finished, he took Crimmens's partner back to the guesthouse, but Crimmens came to me. He grinned when he saw my face.

"What happened, Cole, you mouth off to the wrong guy?"

"I thought you were downtown."

"No more task force. They sent me back to North Hollywood. Is that really Tomaso back there?"

"See for yourself."

"You kill him?"

"He was dead when I got here."

"When did you get here?"

"Five minutes before Giardi and Silbermann."

"We'll see."

"Too bad I didn't get here last week when you and Bastilla couldn't find him. He might still be alive."

"Sit tight, shitbird. You're going to be here a while."

Crimmens left to see the body as Silbermann returned and slid in beside me.

Silbermann said, "Did you kill that guy?"

"Of course not."

"I think you killed him."

"Let me ask you a question. When was the body reported?"

"Forget it, murderer. I'm not telling you anything."

Silbermann didn't speak to me again for twenty minutes. During that time, Crimmens and his partner returned to their car. Crimmens spent most of that time on his phone until the coroner investigator arrived, then the three of them went back to the body. Crimmens almost immediately reappeared as a command-level black-and-white arrived and parked at the mouth of the drive. When the command car opened, Bastilla and Marx got out.

Silbermann's eyes widened and he craned around for a better look.

"Wow, that's a deputy chief."

"He puts on his pants just like you."

"You're retarded."

Marx glanced at me only once, then turned away as another unmarked D-ride pulled up. A tall, thin detective in his mid-fifties got out of the new car and joined Marx in the drive. They traded a few words, both of them glancing at me, then hooked up with Bastilla and Crimmens. The new guy was probably Munson. I wanted to wave and smile, but common sense got the best of me.

Marx and Munson eventually disappeared down the drive, but Bastilla and Crimmens came over to me.

I said, "For a task force that no longer exists, you people spend a lot of time together."

Bastilla stopped on the sidewalk and crossed her arms.

"How did you find him?"

"Aren't you going to smart off about my face? Everyone else does."

"Everyone else probably cares. How did you find him?"

"His former roommate gave me a number for Tomaso's family in Texas. The family told me he moved back here to resume acting. His talent agent gave me the address."

I left Pat Kyle out of it and would not involve her without her permission.

"Did you speak with him?"

"He was dead when I got here."

"Before he was dead, Cole. Did you have a conversation with him before he was murdered?"

"I only learned he was here a couple of hours ago. I called, but all I got was his message, so I came over. I didn't know he was dead. I had no reason to believe he was in danger."

"You remove anything from his apartment?"

"C'mon, Bastilla. You think I was looking for souvenirs?"

Silbermann jumped in.

"The door was open when we arrived. He was right there by the door and all by himself. It's a solid burglary collar."

Bastilla said, "You're Silbermann?"

"Yes, ma'am. Giardi and I arrived on the scene at—"

Bastilla held up her hand.

"You can leave now, Officer. Thanks for your assistance."

Silbermann looked crestfallen, but slid out of the car.

I said, "Why are you and Marx here? I thought the case was cleared."

"What makes you think this poor kid has anything to do with the case?"

I stared at her, but her face had been composed to show nothing.

"Because you and Crimmens were looking for him and now he's dead. Because he was a principal in the

Bennett case, and now we can't talk to him."

"Did you see what was written on his wall?"

"Are you kidding me?"

"The evidence indicates a lovers' quarrel. Did you enter his apartment?"

"So a man we were all looking for last week turns up dead, and you're good with a lovers' quarrel?"

"Did you go in or not?"

"No. I could see he was dead from the door."

If I admitted entering the apartment, she would have a green light to book me.

"Did you disturb the evidence in any way?"

"How could I disturb the evidence if I didn't go in?"

"Do you know or suspect who did this?"

"Probably the same person who killed those seven women. What happened with Ivy Casik? Did you follow up on the man she saw visiting Byrd?"

Bastilla pursed her lips, then shook her head as if she felt sorry for me.

"You're a screwup all the way around, Cole."

"What does that mean?"

Bastilla stepped away and nodded at Crimmens. Crimmens made a little finger wave, telling me to get out of the car.

"C'mon, let's go."

Crimmens turned me around and pushed me against the car.

"Assume the position."

"What in hell are you doing?"

Bastilla said, "Making sure you didn't remove anything from the crime scene. If you refuse to cooperate, you'll be placed under arrest for unlawful entry, burglary, and suspicion of murder."

Crimmens said, "Don't be slow, Mr. Thirty. Just go along."

Crimmens went through my pockets, placing my wallet, cell phone, thirty cents, and a handkerchief on the trunk of the patrol car. He also took my notepad and a black uni-ball pen. While Crimmens searched me, Bastilla slid into the backseat where I had been sitting. She ran her hand along the seam in the seat, then searched the floorboards and under the front seat. She inspected anyplace I could have hidden something if I had something I wanted to hide, then backed out of the car. I wondered what she was looking for.

"Check his socks and shoes. Make sure he didn't put anything in his shorts."

"Why don't you check me yourself, Bastilla? Crimmens might miss my crotch pocket."

Bastilla turned red, but didn't respond.

Marx and Munson returned and stood with Bastilla on the sidewalk while Crimmens searched me. The three of them spoke quietly, then Munson went to his car, making a call on his cell. Marx and Bastilla turned back to us as Crimmens finished.

"He's clean, boss."

"Have you questioned him yet?"

"No, sir."

"Leave us for now, but don't go far. You can have him when I'm finished."

Crimmens immediately joined his partner and the CI on the driveway. Silbermann and Giardi stood with them, too.

I said, "So much for your case being closed, Marx."

Marx studied me with his mouth folded into a hard crease, then put his hands on his hips.

"You're a pathetic excuse, Cole. You should be ashamed of yourself."

"For doing your job?"

His jaw clenched, but he kept going.

"For destroying what little peace of mind the Repkos have. Mrs. Repko told me you assaulted her sons. What in hell is wrong with you?"

"Speak to Mr. Repko. He might tell a different story."

"What's your endgame here? You trying to drum up a fee by getting the families to hire you?"

"I'm trying to drum up votes so I can run for office. I need the money to hire Leverage Associates. Would you recommend their work?"

Bastilla said, "Take it easy, Cole."

"C'mon, Marx, I'm asking if they're any good. I know you work with them. Did they tell you to close the case on Byrd so you could make a big splash on the news?"

Marx turned bright red.

"You arrogant prick."

"Do the Repkos know you interfered with their

daughter's investigation to protect your handlers?"

Bastilla said, "Cole, get back in the car."

I should have gotten back into the car, but I was angry and looking for a reason to knock Marx on his ass.

The driveway and the front of the house were crawling with police. Neighbors in the surrounding houses had come out to see what was going on, and a reporter from the *Times* had shown up. Marx took one step back, then looked around until he spotted Crimmens in the driveway.

"Detective, get over here."

Crimmens trotted over.

"This man is a suspect in the murder of Angel Tomaso. Place him under arrest and take him to your station for questioning."

I said, "Fuck you, Marx."

Crimmens broke into a ragged smile, but Bastilla took Marx by the upper arm.

"Chief, a word, please."

Marx pulled away and stalked over to Munson, and Bastilla went after him. Crimmens stepped into my face and stood with his nose less than two inches away, still with the ragged grin.

"Resist. I'm begging you. Resist."

"I know what you told the Repkos, Crimmens. When this is over, we're going to talk."

Crimmens laughed as he spun me around. He whispered in my ear as he clipped on the cuffs.

"This is better than sex. I'm getting off right now, Cole."

They put me back in the patrol car. Crimmens left to find his partner while Giardi and Silbermann logged my possessions into a plastic bag.

Silbermann said, "I knew you did it."

Bastilla spoke with Marx and Munson privately by their command car, then Bastilla called over Giardi. They spoke for a few minutes, then Munson drove away. Marx got into his command car and Bastilla came back to me.

She said, "Just take it easy."

"This is bullshit. You people don't have a god-damned thing."

She made a shushing gesture.

"I'm handling it, Cole. Take a breath."

"Talk to Casik."

When Crimmens and his partner came back, Bastilla changed their orders.

"Question him here. Don't take him in."

"The chief said take him in."

"The chief changed his mind. Question him, then canvass this neighborhood and do your goddamned job. You have a murder to solve."

She stalked back to the command car, got in beside Marx, then they drove away, too.

I grinned at Crimmens.

"Is it still good for you?"

They kept me in the backseat of Giardi's car for almost two hours, first Crimmens and his partner, then one, then the other, then both together again. They questioned me about Tomaso, the phone calls I placed prior to arriving at his residence, and everything I saw, did, and witnessed once I reached the scene. I kept Pat Kyle out of it. I told them I had checked the exterior doors and windows for signs of forced entry because I knew they would find my fingerprints, but refused to admit I had entered the guesthouse. If I admitted entering, Marx would have an uncontested shot at me for unlawful entry, and I didn't trust he wouldn't book me. I told the truth about everything else. The questions were fair and appropriate, and would have been asked of anyone found at the scene. A criminalist appeared halfway through the questioning to take my fingerprints.

We were going over the same questions for the third time when Crimmens received a call on his cell. He listened a moment before responding.

"Sure, Chief. We're still questioning him."

He listened some more, then held out the phone.

"Chief Marx."

I took the phone.

Marx said, "Listen to me, Cole, and make no mistake. Lieutenant Poitras told me you two were close. I understand you're the godfather to one of his children."

I felt irritated and confused, and suddenly scared.

"That isn't your business, Marx."

"I gave the lieutenant a lawful and direct order when I instructed him to seal Byrd's house and deny all requests for information. Yet there you were, a civilian, present at a crime scene I had sealed, and you were accompanied by the lieutenant—in direct violation of my orders, and in front of multiple witnesses. Are you hearing me?"

I felt the sting of acid on the back of my tongue.

"I hear you."

"I could have Lieutenant Poitras brought up before a review board for administrative punishment. This would effectively end his career."

"What are you doing, Marx?"

"Stay away from the Repkos. Stay away from the good people at Leverage and away from my case. Do we understand each other?"

"Yes."

"Give the phone to Crimmens."

I felt empty, as if I had not eaten in days and would never eat again. Crimmens listened for a moment, then closed his phone.

"Get outta here, Cole. He says you can go."

24

TWILIGHT SETTLED like a murky shawl as I drove away from the crime scene. Marx had taken an enormous risk by threatening Lou Poitras. He would have anticipated I would tell Poitras, which meant Marx was confident he could control the situation however Poitras reacted—probably by doing exactly what he had threatened. But people don't take enormous risks unless they're desperate, which meant Marx was hiding something important. If he wanted to make me back off, then I wanted to get even closer.

I pulled into a gas station on Ventura Boulevard, called Joe Pike, then an attorney named Abbot Montoya. It was late in the day, but I knew Mr. Montoya would take my call.

"How are you, my son? It is good to hear you."

The smile in his voice was warm.

Abbot Montoya was a cultured gentleman in his seventies, but he had not always been cultured and no one in those days would have described him as a gentleman. Mr. Montoya was once an East L.A. gang-banger along with his best friend from those days, another young thug named Frank Garcia. Together, they had risen from the barrio, Abbot Montoya working his way through UCLA Law and Frank Garcia building a food empire worth more than a billion dollars. Frank owned a city councilman named Henry Maldenado. He probably owned others, as well.

"It's good to hear you, too, sir. I have a favor to ask."

"What you call a favor, we call an expression of love. However we can help, it will never be enough."

Frank Garcia had hired Pike and me to find the person who murdered his only child. We did, and they've been like this ever since.

"Do you know anything about a political management firm called Leverage Associates?"

"I know of them. They are a firm of long standing."

"I need background information on them and their clients. One of their clients is an LAPD deputy chief named Thomas Marx. Another is Nobel Wilts."

"Councilman Wilts?"

"Yes, sir. Is Councilman Maldenado a client of theirs?"

"He is not, but it would not matter if he were. Would you like to speak with him about these people?"

"Yes, sir. If he would."

Mr. Montoya chuckled as if the thought of Maldenado refusing was laughable.

"He will be most happy to see you."

"Sir, I can't have Leverage learning of this. The people I ask about, they can't know I'm asking."

"*Para siempre*. Trust me on this."

I lowered the phone but remained in the gas station, thinking how easily I had found Angel Tomaso. Having Jack Eisley as a contact had helped, but a couple of phone calls and there he was. Almost as if Bastilla and Crimmens hadn't been trying. Ivy Casik hadn't been much more difficult, and now I wondered if Bastilla had bothered to follow up. She had ignored me when I asked.

I fought my way down through the Cahuenga Pass into Hollywood, then up again through the soft hills surrounding the Hollywood Bowl, where Ivy Casik lived. The low apartment building was just as quiet as when I met her, the neighboring apartments locked tight against the world. I rang her bell and knocked, the knocking loud in the silent courtyard.

"May I help you?"

A bald man shaped like a pear had stepped into the courtyard. He was wearing oversize shorts and a baggy undershirt and holding a cocktail glass. A small sign beside his door identified him as the manager.

"I'm here to see Ms. Casik."

He shook the glass. The courtyard magnified the tinkling ice.

"She isn't home. Your knocking is quite loud, you know. You don't have to knock so loud."

He tinkled the ice again.

"Sorry. I'll leave a note."

I took out a card and held it against the building to write a note asking Ivy to call.

The man said, "Is this about the police? They were loud, too."

I stopped writing to look at him. When I looked, he tinkled the ice, then sipped his drink.

"Was that Detective Bastilla?"

"I don't know her name."

Her. I put my hand at Bastilla's height.

"This tall. Forties. Latina."

"That's right. This morning."

Another sip. Tinkle.

"You know if they spoke with her?"

"Ivy wasn't home."

He reached out his hand for the note.

"If you'd like, I'll make sure she gets it."

"Thanks anyway. I'll leave it in her box."

I dropped the card in Ivy's mailbox, then wound my way down out of the hills toward home. The drive home seemed long, maybe because there was so much to think about, and so little that made any sense.

I put the car in the carport, let myself into the kitchen, then drank a bottle of water. I had parked in the carport and opened the kitchen door and drank the same bottle of water ten thousand times. The cat wasn't home, but I put out new food for him exactly as I had another ten thousand times. Ten thousand fresh bowls of water. The patterns were reassuring.

I stripped off my shoes and clothes in the kitchen,

threw them into the laundry room, then went upstairs to shower, which is what I did every time I came home after being with a body. My patterns continued, but Angel Tomaso did not have the same luxury. His pattern was a single event that could not be washed away.

I did my best in the shower, then put on fresh clothes, went downstairs, and found Pike in the living room. He was holding the cat in his arms like someone cradling a baby. The cat's eyes were closed. All four of his feet were straight up in the air as if he was drunk.

I said, "I'm going to cook. You want a beer?"

"Sure."

I took two beers from the fridge, set them on the counter, then told him about Angel Tomaso.

"An anonymous caller tipped the police, and the cops arrived while I was with him."

"Think they set you up?"

"They couldn't know I would find him. They couldn't know I was at his house."

"Someone watching the body would know."

I drank more of the beer, then went through the rest.

"They sweated me for a couple of hours, then Marx told me if I didn't back off he would bring Lou up on charges for disobeying his orders. He would ruin Lou's career."

"He threatened Poitras."

"Yeah. For letting me into Byrd's house."

"He actually made the threat."

"Yes."

The corner of Pike's mouth twitched and he leaned against the counter.

"What did he mean, back off?"

I described how Marx was involved with Leverage Associates.

"Marx ran interference for Leverage during the original investigation into the Repko murder. He shut out Darcy and Maddux weeks before Byrd's body was discovered, and those guys never knew he was involved. Darcy also turned up a security vid made in the alley where Repko was murdered. SID couldn't do anything with it, so Darcy sent the disk to a CGI house. Thing is, when Byrd turned up, the task force sucked up the disk before the CGI house finished their work. Now nobody knows what happened to it."

"You think Marx is sitting on it?"

"I don't know what to think. If it showed Byrd committing the murder, Marx would have used it. If it was garbage, why make it disappear?"

"Maybe it showed someone else."

"Maybe. I don't know."

Pike took a careful sip of his beer.

"You're not just talking about Marx, Elvis. You're talking about an entire task force. Someone would be talking about it. You can't keep secrets like that."

"Lindo told me the task force was vertically integrated. Only the people at the top knew the full picture, what Lindo called the inner circle. He said the guys on his team even used to joke about it. Secrets are a lot easier to keep when people don't know what's going on."

"Who ran the show?"

"Marx on top with Bastilla and a dick named Munson. Lindo heard Marx and Munson have some kind of history together."

Pike put down the cat. He slid from Pike's arms like molasses and puddled at his feet.

"If Marx is shading the case, Bastilla and Munson would have to go along."

"He's a deputy chief, Joe. He can make their careers before he retires."

The cat peeled himself off the floor. He gazed at Pike, then came over and head-bumped my leg. I poured some of my beer in his beer dish, and watched him lap it.

Pike said, "So what are you going to do?"

"Dig into Leverage. It's all about Leverage and Marx. While I'm doing that, maybe you can try to dig up something on Munson and Bastilla. Dirty cops leave a dirty trail."

Pike grunted.

"Have you told Lou?"

I finished the rest of the beer.

"You know Lou. If I tell him, he'll jump in Marx's face."

"Uh-huh."

"I have to keep him as far from Marx as I can, but I can't drop this thing now and walk away."

I glanced at Pike, but Pike was impenetrable.

"You understand what I'm talking about?"

"I understand."

"If Marx is so worried about something he's willing to threaten Lou, if I can find that something then I take away his power to threaten."

Pike nodded.

"Do you think I should tell Lou anyway?"

"No."

"Let him decide for himself?"

"Telling him takes the responsibility off you and puts it on him. But you already know that."

"Yes, I know. I've been thinking about it."

"You're going to move forward anyway. We always drive forward."

"That's right."

Pike watched me for a while through the quiet dark glasses, then squeezed my trapezius muscle.

"Lou wouldn't want you to stop. He would think less of you if you did."

I nodded. Sometimes it helps to hear it.

Pike said, "What do you want me to do?"

"You're doing it."

We cooked, and drank more beer, and ate in silence as we watched an ESPN sports recap. Sometime after Pike left, the coyotes began to sing.

I was getting ready for bed when I remembered Pat Kyle. Angel's agent would be questioned the next day. He would almost certainly tell the police Pat had been looking for Tomaso, after which the police would call her. Crimmens would likely be the caller. I didn't like calling so late and didn't want to tell her this would be waiting for her tomorrow, and I didn't like knowing my call would upset her and cost her a miserable night. I didn't want to call, but I did. She needed to hear it from me so she would be prepared. Pat Kyle was my friend. You have to take care of your friends.

25

JOE'S SUGGESTION that someone had been watching Angel Tomaso's guesthouse left me with a wakeful paranoia the rest of the night. An opossum foraging on the deck became a home invasion crew. The soft clicking of the cat door was a lip gloss tube being readied to write. *I loved u.* I locked the doors and windows before shutting off the lights, but woke to check them twice, as if I had only imagined locking them in an earlier dream. The second time up I carried the Dan Wesson, but told myself I was being silly. I covered my head with a pillow. The ostrich approach.

Abbot Montoya phoned at twenty minutes after eight the next morning to tell me the meeting with Councilman Maldenado had been arranged. Maldenado would see me at ten and offer every assistance. Frank Garcia assured it. By eight forty-five, I was showered, dressed, and eating scrambled eggs with cilantro when the doorbell rang. It rang three fast times before I reached the door and found Alan Levy. Levy had never been to my home or my office. Outside of the six or eight times we met when I worked for him, I had never seen him anyplace other than his office or court.

"Alan. This is a surprise."

A sleek Mercedes convertible was parked off the road behind him, but Alan didn't look sleek. He looked awkward and worried, and his bulging frog eyes flickered as if he was nervous.

"I hope you don't mind, me dropping in like this. I thought we could speak more freely outside of the office."

This, from a man who made his living as a criminal defense attorney having the most private conversations in the world.

I stepped back to let him in. Levy noticed my loft, then stared out through the sliders into the canyon. The morning haze filled the house with a milky glare.

"Hey, this is nice. You're very private up here."

"What's up, Alan? I have to leave for an appointment."

He turned from the view and put his hands in his pockets like he didn't know what else to do with them.

"Angel Tomaso was murdered."

"I know."

"I know you know. The police found you with the body."

"Are you here as an attorney, Alan? Are they going to charge me?"

"No, nothing like that, but—"

He managed to look pathetic. I had never seen Alan Levy look pathetic before, but then he suddenly frowned.

"Tomaso was *murdered*. Tell me a young man found himself in a relationship that resulted in murder, I would say that sort of thing happens all the time. But not this particular young man. Not at this particular time. Maybe you were right about there being more to this than the pictures recovered with Byrd."

The frog eyes blinked.

"Tell me what's going on."

"Marx is still working the homicides."

Levy's eyebrows arched in surprise.

"But Marx closed the case. He shut down the task force."

"Marx kept his top people on, what they call his inner circle. The task force might have been officially shut down, but Marx is still kicking rocks. The problem is, I'm not sure whether he's trying to find evidence or hide it."

I told him how Marx was connected to Leverage and how he had interfered with the Repko investigation even before Byrd's body was found. When I described the video disk of Debra Repko's murder, Levy grew irritated and stopped me.

"What did they do with it?"

"No one knows. Marx took it away from the CGI house before the work was finished. It's possible he sent it to the FBI lab, but that's only a guess."

"So the FBI has it?"

"I don't know where it is, Alan. For all I know, Marx is using it as a bookmark. Either way, it was probably garbage like SID said."

Levy told me to go on, and I did, anxious to finish so I could leave for my meeting with Maldenado. When I told Levy about Ivy Casik, he leaned forward.

"This woman claims someone was writing a book about Lionel Byrd?"

"She's claiming Byrd told her someone was writing a book about him. He could have made it up."

Levy considered me for a moment, then took out a pad.

"Is she credible?"

"She knew Byrd had been charged in the Bennett murder and about the trumped-up confession Crimmens used to make his case."

"Have the police interviewed her?"

"They went to her apartment, but I don't know if they reached her. She wasn't home when I went back to check."

"Which officer was that, Marx?"

"Bastilla."

Alan grunted again and wrote something.

"All right. I'll try to see the Casik woman, too. Tell me how to find her."

He copied her name and address as I gave him directions, then tapped at the pad with his pen.

"Here's what I can do. I'll request Byrd's criminal history—not just the arrest record, but the complete history. The DA shouldn't object, and if she does, well, there are others who won't."

"Why the history?"

"Perhaps an officer who arrested him turns up on the task force. Maybe an attorney who once represented him now works for Leverage. You never know what you might find."

I nodded. The big gun rolls into action.

"I'll see if I can find out what Marx is up to. Maybe I can get more information from the inside than we've been able to get from the outside."

We. I didn't bother to correct him.

"Let's get back to Tomaso for a second. Do you know which detective is in charge of the case?"

"That would be Crimmens."

"Ah."

Levy smiled as he made the note, then looked back at me.

"Had they identified any witnesses? Anyone see or describe the killer or a vehicle?"

"No witnesses by the time they cut me free. They had already started the canvass. They were striking out."

"Evidence recovered at the scene?"

"Nothing they mentioned in front of me. Alan, look, I have to get going."

He put away his pad and pushed back from the table.

"I know you have to go, but listen—you should be careful. Byrd had these pictures. That much is an undeniable fact. The man didn't just find them on the side of the road."

"Didn't we go through this before?"

"Yes, but Tomaso has caused me to reconsider. Even if Byrd wasn't a party to the murders, the person who gave those pictures to him was, and Byrd and that person were connected. That man is still out there."

"I know."

"You don't want to end up like Tomaso, do you?"

"Alan, I have to go."

"If Byrd was connected to someone at Leverage, maybe we'll find the connection through his record. In the meantime, stay away from Marx. You should lie low for a while, Elvis. Don't give these people an excuse to arrest you."

"They could have arrested me yesterday."

"They might still change their minds. Give me a chance to find out what they're doing before you get yourself in worse trouble."

We reached the door, and I watched him go to his car. It was a lovely car, and he waved as he got in.

"Hey, Alan. Good to have you aboard."

He twisted around to look at me. He said, "I'm sorry I doubted your instinct."

I smiled as he drove away.

26

MEMBERS OF the Los Angeles City Council had downtown offices on Spring Street, but each member also maintained an office in his or her district. Maldenado's district office was in a two-story strip mall in an area where most of the signs were in Spanish and Korean, conveniently distant from the spying eyes that went with the downtown action. The councilman's office was located above a women's health club. The women entering the club were uniformly beautiful, but this probably had nothing to do with the councilman's location.

I parked underground, walked up to the second floor, and entered the reception area. The receptionist was speaking Spanish to an older couple while two men in business suits waited on the couch, one tapping out a text message while the other read some sort of document. Photographs hanging above the two men and behind the receptionist showed Maldenado with Little League teams, sports stars from the Dodgers,

Lakers, and Clippers, and various politicians. I counted Maldenado with three different California governors and four U.S. presidents. The only person who appeared with Maldenado more than once was Frank Garcia.

The receptionist said, "May I help you, sir?"

The older couple had taken a seat.

"Elvis Cole for Mr. Maldenado. I have a ten o'clock."

"Yes, sir. They're expecting you."

She immediately led me around her desk and into Maldenado's office. She didn't bother to knock or even announce me. She opened the door, let me walk in, then closed the door behind me.

Before entering politics, Henry Maldenado had sold used cars and trucks, and had been good at it. His office was large and well appointed, and reflected his love of cars with models of classic Chevrolets. Maldenado was a short, balding man in his fifties who looked younger than he was, wearing jeans, a short-sleeved shirt open at the neck, and cowboy boots. A bank president's desk sat at the far end of the room, bracketed by a glass wall overlooking the street and a couch. He came around his desk, offering his hand and a charming, natural smile. A second man sat on the couch.

"It's good to see you again, Mr. Cole. If I haven't expressed this before, I want to personally thank you for the help you've given to Frank in the past. He is one of my closest, dearest friends."

"I'm sure. Thanks for making the time, Councilman."

The other man was nothing like Maldenado. He was thin, with a sagging face and steel-colored hair. His sport coat and slacks fit like secondhand clothes draped on a rack. I made him for his late sixties, but he could have been older. He did not stand and made no move to greet me.

Maldenado waved at him as he showed me to a chair facing the desk.

"This is another close friend, my adviser, Felix Dowling. Felix has been working the back rooms of this city longer than either of us cares to admit, isn't that right, Felix?"

Maldenado laughed, but all Felix managed was a polite nod.

Maldenado hitched his pants and hooked his butt on the front of his desk, one foot on the floor, the other dangling in front of me.

"So, Abbot tells me you have some concerns about my friends at Leverage. They're a fine firm. Been in business for many years. Just a fine group of people."

"That's good to hear. I'm hoping you can answer a few questions about them."

"Well, I'll tell you, I don't know much about those folks, but Felix here, well, Felix knows just about everything about everyone in this town, so that's why he's here. He knows where the bodies are buried, I'll tell you that."

Maldenado laughed again, but Felix still didn't join him.

Felix said, "Why don't you freshen your coffee, Henry?"

Maldenado glanced at his cup and appeared surprised at how empty it was.

"You know, I'll do that. I'll be right back, but you boys don't wait for me."

Maldenado closed the door on the way out. I glanced at Dowling, and Dowling seemed to be sizing me up. The office felt different with Maldenado gone, as if it suddenly belonged to Dowling and maybe always had. I let him look.

He said, "So. You're the boy got the sonofabitch who killed Frank's daughter."

"My partner and I. I wasn't alone."

"She was a sweet kid. I met her a couple times."

I nodded.

We looked at each other some more.

He said, "Okay. What's up?"

"I believe Leverage Associates might be acting to suppress or subvert a murder investigation. Would they do that?"

He shrugged with no more reaction than had I asked if they validate.

"Would they? In my experience, people will do damn near anything. If you're asking whether they've done that kind of thing in the past, my answer would be no. I've never heard them to be associated with anything that extreme. They've had clients get into trouble, sure, but never like that."

He stopped, waiting for the next question.

"Are you familiar with their client list?"

"Sure. They have five or six on the council, couple of commissioners, on up the line. Right now, I'd call it fourteen clients holding office and another thirty or so contenders."

"Could you get information about those individuals if I wanted it?"

"Yes. You want their entire list?"

"Yes, sir."

"Done. What else?"

The door suddenly opened. Maldenado took half a step in and froze in the opening. Dowling and I glanced at him, but he backed out of the room, closing the door.

Dowling said, "Forget him. What else?"

"Do you know the name Debra Repko?"

"No."

"She worked at Leverage as a first-year associate. That's a training position where—"

"I know what it is."

"She worked with several clients while she was there. Maybe a lot of them. Could you get their names?"

"That one I can't promise you. I can get some names, no doubt, but I'll have to see. Was she screwing somebody?"

"She was murdered almost two months ago. When her case was being investigated, Leverage didn't want their client list made public or the clients questioned. They had a deputy chief named Marx crowd out the detectives."

Dowling seemed interested for the first time.

"Thomas Marx?"

"You know him?"

"Never met, but he wants into politics. A lot of these guys do. He's had a few conversations."

"It's beyond the conversation stage. He's signed up at Leverage."

Dowling seemed surprised.

"Marx is with Leverage?"

"They think they can position him for a shot at the council."

Dowling stared with the same surprised expression, then suddenly barked a single sharp laugh.

"Of course. Wilts is with Leverage."

Casey Stokes had mentioned that Wilts thought Marx had what it took to get elected. I thought Dowling was saying the same, so I nodded along.

"That's right. Someone told me Wilts was a big supporter."

Dowling made the bark again.

"Bet your ass he is. Marx was Wilts's fixer. How do you think Marx got to the top of the glass house?"

The glass house was Parker Center.

"Marx took care of Wilts for years, and Wilts took care of Marx. Guess he still is. Wilts must have brought him in."

Wilts had been at Marx's press conference, but I had seen Wilts at dozens of press conferences over the years and thought nothing of it. I had not known their relationship was deeper, or longer, and now a nervous tension grew in my belly. Debra Repko's final event was a dinner for Nobel Wilts.

"What kind of trouble did Wilts need fixed?"

"Those days, Wilts was a notorious drunk. I'm talking blackouts. He was always getting pulled over or crashing his car. Couple of times he got out of hand with a broad. Whatever. He'd call Marx, and Marx would make it go away. That's what fixers do."

"And Wilts returned the favors?"

"Leverage wouldn't be interested in a stiff like Marx unless he was holding an ace. I'm guessing Wilts brought Marx in as his successor. The old man must be thinking about calling it quits."

"As simple as that? Wilts tells Leverage Marx is his boy and Leverage takes him aboard?"

"Well, Leverage isn't doing it because they like his smile. This stuff costs money."

"So who's paying the tab? Wilts?"

Dowling made a flicking move with his hand.

"Nah, he probably pressed one of his backers into footing the bill. They make the investment now, they get the favors later. Politics is like Oz, only you never see the magician behind the curtain."

"Can we find out?"

He thought about it a moment, then checked his watch.

"I'll have to get back to you. Anything else? Henry has a full day."

I thought about what he had told me and all that went with it. Marx was no longer just a cop shading an investigation for publicity; now he was a cop who covered up crimes. I wondered how many crimes he had covered, and if Wilts was his only angel.

"One more thing, Mr. Dowling. How far back do Marx and Wilts go?"

"Gotta be fifteen or twenty years. Fifteen, for sure. I can tell you exactly how they got together. I heard it from someone who was there. You do what I do, you hear things, you learn from what you hear."

He went on without waiting for me to ask.

"Wilts was still a supervisor, before his first run at the seat. Found himself shit-faced at Lenny Branigan's, but that didn't stop him from trying to drive. He didn't make it half a mile. Sideswiped a line of parked cars, just raked right down their sides knocking off the mirrors, and ended up on the sidewalk. When he came to, Marx was wiping the blood from his face, had to be about three in the morning. Marx wasn't even on duty that night, just happening by, and one thing led to another. Marx drove Nobel home, then brought his car to a boy in Glendale who worked fast for cash. I've used him myself. You know who told me this story?"

I shook my head.

"Wilts. Wilts said, you need a boy you can trust, you call this boy Marx. He was looking out for Marx even then, figuring I'd use him."

"Did you?"

Dowling smiled.

"I have my own fixers."

Dowling glanced at his watch again.

"Anything else?"

"No, sir. I guess that's it."

"Okay. You talk to Frank, tell him Chip Dowling sends his respects."

"Yes, sir. I will."

I thought of a final question when I reached the door.

"One more thing—"

He nodded.

"What's the worst thing Marx ever fixed?"

"I don't know the worst thing he fixed. All I know is the worst I've heard about."

I let myself out.

27

I SAT in my car in the strip mall parking lot, watching the women come and go without seeing them. The heat was suffocating. It baked down from the sky and bounced up from the parking lot and soaked into the car until the car became part of the oven. The heat came from all sides, and didn't let up, but I still did not move. I didn't like what I had learned from Dowling or what those things led me to think.

The manila envelope with the articles and files I had collected was behind the passenger seat. I fingered through the printouts until I found the one I wanted, and reread it.

Marx had investigated the murder of the first victim, Sondra Frostokovich, almost seven years ago. Described as an administrator for the city, her body had been found by workmen in an empty building on Temple Street, four blocks from where she worked in the city administration building. She was twenty-four years old, and had been strangled to death with an extension cord. Lindo had pointed out the blood dripping from her nose in the death album Polaroid. Three drops that, when compared to the coroner investigator's crime scene pictures, established the Polaroid had been taken within moments of her death. When I closed my eyes, the frozen image returned to life, and the red pool continued to grow.

The short article provided no personal information of any kind. No family members, spouse, or children were mentioned, nor was a place of birth or school affiliation. The article ended with the plea from Marx for anyone with knowledge of the crime to come forward. He had almost certainly worked the case with a partner, but the only officer identified was Detective-Sergeant Thomas Marx of Central Bureau Homicide.

It was a long road from sergeant to deputy chief, and Marx had traveled that road in only seven years.

I dialed Information and asked for any listing in any city area code for Frostokovich. It took a moment, but the operator found five listings scattered over three area codes—two male, one female, and two showing only initials. Good thing Sondra wasn't a Jones or Hernandez.

I called Edward Frostokovich first, but got no answer, not even a message machine.

Grady Frostokovich was my second call. He answered on the fourth ring, sounding young and polite. I identified myself, and asked if he knew of or had been related to a Sondra Frostokovich.

He said, "The one who was murdered?"

"That's right. I'm sorry to disturb you like this."

"Hey, no worries, I barely knew her. They found the guy. All this time later, they got him. How cool is that?"

"I'm looking into the original investigation back at the time of her murder. Think you could help with that?"

"Well, I would if I could, but she was my cousin, you know? Our family isn't the closest family in the world."

"Was Sondra from here in L.A.?"

"Oh, yeah. They lived in Reseda."

"Are her parents or sibs still here?"

"That's my Aunt Ida. Uncle Ronnie died, but her mom was Aunt Ida. You should talk to Aunt Ida."

There was an I. L. Frostokovich on my list.

"Is that I. L. Frostokovich?"

"Yeah, that's her. She's really nice. My mom hates her, but she's really nice."

Grady was right. Ida was nice. I explained I was working with the family of the seventh and final victim, Debra Repko, and asked if she would be willing to tell me about her daughter. Five minutes later I was heading for Reseda.

28

IDA FROSTOKOVICH lived in a small tract home in the center of the San Fernando Valley, north of the Los Angeles River and fifteen degrees hotter than the basin side of the city. When Ida was a child, orange groves covered the valley floor as far as she could see with Zen perfection—identical rows of identical trees, each tree identically distant from its neighbors; row after row of low green clouds heavy with orange balls that smelled of sunshine. She remembered those times, and thought often of the trees, but during the boom years after the Second World War, the groves were bulldozed and the trees replaced by row after row of small, low-cost houses. Most of the houses were much the same in size and shape as the thousands of other houses there on the valley floor, but none of them smelled like sunshine.

Ida had probably let the house go after losing both her daughter and her husband. The small stucco house with its composite roof, faded paint, and ragged yard seemed weary. A single orange tree from the original grove stood in the front yard like a lonely reminder of better times. Two more trees were in her backyard, the crowns of the trees visible past the roof. I circled the block twice before I stopped, checking to see if someone was watching her house, but found no one. The paranoia.

I was walking up the drive when she opened the door. Ida had been waiting for me to arrive.

"Mr. Cole?"

"Yes, ma'am."

"Come in where it's cool."

Ida Frostokovich was a sturdy woman with big bones, a fleshy face, and nervous hands. Like the Repkos, she had created a shrine to her daughter, which I saw as soon as I entered. A poster-size portrait of Sondra hung on the wall over the television, with smaller pictures around it and still more pictures on a nearby credenza. The pictures preserved Sondra's life from birth to death, and dominated the room. I had seen similar shrines when I returned from the war and sought out the parents of friends who had died. A husband or wife could be lost and you would never know they were gone, but losing a child left an emptiness so large it screamed to be filled with memories.

"You say the Repkos want to know about the original investigation?"

"They're trying to understand why it took so long to catch this man."

She settled into a Barcalounger and cupped one

hand with the other, but the hands never quite rested.

"Oh, I understand, believe me, and I don't blame them. If the police would have caught this lunatic sooner, their daughter would still be alive."

"Something like that. Were you satisfied with the way Sondra's investigation was handled?"

"Ha. Seven years, and they still wouldn't have him if he hadn't blown his own brains out. I guess that should tell you something about my satisfaction level."

"Who notified you of the discovery in Laurel Canyon?"

"A Detective Bastilla. She told me the newspeople might come around, but they didn't. No one came. I guess it was too long ago, what with so many others."

"I'll get back to the police in a minute, but first let me ask you this—do you know of a firm called Leverage Associates?"

"I don't believe I do. What is it?"

"They're a political management firm downtown. Debra Repko worked for them."

"Ah. Uh-huh."

She nodded without comprehension, probably wondering what this had to do with anything.

"Sondra and Debra had a lot in common. More with each other than with the other five women. They both had college educations. They both worked downtown in fields involved with the government. Was Sondra interested in politics?"

"Not my Sondra. She was an account administrator

with the planning commission. She called herself a bean counter."

"She ever attend political events, like a fund-raiser or dinner?"

"Oh, my, no. She hated that kind of thing. Is that what the Repko girl did?"

"She was at a political dinner on the night she died."

"Sondie was off having fun with her friends. At least she was enjoying herself."

"Do you remember how the police handled the original investigation?"

"Every word. I lie in bed at night, remembering. I can still see them sitting here, right where you're sitting now."

"The detective conducting the investigation was Chief Marx?"

"At the beginning, but he left. Then it was, oh, I think it was Detective Petievich. A Serbian, that's why I remember. Ronnie was so glad when a Serb took over. Frostokovich is a Serbian name."

"How long was Marx involved?"

"Four or five weeks, was all, then he disappeared. Got a promotion, they said."

"After four or five weeks."

"Ronnie was just furious, but he calmed down. Marx and that other one hadn't caught anyone, so we thought the new people might get results."

"Who worked on the case with Marx?"

"Let me think—"

She stared at the ceiling, trying to remember.

"That was Detective Munson. He never said much. Ronnie called him The Zombie. Ronnie was always making up names like that."

I tried not to show a reaction.

"Did Munson stay on the case with Petievich?"

"For a while, but then he moved on, too. They all moved on, sooner or later."

"But Marx and Munson were the first investigators?"

"The day they found her body. They sat right where you're sitting."

"Did they have a suspect?"

"Oh, no. That first day they asked if *we* knew who did it. I will always remember that, them asking if we knew. Ronnie went straight up right through the roof. He told them if he thought anyone was going to kill Sondie, he would have killed them before they had the chance."

"Was there anyone you suspected?"

"Well, no. Why would we suspect anyone?"

"Maybe something Sondra had said."

The nervous hands held each other. It was a sad move, as if her hands were keeping each other company.

"No, nothing like that. We were shocked. It was like being swept away by a wave. We thought they must have made a mistake."

"Did they ask many questions?"

"They were here for hours. They wanted to know if

Sondra was seeing anyone or had complained about anyone, that kind of thing. Sondie had gone out with her friends from work that night, so the police wanted to talk to them. We had to look up their names and numbers. It just went on and on like that."

She suddenly smiled, and her face was bright with living energy.

"Would you like to see?"

"See what?"

"Her friends. Here, they took a picture together—"

She pushed up from the well of the Barcalounger and waved me with her to the credenza.

"Carrie gave this to us. Ronnie called it The Last Supper. He would cry like a baby when he looked at it, but then he would call it The Last Supper, and laugh."

She grabbed a framed snapshot from the forest of pictures on the credenza and put it in my hands.

"They took this at work that day. That's Sondie, second from the right, that's Carrie, that's Lisa and Ellen. They used to cut up and have so much fun. They went out together that night after work."

I stared at the picture.

"Her friends at work."

"Well, the girls, not the gentlemen."

The four young women were standing shoulder to shoulder and smiling in a professional, businesslike manner. They were in what appeared to be a city office, but they were not in the picture alone. A middle-aged African-American man stood at the left end of their line, and Councilman Nobel Wilts stood to their right. Wilts was next to Sondra, and appeared to be touching her back.

Ida tapped the African-American man.

"Mr. Owen here was Sondie's boss, and this was Councilman Wilts. He was so kind to her. He told her she had a bright future."

I couldn't take my eyes off the picture. I stared at it as if I was falling into it.

"I thought her job wasn't political."

"Well, it wasn't, but they worked in the budgetary office, you know. The councilman stopped by for one of the bigwigs, but took time to tell them what a great job they were doing. Wasn't that nice of him?"

I nodded.

"He was very impressed with them, Sondie in particular. He even remembered her name that night."

I let go of the picture and watched her put it back on the credenza. She placed it perfectly onto a line in the dust.

"Did she see him again that night?"

"At dinner."

"Sondie and Wilts had dinner."

"Sondie and her friends had dinner. They bumped into the councilman at the restaurant, and he was just so nice again. He told them how much he enjoyed meeting them, and he even remembered Sondie's name. I have voted for that man ever since."

"When did Carrie give you the picture?"

"Must have been a year or so after what happened.

She found it one day and thought we'd like it."

"Did Marx and Munson see it?"

"They were long gone by then."

I studied the picture in the little forest of pictures on the credenza, and knew by the smudged dust lines it had been moved more than once.

"Did Detective Bastilla see it when she was here?"

Her smile grew even brighter.

"She thought it was so pretty of Sondie. She asked if she could have it, but I told her no."

I took Ida's hand and gave her an encouraging squeeze.

"I'm glad you told her no, Ida. It's a good picture. Let's keep it safe."

29

THE DAY shift ended at three. Uniformed officers punched on and off duty pretty much with the clock, but homicide detectives required more flexible hours. Interviews were arranged when citizens could make the time to be interviewed; file or evidence transfers often meant sitting in traffic for hours; and reports, records, and case notes still had to be typed and logged by the end of the day.

I arranged to meet Starkey a block from Hollywood Station when her shift ended and phoned Alan Levy while I waited. I wanted to see if he had learned anything about Marx from his inside sources, and I also wanted to know how Bastilla had handled Ivy Casik.

Levy's assistant answered.

He said, "I'm sorry, Mr. Cole. Alan's out of the office today."

"I know. We saw each other this morning. Do you know if he's spoken with Ivy Casik?"

"No, sir, I don't. Would you like to leave a message? I expect he'll call in later."

"Yeah. Ask him to call me. Tell him I've learned some things about the task force."

I gave him my cell number, then put away my phone.

Starkey left Hollywood Station at ten minutes after four and walked south, looking for my car. She was wearing a navy pantsuit, tortoise-shell sunglasses, and twining ribbons of cigarette smoke. A black bag hung on her right shoulder. When she saw me, I raised a hand. She flicked her cigarette to the street, then opened the door and dropped into the car.

"Is this a date?"

"I need to talk to you about something."

I pulled a U-turn away from the curb, driving away from the station.

"I'm going to call it a date so I'll feel better about myself. Here you are, picking me up, and now we're going someplace nice. You see?"

I didn't say anything. I was trying to work up how to ask what I needed to ask. It would put her in a bad place, but I didn't know what else to do.

Starkey sighed dramatically at the silence.

"Not the most charming date conversation I've had, but I guess it will have to do."

"Lindo told me the task force still has a locked evidence room down on Spring Street. You know that layout pretty well."

"So?"

"You know which room he's talking about?"

She looked at me with something like a scowl.

"They cleared out the offices they were using. They probably already shipped their files to storage."

"They haven't. Bastilla and Munson are still using the room. Lindo told me he's seen them."

She studied me some more, and now she looked uncomfortable and suspicious.

"What exactly are you asking me, Cole?"

"I'm asking if you know where they're keeping their files."

"Every task force they house down there uses the same room—and it's not a *room*, Cole, it's a fucking *closet*. Of course I know where it is. I spent three years down there."

"Will you tell me how to find it?"

"The *closet*?"

"Yeah. I want to look at their files."

"Are you stupid?"

"I need to see what they're hiding."

She held up her hands.

"You're serious? You're telling me you want to illegally enter an LAPD facility and break into official police files? You are actually asking me to help you do that?"

"I don't know who else to ask."

"That's a police building, you moron. It's filled with police officers."

"I still have to do it."

"You're beyond stupid, Cole. They don't have a

word for what you are. Forget it. I am so pissed off right now—"

I drove another block, then pulled into a parking lot where a group of teenagers crowded a falafel stand. I parked behind the stand, but left the engine running. The smells of cumin and hot oil were strong.

"I know what I'm asking, but I have to keep Lou out of this for now and I don't want Lindo to know. I believe Marx, Bastilla, and Munson aren't trying to find the person who killed those seven women. I believe they know who that person is, or suspect they know, and they're trying to protect him."

Starkey's face softened. The hard vertical line between her eyebrows relaxed as the weight of what I was saying settled, but then she shook her head.

"Marx might be an asshole, Elvis, but he's a deputy chief of police. Munson and Bastilla—they're top cops."

"They appear to be protecting Nobel Wilts."

The tip of her tongue flicked over her lips.

"The city councilman. *Councilman* Nobel Wilts."

"Yes."

"You're telling me you believe a city councilman killed these women. That's what you're saying. Am I confused?"

"I don't know. I'm not telling you Wilts is the killer because I don't know. I've been digging into Marx, not Wilts, but you can't rule out Wilts just because he looks normal. A lot of these guys look normal."

"Thank you, Cole, I know that. I studied fucked-up

people when I worked on the bombs. High-functioning people are just as fucked up as everyone else—they just hide it better. What do you have?"

I described Marx's history as a fixer for Wilts, and how at least two of the fixes were for assaults against women. I went through everything Ida Frostokovich told me about Wilts meeting her daughter on the day Sondra was murdered, and described how Marx and Munson had been the original investigators. I told her how Marx had run interference for Leverage Associates when Darcy and Maddux were investigating Debra Repko's murder, and that Wilts was a Leverage client and had arranged for Leverage to manage Marx's run for the council. Starkey grew pale as the overlaps added up, and made only a single comment when I finished.

"Jeez."

"Yeah. That's what I said, too."

Starkey rubbed hard at the sides of her face, then studied the kids around the falafel stand as if she thought she might have to pull them out of a lineup.

"I guess it's possible. You don't have any proof?"

"Nothing."

"You think Marx and these guys are hiding the proof."

"They're lying. Things that might be proof are disappearing. People who should be involved are being cut out. You tell me."

"If they're protecting Wilts, you're not going to find

anything in their files. They would destroy incriminating evidence or doctor it."

"Maybe I'm hoping something incriminating will be there. If Marx showed Wilts as a person of interest in the Frostokovich murder, maybe I'm wrong about the cover-up. Maybe it's something else."

Starkey laughed, but it was sickly and weak.

"Right. And you want to be wrong."

"Like you said, the man's a deputy chief of police. It's okay if he's a political asshole, but it's not okay if he's protecting a murderer. The only way I can know what they're doing is to see what they're doing with the information."

Starkey nodded, but she was still thinking it through.

"So you just want to see."

"The murder book Marx started on Frostokovich should contain statements by the girls she had dinner with on the night she died. They would have mentioned bumping into Wilts, and Marx should have followed up by asking Wilts if he saw anything that night. I also want to see what these blind tests they're running through SID are about, and what happened to the DVD from the Repko case."

"All right, listen—here's what I can do. That's very specific. That's just looking in some boxes to see what's what, right?"

"It won't take long."

"I'll have Lindo do it. He'll bitch, but he'll do it. He can go in early and take a look when no one's around."

"They keep the room locked."

"Cole, wake the fuck up—the department uses these offices every time someone squirts a new task force out their ass. They don't change the locks. I know five different people down there who have keys to that room. I used to have them myself."

"Lindo can't be involved. If Lindo looks, I'll have to tell him what to look for, and he'll figure it out. The more people who know, the greater the chance Marx will find out."

"There are ways to do this, man. There are people we can talk to."

Starkey wasn't liking it, and I couldn't blame her. I twisted sideways, the better to face her.

"I know what I'm asking. You tell me you can't get involved, that's fine. I mean it."

"Oh, that's big of you, Cole. That is amazingly generous. If I decline to help you commit a crime against my employer, which just happens to be the Los Angeles Police Department, me being a sworn officer and all, you won't hold it against me. How did I become so lucky?"

I felt myself flush.

"I didn't mean it that way. I'm talking about a city councilman and a deputy chief who might be abetting the deaths of seven women. I can't bring something like this forward until it's tied up so tight Marx and Wilts can't use their influence to duck it."

Starkey rubbed at the sides of her face again.

"God, I'm hungry. A real date would've fed me before he fucked me."

I straightened behind the wheel, even more embarrassed.

"Let's forget it. I shouldn't have asked."

"No, you shouldn't have asked. Jesus Christ."

"It's my play. I didn't want you involved."

Starkey glanced at me, then studied her watch. She reached into her purse, took out a cigarette, and lit up even though I don't let people smoke in my car.

"Looks like I'm involved whether you like it or not. I'll get you in there myself."

She waved her cigarette to fan the smoke.

"Don't just stare at me, Cole. Buy us a couple of falafels and let's get going. Traffic's gonna be a bitch."

30

THE CRIMINAL Conspiracy Section's primary task was investigating bomb events. Most of the time when the bomb squad investigated a suspicious package, the package turned out to be someone's abandoned laundry or a forgotten briefcase. But if the bomb squad determined the package to be an improvised explosive device, the CCS was tasked with identifying and investigating the person or persons who built the bomb. Such events could happen at any time, which meant CCS detectives might be working at any hour.

As we made our way through prime rush-hour traffic, Starkey sketched out her plan.

"Everyone bags it around four except for the duty officer. The D.O. hangs around doing paperwork, but that works for us. As long as the D.O.'s on duty the squad room is open. We just need to give everyone else time to leave."

"Okay. Then what?"

"I am going to get us into the building. Then I'll show you the file room and keep the duty officer busy while you see what you can find out about their investigation. How easy is that?"

"Okay. But what if they had a call-out and everyone's working?"

Starkey made an irritated grin.

"Then I guess we don't do this tonight, do we?"

"Guess not."

"They don't grow'm for brains where you come from, do they?"

"Guess not."

"See the drugstore ahead on the right? Pull over and give me twenty bucks."

Starkey returned a few minutes later with a two-pound box of chocolates and a fresh pack of cigarettes. We continued downtown, though neither of us said very much after we bought the candy.

When we reached the Spring Street building, Starkey directed me to a public parking lot across the street where an attendant made me pay in advance, but let me park it myself. Parking was easy at the end of the day, offering plenty of spots with a view of the building's entrance. We watched as the detectives and plainclothes officers who worked in the building left. After a while Starkey checked the time, then glanced at me.

"Get rid of your gun."

"It's under the seat."

"You have a camera?"

"Yeah."

I had a small Sony digital in case something was in the files I wanted to record.

Starkey said, "Leave it. We don't need attention at the security station. Leave any pens, coins, anything like that."

I left it all, then walked with her across the street toward the entrance. A trickle of plainclothes officers were still leaving, but most were already gone.

Starkey said, "Looks good. Let's do it."

She took my hand, twined her fingers through mine, and gave me a beaming smile.

"Make a dimple for Mama. That's it, Cole—look like you're pleased with yourself."

Starkey pulled me into the lobby and focused her attention on a muscular uniformed officer seated at the security station. A metal detector was set up beside him, but Starkey stepped around it without hesitating, and headed straight for the elevators.

"Yo, Manuel! You better wake up back there. They might make you start working for a living."

Manuel gave her an easy smile.

"Yo, Bombs. Where you been, girl?"

Starkey raised our hands to show him how our fingers were wrapped together.

"Puttin' this smile on my man's face. Did Beth get back yet?"

Beth Marzik had been Starkey's partner at CCS.

"No idea, babe. She might've come in through parking."

Manuel glanced at me but didn't seem overly concerned.

Starkey pulled me steadily toward the elevator as if the building belonged to her, walking backwards to keep up the patter with Manuel. She waved the candy at him with her free hand.

"Her birthday's next week. Make her share, man. Don't let her keep it all for herself."

"I'm on it, Starkey. You be good."

"Not in this life."

Starkey backed me into the elevator as the doors closed. We stood silently for a moment, breathing.

I said, "You're something."

"Aren't I?"

I realized we were still holding hands, and let go.

"Sorry."

We rode in silence to the fifth floor, then Starkey took my hand again as the doors opened onto a short hall.

"Just follow my lead. If we walk into something I can't handle, all we have to do is walk out."

"I'm good."

"Your hand is sweating."

"That's called fear."

"Jesus, dude. Chill."

Starkey's hand was cool and dry. I guess if you de-armed bombs for a living, sneaking into the police department wasn't impressive.

I followed her past a placard that read CRIMINAL CONSPIRACY SECTION into a large modern room divided into cubicles. The cubicles appeared deserted. Starkey raised her voice.

"Knock, knock, knock! I knew this place would fall apart when I left!"

A balding man stepped from a doorway at the far end of the room. He was short and neat with a tie on his short-sleeve shirt, and appeared to be holding a napkin.

"Carol?"

Starkey hit him with the smile and tugged me toward him.

"Hiya, Jorge. How'd you get stuck with the duty?"

The man seemed awkward and surprised, but he was probably always awkward around Starkey. He wiped his hands as we approached.

"My turn in the rotation, is all. What brings you by, Carol? Everyone's gone."

Starkey waved the box of candy.

"Marzik's birthday next week. I'm going to leave it on her desk so she'll be surprised in the morning. Hey—I want you to meet someone. This is my boyfriend, Axel. Ax, this is Jorge Santos. Everyone calls him Hooker."

Axel.

I smiled politely and shook Jorge's hand. He had been eating in a small interview room where two open Tupperware containers and a cup of coffee were still on the table. A copy of the LAPD union newspaper, the *Blue Line*, was open beside the food. Enchiladas.

Starkey glanced at his food.

"Oh, hey, man, we didn't mean to interrupt your dinner."

"That's all right. I heard you got onto Homicide. How do you like it?"

Starkey shrugged, and glanced back at the squad room.

"It's okay, I guess. Anything shaking tonight?"

"Same old same old. You know how it is—weeks of boredom, seconds of terror."

"Yeah. Listen, Ax here needs to use the head, so I'm going to show him, okay? Is Beth at the same desk?"

"Oh, sure, right next to your old desk."

Starkey slipped her arm around my waist and gave me a squeeze.

"Now you get to see where I used to work, honey. Isn't that exciting?"

"Exciting."

She showed him the candy again.

"I'll drop this on her desk and get Ax squared away. Can I bring you a fresh coffee?"

He visibly brightened.

"That would be nice, Carol. Thanks."

"Right back. Keep eating, Hook. Really. Don't let your enchiladas get cold."

Starkey quickly found the desk she was looking for, put the chocolates beside the phone, then quietly opened a ceramic cookie jar with a unicorn on the lid.

She made sure Santos was back in the interview room, then lowered her voice.

"Marzik's kept her keys in here for years."

She fished inside, took out a ring of keys, then led me past a coffee room into an adjoining hall. The hall opened into another large room. This room was smaller than the CCS squad room, with half the number of cubicles, and was also deserted. The lights were on, which surprised me, but we were moving too fast to think about it.

"The task force guys were in here. C'mon, I'll let you in—"

Starkey checked again to make sure Santos wasn't watching, then trotted across the room with me behind her. Unlike the CCS cubicles, which were marked by clutter and family photographs, these cubicles were stripped and lifeless. The men and women who had sat at these desks cleaned out their possessions when the task force disbanded, and now the cubicles seemed desolate.

Starkey unlocked a door behind the cubicles, pulled it open, and stepped away.

"I'll put the keys back and keep Hooker busy as long as I can, but don't dawdle, okay? Look fast and get the hell out."

I stepped inside as she hurried away.

The file room was small and cramped, with three rows of metal Ikea shelves the CCS detectives had probably put up on their own time. Cardboard file boxes were lined on the shelves, along with a vinyl log used to keep track of who had which reports. The boxes on the middle shelf were labeled with the names of the victims, and should have contained everything

I wanted to check. I pulled down Frostokovich first, and knew it was bad even before I took off the top. Yellow hanging folders held a few scattered files and documents, but most of the folders were empty and the murder book was missing. I pushed the box back onto the shelf, then opened the Evansfield box to see if it had been cleaned out, too, but it was heavy with files and the murder book was wedged in behind the folders.

I checked each of the other boxes and worked my way to Repko, but, like Frostokovich, most of its files and murder book were missing. I looked through the remaining files for information about the video disk, but if the disk had ever been in the box all signs of it and Debra Repko's employment at Leverage Associates were missing.

I was checking the log when I heard Starkey call from far away.

"Hey, Ax! Did you get lost, honey? Where are you?"

I straightened the boxes, snapped off the light, and stepped out of the closet as Starkey appeared in the hall. She waved frantically for me to join her and lowered her voice as she pulled me down the hall.

"Munson's coming. Hooker told me he was just up here, and he's coming back—"

"The murder books are missing."

"Whatever. We're out of here, Cole."

We made sure the squad room was clear, then hurried toward the elevators. I hit the button, but Starkey moved past, pulling me with her.

"Forget it. We're taking the stairs."

She pushed through a stairwell door, and we hurried down the stairs, neither of us speaking. Every time we turned a corner I expected to see Munson on his way up, but we made it to the bottom without passing anyone.

Starkey stopped when we reached the lobby landing and took several deep breaths, calming herself. I touched her arm.

"We're okay. It's going to be fine."

"I'm not scared, Cole. I *smoke*."

She sucked a last deep breath, then took my hand and we stepped into the lobby. A man and a woman were waiting at the elevator, and Manuel was still looking bored at the security station. We held hands as we crossed the lobby as if it was the most natural thing in the world.

Manuel said, "Take care, Bombs. Be seein' you."

"You, too, Manny. I'll try to stop by more often."

I didn't realize her hand was damp until we were on the sidewalk.

31

WE KEPT our faces down as we walked to the corner, then crossed with the light to the parking lot and got into my car. When I put the key in the ignition, Starkey touched my hand.

"The murder books are missing?"

"Pretty much everything they had on Repko and Frostokovich is missing. The file on Trinh seemed light, but I don't know enough about that case to be sure. The log says everything should still be in the files, but it isn't."

"Hooker told me Munson carried out a box just before we got there. He said Bastilla took something yesterday."

"The last date in the log was the day Marx closed the case. Nothing has been signed out since."

"So they're just taking it."

I nodded, but I wasn't sure what to do about it. I reached for the key again, but Starkey stopped me.

"Let's wait."

"I'll take you back."

"I don't need to go back. If these bastards are covering for a murderer, I want their asses on a string. Let's see where he goes."

"He'll probably go home."

"Then let's follow him home and figure out what to do later. Maybe we can break into his car."

"Are you serious?"

"Roll down your window, Cole. I'm going to smoke."

Munson pulled out of the building two cigarettes later in a red Mustang GT. He stayed on the surface streets in no apparent hurry, passing under the freeway and away from the skyscrapers. We had followed him less than a mile when his blinker came on.

"You see it?"

"I got it."

The Mustang turned into the parking lot of one of the oldest steak houses in Los Angeles, Pacific Dining Car. Built in the twenties, the restaurant was housed in a railroad dining car. I pulled to the curb so we could watch.

Munson got out of his car with what appeared to be several loose files, left his car with the valet, and entered the restaurant. A crowd waiting to be seated was huddled around the door, but Munson wound through them as if he already had a place waiting. The restaurant had preserved the dining car's ambience by maintaining the big touring windows through which dining passengers had enjoyed passing scenery, so it was easy to watch Munson make his way through the restaurant. He went the length of the car, then slipped into a booth where two people were seated. Marx and Bastilla had been waiting.

Starkey and I got out of my car for a better view. The valets glanced over at us, but probably thought we were deciding whether to try out the restaurant.

Marx glanced at the files as Munson said something, then Marx brought a briefcase from under the table. He put the files into it, then put it away and motioned a waiter over.

The head valet was openly watching us now, and growing suspicious. It wouldn't be long before he alerted someone in the restaurant.

"Keep an eye on them. I'm going to pull around the corner for a better spot."

I moved my car into the shadows beneath a sycamore tree, then got out with my camera. The telephoto images would be grainy in the dim light, but the identities of the three people in the restaurant would be clear. The head valet didn't like seeing me with the camera, but couldn't do anything about it. Maybe he thought I was a paparazzo.

Starkey and I settled into my car and watched Marx and his inner circle share red wine and steaks for one hour and ten minutes. Then Marx paid the tab. The valets brought Munson's Mustang first, then a light-colored Toyota, then a dark Lexus sedan. When the cars were lined up nice and neat, Marx put his briefcase into the Lexus. Bastilla took a manila envelope from her car and gave it to Marx, who tossed it in with the briefcase. Munson took a cardboard file box from the Mustang's trunk, and put it into the back of Marx's Lexus. I photographed all of it. Everything was going with Marx.

Starkey said, "What do you think he's going to do with it?"

"I don't know. Maybe nothing. We still don't know what they have."

Her stare was languid and thoughtful through vines of smoke.

"Change it, more likely. You don't destroy that many records—a couple of files, maybe, sure, anyone can lose a file—but you can't explain it if that much stuff goes missing. So you change it. Take out the parts you don't like. Retype the pages if you have to. Then you put everything back in the system and hope nobody notices."

I was staring at her when she finished. She saw me staring, and shrugged.

"Just saying."

Marx didn't say much when they finished. They slipped into their cars, and pulled into the oncoming traffic. Starkey and I followed Marx.

He climbed onto the Pasadena Freeway almost right away and never once exceeded the speed limit. The traffic was heavy, but smooth—the lanes flowing with on-their-way-home-from-work freeway professionals who made this same drive at this same hour every day of the week. We crossed the river and cruised up through Montecito Heights, where the Pasadena officially becomes part of Route 66. Marx led us into South Pasadena, where the freeway ends, then along surface streets into the soft residential slopes of Altadena. We entered a neighborhood of neat, modest homes set among pepper trees that cast jagged shadows on the lawns. When his blinker came on, I cut the lights and pulled to the side.

Starkey said, "You think this is where he lives?"

"I don't know. Looks like it."

"Maybe he's just dropping off the stuff."

"Can you drive a stick?"

"What are you going to do?"

"I'm going to see. When I get out, get behind the wheel. Be ready to go."

The Lexus turned past the dark shoulder of a camellia bush, then lights flashed across a lawn. I got out, and ran hard to the camellia at the head of the drive. A small ARMED RESPONSE security patrol sign stood beside the bush. The garage was open, and bright with interior light. His sedan shared the garage with a silver Lexus SUV. Marx was lifting the box from his back-seat when I reached the camellia. An interior door from the garage into the house was open, and a woman wearing black pants and a loose T-shirt was waiting at the door. She was a nice-looking woman about Marx's age, and interacted with him the way a wife would interact with her husband.

Marx placed the box on the trunk of his car, sat his briefcase on the box, then put the manila envelope on top of the briefcase. When the stack of goods was manageable, he carried the box into the house. The woman stepped to the side to let him pass, then touched a button on the wall. I wondered if she knew what was in the box. I wondered if she cared.

The light in the garage went off.

The door rumbled down.

Marx was home.

His secrets were with him.

I called Joe Pike.

I SLIPPED into the shadows beneath a pepper tree, then made my way alongside Marx's house into his backyard. I took it slow, thinking there might be a dog or lights rigged to a motion sensor, but there was neither.

The backyard was lush and comfortable even at night, with a giant avocado tree spread over a patio. Fallen fruit littered the ground and filled the air with a pungent scent. The kitchen and what appeared to be a family room were on the garage side at the back of the house, and opened onto the patio. Marx had a very nice outdoor kitchen, with an enormous gas grill and a Big Green Egg smoker. The woman I took to be Marx's wife was in the kitchen. Marx entered the family room from the opposite side of the house, then disappeared through a door. He wasn't carrying the box or files or his briefcase, and no one else was visible inside the home.

Windows glowed with dim light on the far side of the house, so I moved past the patio. The first set of windows revealed a small bedroom that looked as if it hadn't been used in years. A bathroom came next, then the corner room. Marx was using the corner room as an office. The light was on. I moved closer to see if the box and files were in his office, but Marx came in before I reached the window. He went to his desk, looked down at something, then abruptly stepped into a closet. I couldn't see what was inside or what he did, but then he backed out, closed the door, and left his office. He turned out the light as he left.

I drifted back to the patio, saw that Marx was now in the kitchen with his wife, then returned to his office. I took out my penlight, cupped the lens with my hand, then turned it on, letting a sliver of light between my fingers. I examined the windows on both sides of his office, looking for alarm contacts. Most of the houses in the area had the ARMED RESPONSE sign like Marx, but most of them didn't have wired alarms. Neither did Marx. Like most other people in upper-middle-class neighborhoods, Marx had subscribed to the patrol, but hadn't popped for the hardware.

I shut the light, then continued around the house and made my way back to the street. When I reached the car, Starkey climbed over the console into the passenger seat.

"Jesus, what took you so long?"

"Marx brought the files inside. I wanted to look around."

I started the engine, then one-eightied toward the freeway.

Starkey said, "Damn. I'd love to see what he took."

I nodded, but didn't respond.

She said, "What are we going to do?"

"Go home. I'm taking you back to your car."

"That's it?"

"What do you expect me to do, kick down the door and beat him until he confesses? I need to figure out what to do next."

I made small talk as we drove back to Hollywood, and almost everything I said was a lie. I knew exactly what I was going to do, but I didn't want Starkey to know and I didn't want her to be part of it. She had already risked enough. And as with Pat Kyle, you have to protect your friends.

I dropped Starkey outside the Hollywood Station, let her believe I was heading home, then drove back to Altadena. Joe Pike had made good time. He was waiting at a mini-mart not far from Marx's home, his spotless red Jeep glittering in the fluorescent light beside the gas pumps like a jewel.

I pulled up next to him. Headlights coming down from the hills approached, flickered on our faces in a momentary illumination, then passed.

"You know what I'm going to do?"

"Sure. You're going to break into his house. Anyone inside with him?"

"His wife. We'll wait until tomorrow when the house is clear, then I'll go in. You okay with it?"

Pike didn't hesitate.

"Sure. Does Starkey know?"

"No. Better if she doesn't."

"Okay. Let's scout the area, then figure out how we're going to do this."

We planned our action at three that morning, huddled together over all-night mini-mart coffee and white-bread sandwiches of processed cheese. Then we crept into position and waited.

33

MARX BACKED out of his garage at ten minutes after eight the next morning. I was across the street, sitting behind a stunted fig tree at the corner of his neighbor's house. I had moved into position when the first grey fingers of morning pushed off the night. Pike was parked two blocks away beside a house that was being remodeled. Marx would drive past him if he headed for the freeway.

I hit the speed-dial for Joe.

"He's getting into his Lexus. He's wearing his uniform and he's alone. His wife is still home."

I shut my phone and waited. Pike called back two minutes later.

"I'm three cars behind him, southbound. Looks like he's heading for the freeway."

"Okay."

Pike would follow him to the freeway before turning back. Marx might have loaded the files back into his car, but I couldn't know that until I entered his house, so I sat in the fig tree and waited. I figured Marx would be gone for most of the day, but I was concerned about his wife. I wouldn't enter the house as long as she was present, and she might be one of those women who never left home. A housekeeper or guest might arrive, which would be even worse.

I waited.

My cell phone vibrated a few minutes later, making a soft buzz against my thigh. I thought it would be Pike, but it was Levy. He sounded excited and filled with interest.

"I think you're right about Deputy Chief Marx, Elvis. He's been virtually absent from his office this week. He's turned his regular duties over to his assistants."

"He's been busy. Bastilla and Munson have been removing task force files and giving them to Marx. Marx has been bringing them home."

Levy was quiet, then cleared his throat.

"Which files?"

"I'll know when I see them. I'm outside his house."

"Outside his home?"

"In a fig tree. I can't speak any louder."

Levy cleared his throat again.

"You shouldn't be telling me this. I'm an officer of the court."

"Did you talk to Ivy Casik?"

"I couldn't find her. I went to her apartment twice yesterday, but she wasn't home. Do you know if Marx or his people reached her?"

"Not yet. Maybe I'll know when I see the files."

"Right. Well. Good luck."

Levy sounded uncomfortable.

I ended the call and went back to waiting. Pike called again almost two hours later, at five minutes after ten.

"Want to switch places? Let you stretch your legs."

"I'm good. I kinda like it here in the tree."

"Your call."

The day wore on with glacial slowness. The mail was delivered, cars passed, and UPS dropped off a package. I was beginning to think I should have hijacked Marx's car when the garage door shivered open at twenty-six minutes after two and Marx's wife got into her SUV. I pressed the speed-dial as the engine started.

"She's coming out."

I had described her car the night before, but now I read off the license plate. The SUV backed into the street, then drove away in the same direction as Marx.

"Heading your way."

"You going in?"

"Soon as she's clear."

I waited for three cars to pass, then stepped from beneath the fig tree and crossed the street. Mrs. Marx might be leaving for the rest of the day or only running out for a bottle of milk, but either way I didn't hurry. I walked down their drive as if I were an old family friend, continued along the side of their house, and went directly to the kitchen door. The locks didn't take long, a Master deadbolt and the inset knob lock, six minutes top to bottom. I called Pike again when the tension bar slid home.

"I'm good. I'm going in."

I pulled on a pair of latex gloves and opened the door. I listened for a moment, then stepped inside. The house was cool and smelled of scented soap, but I didn't like being there. I wanted to see what I needed to see, then get the hell out. I crossed through the kitchen, listened again, then hurried directly to the office.

A mahogany desk was angled in the corner, facing built-in cabinets, the closet, and a small TV. The unmistakable three-ring navy binder of a murder book sat on his desk. It hadn't been on his desk last night, but now it was, as if he had looked at it this morning before leaving for work. The handwritten label on the spine read *Trinh*.

His desk and the area around the murder book were immaculate, with a desktop PC, a cordless phone, and a short stack of papers beside the keyboard. I fingered through the papers, but found nothing related to the case. Folders inside the desk drawers were labeled for personal things like insurance policies and utility bills. I went to the closet, and there was the rest of it. The box Munson gave to Marx was on the floor. Several thick folders held together by rubber bands were stacked on top, and two more murder books were on the floor beside the box. Repko and Frostokovich.

I felt a twinge of sadness when I saw them.

"Hello, Debra."

I photographed the box and the murder books, then snapped a wider shot to establish the material was in the closet. I dragged the box into the room, put the murder books on top, then took more pictures from angles that included Marx's desk and personal possessions, and the Trinh murder book on the desk. I wanted undeniable proof the missing files were in Marx's home.

When I had enough pictures, I opened Sondra Frost-okovich's murder book. I was reading the first page, all good to go and work my way through the entire thing, when my cell phone vibrated.

Pike said, "Marx and Munson just passed, inbound. Thirty seconds."

He didn't waste time with more words. I had been in the house less than eight minutes, and now I was done. I had wanted to read through the material, photograph those things I found incriminating, and leave the files undisturbed to buy myself more time, but now I couldn't play it that way. It was a lot of paper but I took it. The box was only half full, so I shoved in the loose folders and murder books, and carried it into the bathroom adjoining Marx's office.

The garage door rumbled on the far side of the house as I stepped into the hall. I carried the box into the bathroom, set it on the toilet, and pushed open the window. The front door opened as I climbed out. Marx said something I didn't understand as I reached back inside for the box.

I closed the window, slipped into the thick bushes between Marx's house and the next, and hit the speed-dial for Pike. He answered like this:

"I'm here."

"Never a doubt."

I pushed through the hedges into the neighbors' yard and saw Pike's Jeep in the street. I probably should have walked, but I ran as hard as I could without looking back and without caring who saw me.

I jammed into Pike's Jeep with the box in my lap, and Pike gunned away, the door snapping shut so hard it hammered my elbow.

Pike said, "Close."

My eyes burned as I laughed. It was a stupid laugh, like a barking dog. I couldn't stop until Pike gripped my arm.

34

THE CANYON behind my house was pleasant during the midday hours, with a slight breeze that brought out the hawks to search for rabbits and mice. Somewhere below, a power saw whined in the trees, punctuated by the faint tapping of a nail gun. Someone was always building something, and the sounds of it were encouraging. They sounded like life.

We put the file box and murder books on the dining table, then drank bottles of water. We ate muffins slathered with strawberry jam, standing over the murder books as if we were stealing time to eat like we had stolen the files.

We split the material between us. I skimmed the Frostokovich murder book first, and immediately saw that pages had been removed. Every murder book begins with an initial report by the original detectives who caught the case, identifying the victim and describing the crime scene. Marx and Munson had signed off on the opening crime scene report. Reports relating interviews with the workmen who discovered her body came next, followed by their initial interview with Sondra's parents, Ron L. and Ida Frostokovich. If Marx and Munson interviewed Sondra's girlfriends about the dinner they shared, the report of that interview was now missing. A twelve-page gap in the page-numbering sequence followed the interview with Sondra's parents. The medical examiner's six-page autopsy protocol was intact, but another three pages after it were missing. I didn't bother to flip through the rest of the book.

"They gutted this thing. We've got missing pages all through here."

Pike was fingering through the files in the box. He grunted, then lifted a ziplock bag containing a silver DVD. The name REPKO was written directly onto the DVD and clearly visible through the transparent plastic bag.

Pike said, "Your missing disk."

A folded letter was stapled to the bag. Pike read it, then passed it to me.

"They sent it to the FBI. SID had it right. The Feds couldn't get anything off the disk, either."

The letter was from the FBI's lab in San Francisco and was addressed to Deputy Chief Thomas Marx. It confirmed what Pike had just told me.

"But why send it at all? If Marx thought it would clear Byrd or implicate Wilts, why not just destroy it?"

Pike grunted again, and we went on with the files.

The Trinh murder book was also missing material, though not as much as Frostokovich, but the Repko book had been looted. Most of the documents and large sections of each report were missing.

I put the murder books aside and picked out a thin file marked REPKO-PDA/PHONE LOG. The first page was a letter from the president of a cellular service provider addressed to Marx regarding Debra Repko's missing PDA.

> *Dear Chief Marx,*
>
> *Per your personal request today and with the understanding that this communication is off the record until such time as our attorneys receive the proper court instruction, please find the call record covering the prior sixty-day period for the above referenced cell number, which is held in contract by Leverage Associates. As discussed, I am trusting in your good word and discretion that our cooperation will remain undisclosed.*
> *If I can be of further assistance in this matter, please do not hesitate to call my personal line.*
>
> *Sincerely.*
> *Paulette Brennert, President*

The date indicated that Marx had requested the call log almost a week before Byrd's body was found.

I said, "Get this—Marx knew about Debra Repko's PDA. Darcy and Maddux didn't even know about it, but Marx knew and requested the call history."

"Didn't you ask Bastilla about it?"

"This is from before that. Bastilla must have been pretending."

Pike moved closer and turned the page.

The next five sheets were the call logs listing the numbers to and from Debra's PDA during the period prior to her death. Handwritten notes in blue or black ink were by each call and most of the calls were identified as being to or from Leverage employees. A few of the calls were simply marked as family, but six of the calls were highlighted in yellow marker. The six highlighted calls had all been made in the ten days prior to her death, and all were to or from the same number. The highlighted number had not been identified. I kept reading.

The next page was a spec sheet showing a picture of a simple basic cell phone manufactured by Kyoto Electronics. It was an inexpensive model that did not fold or take pictures, and likely offered very few features. An accompanying letter was attached to the spec sheet.

Detective C. Bastilla,

The cellular number in question is a prepaid number assigned to a cell phone (Model AKL-1500) manufactured by Kyoto Electronics. (See enclosed picture.) Our records indicate that the phone unit, cell-service activation, and additional talk-time minutes were purchased by cash. For this reason, we are unable to provide information about the purchaser.

Due to legal and liability requirements, we are unable to provide call-log records for the above-referenced number until in receipt of an appropriate court order. Once in receipt of such order, we will be happy to comply.

> *Sincerely,*
> *Michael Toman*
> *Operations Manager*

Pike said, "She had two conversations with the highlighted number on the day she was murdered."

"Joe. Bastilla was trying to identify the caller."

"Looks that way. Looks like they were trying to identify someone else, too."

Pike drew out a folder that was thick with documents about Wilts, but none of the reports and files were anything I expected. This file was labeled FBI, and contained a letter from Marx to the FBI director in Washington, D.C. It was marked PERSONAL & CONFIDENTIAL. A short list of phone numbers was attached, including the number that had been highlighted in yellow.

This letter will serve as my official request that your agency obtain the proper court instruction for, and initiate and maintain, recorded phone monitors on the attached Los Angeles area code phone numbers, and do so independent of and without the knowledge of my own agency, the Los Angeles Police Department, or any other local personnel, officials, or local judicial members. As Councilman Nobel Wilts is believed to have knowledge of or possibly have committed multiple homicides over a seven-year period, I cannot stress enough the need for utmost security in this matter.

I stared at the page, but the words had lost focus. I pushed past a growing sense of frustration and checked the date. Marx had faxed his request to the head of the FBI only eight days ago—two days before he told the world that Lionel Byrd had committed the murders.

I said, "Joe."

I gave him the page.

"They aren't protecting Wilts. They're investigating him. It's an active investigation."

We were reading through the rest of the files when the first car arrived. They didn't scream up Code Three with the lights and sirens, and SWAT didn't rappel from hovering choppers. Gravel crunched outside my door, followed by the soft squeak of brakes.

Pike went to the window.

"It's Marx."

The Inner Circle had arrived.

35

MARX AND Munson unfolded from his Lexus. Bastilla eased up from the opposite direction with a black-and-white Metro car behind her. They saw me at the same time, but no one shouted or tried to knock me down.

Marx was calm, but somehow larger, as if swollen with tension.

I said, "You heartless sonofabitch. You told those people it was over."

Munson flicked his fingers, telling me to move out of the door.

"Let's go in, Cole. We need to have a little talk."

"Do you have a warrant?"

Bastilla said, "You're in no position. Act like an adult."

The uniforms stayed in their car, but the rest of them came inside. Marx glanced at Pike, then frowned at the files and murder books spread over the table. He told Bastilla to gather their stuff, then frowned at me.

"Have you read these things?"

"Enough to know what you're doing. I pushed this thing because I thought you were protecting him."

"Now you know you were wrong. You should have just let it go, but no, you couldn't mind your business."

"Yvonne Bennett made it my business, Marx. So do the Repkos and Ida Frostokovich and the other families you've lied to. You told those people it was finished. They've buried their children, but they're going to have to dig them up again. What in hell were you thinking?"

He hooked a thumb at Pike.

"How many people besides you and this one know what we're doing?"

"A few."

"Poitras is probably helping you, isn't he?"

"Poitras doesn't know anything."

"We need their names."

"Forget it, Marx. There's no chance in hell."

Munson had gone to the sliders.

"Sweet. You got your privacy, you got your view, you have your stolen police property. Not everyone would have the balls to break into a deputy chief's house."

"You have me confused with someone else."

Munson laughed. He was probably a pretty good guy and I would probably like him if he was someone else.

"Please, Cole. Really. Who else could it be, the way

303

you've been dogging us. Now we have this problem."

Pike, floating between the dining room and kitchen, said, "We don't have a problem."

Munson hit Pike with the grin.

"Look at Pike here. Pike looks like he wants to shoot it out. What do you say, Chief? We could kill'm, say they resisted arrest."

Bastilla glanced up from stacking the files.

"You're not helping."

"That was humor. They know I'm kidding."

Marx looked at me with the unfocused eyes of someone who had considered it and hadn't been kidding.

"We could have gotten the warrants and brought along some boys from Metro, but we didn't. I can't force you to cooperate, but we have to contain this. If Wilts finds out, we may never be able to make the case. That meant lying about our investigation, but now this is where we are, and you're here with us."

"You believe Wilts killed those women."

"Yes."

"Then why close the case on Byrd? Why tell those families it was over?"

"Because that's what Wilts wants us to think."

Munson pulled a chair from the table and swung his leg over it like he was mounting a horse.

"We believe he engineered Byrd's death so we would close the Repko case—probably because he was scared we might find something on the security disk. He forced our hand with this damned death book. When we realized that's what he wanted, we gave him Byrd to buy ourselves more time."

Pike said, "Why Byrd?"

Munson shrugged.

"Byrd was already connected to one of the victims—Yvonne Bennett. He's gotta be thinking, when we find Byrd with this picture of Bennett, we'll think it's a slam dunk. If you're asking how Wilts and Byrd are connected, we don't know. Wilts might have picked him because of the Bennett connection, but maybe they knew each other."

I said, "That's a helluva risk to take, thinking you'll call it quits just because Byrd has the book."

Marx's lips pressed into a hard line.

"Well, Cole, I guess he thought it was worth the risk, didn't he? Repko wasn't some streetwalker—he screwed up by killing someone close to him, which was a mistake he hadn't made since Frostokovich."

A knot of anger grew in my shoulders.

"Have you bastards known he's been killing people for seven years?"

Munson made a grunting laugh that caused Bastilla to glance up, but Marx glowered.

"Of course not. Only since the book."

"You must have known since Frostokovich."

"Goddamnit. I took care of some things for him, but nothing like this. He was a nasty bastard, all right, but I was investigating one of my friends. You never think someone you know could do something like this."

"So you let it go? You fixed it for him?"

"Fuck off, Cole. The girl's friends told us about running into him that night at dinner, so we questioned him. He told us he went to an apartment he kept over by Chinatown after seeing them at dinner. Alone. So we had the coincidence of the meetings, and we knew he was a prick, but that was it. We couldn't clear him, but we couldn't find anything solid. You can't make a case on coincidence, so we all went on with our lives. After a while I told myself it was silly to suspect the guy. Hell, he was my friend, and all we had was the coincidental meeting."

Pike said, "Until Repko."

"Repko got us started, but it was really the book. When we saw Frostokovich everything came back. Wilts knew some of these girls. Wilts was the common demoninator."

Munson picked up where Marx left off by explaining they had discovered a connection between Wilts and the fourth victim pictured in the book, twenty-five-year-old prostitute Marsha Trinh. In reviewing her arrest record, it was learned she was one of five prostitutes Wilts had hired for a private party to influence prominent supporters one month before her murder. This contact put Wilts with three of the seven victims. Three out of seven was convincing.

Munson said, "We still have a long way to go, Cole. We can't have you drawing attention to this. The man has to believe he's safe."

"How close are you?"

"We would arrest him if we had something. We don't."

"You think he's a flight risk?"

"You never know, but no, I don't think so. People like this, they think they can beat you and some of them do. They get off by thinking they're smarter than us. He wanted us to think Byrd is the guy, and right now he believes we bought it. That's why we played it the way we did. As long as he believes he's safe, we have a shot at making a case. You cannot kill seven people without making a mistake. It cannot be done."

Munson nodded like he believed it, then stared at me.

"We're busting our asses to make this case, but right now our biggest problem is you, asking around at Leverage, scaring the shit out of the Casik girl, getting Alan Levy worked up—"

I raised my palms, stopping him.

"Waitaminute. How did I scare Ivy Casik?"

Marx scowled at me.

"That's why I hate goddamned private operators like you—you don't know how to handle yourself."

I looked at Bastilla.

"What's this about, Bastilla? Did you find her?"

"I didn't have to find her. She called. She wanted to file a complaint against you."

"For what?"

"She said you accused her of being a drug dealer."

"I asked if she picked up the oxys for Byrd."

"She heard it as a threat."

"What did she say about the reporter?"

"There wasn't a reporter, you dipshit. She made it up to get rid of you. Then she got worried she might get into trouble, so she called us to straighten it out."

I flashed on Ivy Casik. I wondered if Levy had found her and if she had told him the same thing. Then Bastilla put the last of the files in the box and stacked the murder books on top.

"That's everything, Chief."

Marx nodded, then studied me again. His brow was so deeply furrowed it looked like rows of midwestern corn.

"So what are you going to do? Can we get some cooperation here?"

I glanced at Pike, and Pike nodded.

"I don't like it, but I understand what you're trying to do. I'm not going to sit out the game, Marx, but I won't spoil the play. I'm better than that."

"We'll see."

Marx put out his hand. The gesture surprised me, and maybe I hesitated too long, but I took it. He left without saying anything else, then Munson followed with the files. Bastilla was trailing after Munson when I stopped her at the door.

"When you bust Wilts, everything about the chief's prior relationship with him is going to come out. It isn't lost on me that he knows that."

She arched her eyebrows, and it was as cool a move as anything I had ever seen.

"How nice for you, Cole."

We listened to them drive away, then I went to the phone and called Alan Levy. Jacob answered again.

"Sorry, Mr. Cole, he isn't in. Would you like to leave another message?"

"This would be easier if you gave me his cell."

Jacob wouldn't give me the cell, but he promised to page Alan and then hung up.

I put down the phone and turned to Pike.

"Let's go see Ivy. If I scared her, wait 'til she sees you."

"You don't think she lied?"

"I think she's lying to someone. The question is who."

We were moving for the door when Alan Levy returned my call. Jacob had come through with the page.

36

SPEAKING WITH Levy left me conflicted. Alan was trying to help, but I had given Marx my word and understood his need for secrecy, so I did not tell Levy that Wilts was a suspect. I told him about Ivy Casik instead.

"I spoke with Bastilla again. She told me Ivy made up the story about the reporter."

"Where did Bastilla find her?"

"She didn't. Ivy called her to complain about me."

I related what Bastilla told me.

Alan made grunting noises as he listened, then sounded doubtful.

"She claimed you threatened her?"

"She was surprised when I approached her, but I didn't threaten her or do anything to scare her. She told Bastilla she made it up to get rid of me."

"Does Bastilla believe her?"

"It sounded that way. Ivy called Bastilla, not the other way around. She wanted to file a complaint."

"Did she tell them anything new about Byrd?"

"I don't think so. Bastilla didn't say that she did."

Alan fell silent for a moment.

"We should speak with this woman. I went over there again today and she still wasn't home."

"Pike and I were leaving for her apartment when you called."

"Good. If you find her, let me know. I think this girl knows more than she's telling."

"I do, too, Alan."

"Let me give you my cell number. You won't have to go through Jacob."

He gave me the number, then Pike and I locked up the house. We took both cars in case we had to split up, driving in a loose caravan down through the canyon and east to Ivy Casik's apartment.

The modest apartment house held the same watchful silence it had on my earlier visits, as if the building and people within it were sleeping. The afternoon stillness trapped the scent of the gardenias in the courtyard, reminding me of the cloying smell of a funeral parlor.

Pike and I knocked on Ivy's door, but, like before, she did not answer.

Pike said, "Creepy place."

"Pod people live here."

"Maybe she's at work."

"She's a website designer. She works at home."

Pike reached past me and knocked again. Loud.

I pressed my ear to the door, listening for movement

inside her apartment. A large window was to the left of the door, but Ivy had pulled her drapes. I cupped my face to the window, trying to see through a thin gap in the drapes, but couldn't see much. The lights were off, but my view was only a thin slice of the interior. The memory of Angel Tomaso's body was fresh, and I suddenly feared I might find Ivy the same way.

"You with the noise again."

We turned, and saw the pear-shaped manager in his door. He blinked at me, then saw Pike and blinked again.

He said, "Oh, my."

The little pug waddled out between his feet and stood in the courtyard, panting.

I said, "Sorry. The sound really echoes in here, doesn't it?"

"Is this about the police again?"

He wore the same thin cotton shirt and baggy shorts, and still held a cocktail glass. It might have been the same glass. His legs were lumpy with cellulite and very white.

I said, "That's right. We need to see her."

"You and everyone else. Someone was here earlier, too, banging away at the door."

That would have been Levy.

"Was she home?"

"She travels a lot, you know. I don't think she saw the note you left in her box."

He tinkled the ice again, pissed off I had left the

note in her mailbox instead of with him, and frowned at the dog.

"Go make piddle."

The little dog's round face curled into a smile, then it waddled back into his apartment.

"She doesn't tell me when she's coming and going. If you'd like to leave a note with me this time, I'll make sure she gets it."

I glanced back at her apartment, wondering what was behind the door.

Pike gestured at the surrounding apartments.

"She friendly with any of these people? Maybe they know where she is."

He sized Pike up and down, and tinkled the ice again. He put out his hand.

"I'm Darbin Langer. Yours?"

"Pike."

Langer hadn't bothered to introduce himself to me.

He shook his head, answering Pike's question.

"I doubt it. She isn't the friendliest person, and we like our privacy here. We like a quiet home without all this coming and going and knocking. They're all at work anyway, and I'd ask you not to pound on their doors."

"How about I slip a note under her door. Maybe that would work better than leaving it in her box."

He frowned, pissy again, then turned back into his apartment.

"Whatever. Just stop with the noise."

Pike and I returned to her apartment but I had no

intention of leaving a note. I left Pike by her door, then circled behind the building, trying to see inside.

Climbing roses trellised the walls, bracketing a tall hedge that formed a narrow path leading around the sides of the building. The rose vines drooped over the path, brushing my face like delicate fingers. The stillness and silence felt eerie. I followed the path around the building, peeping in Ivy's windows like a neighborhood pervert, with the creeped-out feeling I was about to see something I didn't want to see, like Ivy with a slashed throat.

The back and side windows were off her bedroom, and here she hadn't been as careful when pulling the drapes. The first window was completely covered, but the drapes covering the second window hung apart with a gap as wide as my hand. The room inside was dim, but revealed a double bed and a doorway to the hall leading out to the living room. The room was bare except for the bed, with no other furniture, nothing on the walls, and no bodies in evidence. Ivy might have been hiding under the bed, but probably wasn't.

The bathroom was next, with one of those high windows so neighbors can't see you doing your business. I gripped the ledge and chinned myself. Being high the way it was, drapes weren't necessary, so nothing covered the window. Ivy wasn't crouching in the bathroom, either. I let myself down, went on to the living room, then returned to the bathroom. I chinned again, and squinted inside. The bathroom was old like the rest of the building, with a postwar tub and cracked tiles seamed by darkened grout. The floor was a dingy vinyl that had probably been yellowing since the sixties. Something about the bathroom bothered me, and it took a moment to realize what.

I let myself down and returned to the courtyard.

Pike said, "Clear?"

"She told me she rented the room on Anson because they found mold in her bathroom, but this bathroom hasn't been touched in years."

We went back to Langer's apartment. He opened the door wide. Still with the glass in his hand.

"Oh. Back so soon?"

"Did you have a mold problem in Ivy's apartment?"

He squinted as if we were trying to trick him.

"Mold?"

"Did you remodel her bathroom to get rid of mold?"

"I don't know what you're talking about."

"Ivy told me mold was found in her apartment a couple of months ago. She had to move out for a few weeks while it was remodeled."

"We've never had mold. I don't know what you're talking about."

"Did she move out?"

"Well, she was gone for a while, but she didn't move out. She was working."

"I thought she worked at home."

He wiggled the glass again, only now the ice was melted. The wiggle was silent.

"No, she works with the films. A makeup artist, I think, or doing their hair. That's why she's gone so much. The location work."

Pike grunted.

"Websites, huh."

I looked back at her closed apartment door. The little courtyard grew stifling hot and the gardenias smelled like ant poison.

"Mr. Langer, how long has Ivy lived here?"

He looked from me to Pike, then back to me, and now his bald head wrinkled. He was getting nervous.

"About four months now. Why do you want to know that?"

Pike said, "We'd like to see her apartment, please."

Langer's eyes flickered to Pike, and he shifted from foot to foot.

"Just let you in? That wouldn't be right. I don't think I can let you in."

He wiggled the silent glass nervously.

I said, "The police and I were here to question Ivy about a man involved in a multiple homicide—"

"A murder?"

"That's why all these people have been coming around, only now it looks like Ivy's been lying about some things. We can't wait for her to come back."

I glanced back at her apartment.

"She might already be back. She might be in there right now."

He glanced at her apartment, too, and Pike stepped very close to him.

"Let us in, Mr. Langer."

Langer hurried away for his key.

37

THE DAY I questioned Ivy Casik about Lionel Byrd, her apartment had seemed efficiently minimalist and neat, but now it felt empty, as if it were not a place where someone had ever lived. The couch, chair, and cheap dinette set were lifeless and anonymous like rental castoffs. The kitchen drawers held only three forks, three spoons, and a can opener. The double bed was as absent of life as an abandoned car, and the closet was empty. If there had been a hard-line phone, she had taken it.

Langer let us in, then clenched his hands as we searched.

Pike said, "She's gone. Nothing here to come back to."

Ivy Casik had lied to me and the kid at the store and Langer and Bastilla. She had lied well and thoroughly, and I wondered if she had also lied about her name.

I asked Langer if she paid the rent by check, hoping

he might have one for the banking information, but he shook his head.

"Cash. First, last, and the security deposit. She paid six months in advance."

"What about a rental agreement?"

Pike and I were still looking through her apartment when Langer returned with the agreement. He was so nervous now, his jowls were shaking.

"It has her cell phone number, but I called and it wasn't her. I got somebody named Rami."

Pike said, "She gave you a false number. Like everything else."

Langer held out the rental agreement, as if we would understand just by seeing the number.

The contract was a form document you could buy in any stationery store, obligating the tenant to pay a certain amount every month and to be responsible for any damages. Spaces were provided for background information, prior residences, and references.

"Is this your handwriting, or hers?"

"Hers. It's so much easier if you let them fill it in themselves. We sat at the table, talking."

Her handwriting was slanted to the right and had been made with a blue ballpoint pen. An address in Silver Lake was the only former residence listed, and was probably false. Spaces for her driver's license and Social Security numbers were filled in, but they, like the cell phone number, were probably false. I copied the numbers anyway. I planned to call Bastilla, and then Mr. Langer would have more people knocking on doors and filling his courtyard with noise.

The spaces for banking and credit information were blank.

"You didn't require any of this?"

"She was paying with cash. She seemed so nice."

The dog waddled in through the open door and wandered between us. Pike petted the little round head. The dog licked his hand.

Everything was written in blue ink, except for the make and model of her car. The information about her car was written in a cramped hand using black ink.

"Did you write this?"

"Uh-huh, that's me. People never remember their license. I saw her getting into her car one day, so I went out later and copied it."

Her car was a white Ford Neon with a California plate, and was likely the only true information we had unless she had stolen the car. I remembered seeing the Neon on the day we met.

"Are the police coming back?"

"Yes, sir."

"I didn't do anything wrong, did I?"

"You were lied to like everyone else."

We thanked him for the help, then went to our cars to phone Bastilla. She didn't seem particularly impressed.

"We talk to you about this a half hour ago, and you're back on the case?"

"I told you I wouldn't sit it out, Bastilla. Are you interested in this or not?"

"So she's a liar, Cole. People lie all the time."

"She's the only person we've found with a confirmed relationship to Byrd, and she's been lying to
everyone, which means maybe she lied about Byrd,
too. Doesn't that bother you?"

"Yes, it bothers me, but right now it doesn't mean
much one way or another. This guy you spoke with,
the manager, is he still on the premises?"

"Yeah. In his apartment."

"Okay. Tell him to stay put. I'll see what the DMV
has on her before we roll out."

I closed my phone, then looked at Pike.

"They're coming out to see Langer."

"Cool. Let's kick back and wait."

I laughed, then opened the phone again and called a
friend at the DMV. I read off the Neon's plate, asked
for the registration information, and had it in less than
a minute. The Neon was registered to a Sara K. Hill
with an address in a small community called Sylmar
at the top of the San Fernando Valley.

"Does the vehicle show stolen?"

"Nope. No wants, warrants, or unpaid citations.
Registration is in order and up to date."

I put down the phone and told Pike.

He said, "Maybe that's her real name."

Sara K. Hill was listed with Sylmar Information. I
copied her number, then dialed. A woman answered
on the sixth ring, her voice sounding older and coarse.

I said, "May I speak with Ivy, please."

"You have the wrong number."

She hung up.

I called her again, and this time she answered after only two rings.

"Me, again. Is this Sara Hill?"

"Yes."

"Sorry to bother you, but I'm trying to find Ivy Casik."

"Well, good luck to you. I don't know anyone by that name."

She sounded more irritated than anything else.

"I think maybe you might. She's driving your car."

Sara Hill's voice grew careful.

"Are you from the credit card?"

"No, ma'am. I'm not from the credit card."

Her voice was still careful.

"Who did you want?"

"A tall girl, straight hair, in her mid-twenties—"

Sara Hill cut me off.

"I don't know anyone like that! Don't call here again!"

The line went dead again, but this time we didn't call back. Pike went to his Jeep, I climbed into my car, and we drove north through the Cahuenga Pass toward Sylmar.

38

SYLMAR WAS a small rural community at the foot of the Newhall Pass, where the San Fernando Valley died against the mountains. The main streets were lined with outdated strip malls and fast-food outlets, but remnants of truck farms and plant nurseries were scattered across a landscape gone largely undeveloped thanks to the ugly convergence of freeways, railroad tracks, and power stations. It was the kind of area where signs offered FEED and TACK.

Pike followed me to a small house in a ragged neighborhood between the Golden State Freeway and the railroad. The yards were large the way they tend to be in rural areas, and burned dead by the heat. More than one house sported rusted-out cars and chain-link fences so old they sagged from the weight of the air. Even in that shabby neighborhood, Sara Hill's house looked tired and sad.

The white Neon was not in her drive, so we cruised the area to see if it was parked nearby or hidden in someone's yard. When we returned to the house, we parked on either side of the street, then Pike trotted down the drive to cover the rear. I found three letters and some throwaway flyers in the mailbox. The letters were addressed to Sara Hill. We had the right place.

I brought the mail to the door, rang the bell once, then knocked. A few seconds later, Mrs. Sara K. Hill called from behind the door.

"Who is it?"

"I phoned about Ivy Casik."

"Go away. I don't know anything about the credit, and I ain't got nothin' to say about it."

"I have your mail."

Her voice rose.

"Put it down. Stealin' mail is a federal crime. I'll call the police."

"I'm the police. Open the door and I'll show you my badge."

Lying is often the best policy.

Sara Hill threw open the door. She was a large woman with angry eyes and swollen joints, and she filled the frame with her bulk. She wore a thin house-dress frayed at the hem, and rested her weight on a cane. I tried to see past her, but couldn't.

"You're not from the credit?"

"I don't know anything about the credit. See?"

I held up my license. It didn't look anything like a badge, but she probably didn't understand what she was seeing.

"You gimme that mail. I don't like the look of you one bit. You look like your voice."

I held up the mail but didn't give it to her.

"The Neon."

"You're not from the credit?"

"No, I am not from the credit. I'm trying to find the woman who is driving your car. She may have knowledge of a crime and she might be in danger."

The angry eyes softened into something fearful, as if she was used to bad news and figured she was about to get more.

"She didn't have an accident, did she? I don't think I could take that right now."

"Do you know a young woman named Ivy Casik?"

"I don't know any Ivy Casik. My daughter is Jonna Hill. She has the car, but I guess she could've loaned it out. What happened?"

I tried to see past her again, and held up my hand to indicate Ivy's height.

"This tall. A big girl, athletic, with straight hair. A heart tattooed here on her arm."

Her eyes fluttered with even more fear, then she pivoted on the cane and grabbed the wall for support as she headed into the house. She pointed the cane at something deep in the room I could not see, so I followed her.

The small living room was as ragged as the yard, with threadbare furniture that smelled of sour flesh and pickles. An ancient console television sat under the window, but it probably hadn't worked in years.

She was using it as a table. A small Hitachi portable was on the console, along with a couple of pictures. She jabbed the cane toward one of the pictures.

"That's Jonna right there. Don't you dare tell me something bad."

The picture was yet another high-school graduation portrait, the kind every school in America takes during senior year so they can sell different sizes to you and your family. Jonna was Ivy, of course, only younger, with naturally dark hair. I had seen a lot of these graduation pictures in the past week, but Jonna Hill's picture was not the last. A picture of Yvonne Bennett was beside it.

I stared at Yvonne for a while, then looked at Sara Hill. The only part of her I saw in her daughters were the eyes. Seeds of anger were deep in their eyes.

Joe Pike stepped out of the kitchen, as quiet as air moving through air.

"She's not here."

Mrs. Hill staggered sideways in surprise, catching herself on her cane.

"Jesus Lord, what is this? Who are you?"

I gave her a gentle smile.

"It's all right, Mrs. Hill. He's the police, too. We just wanted to make sure everyone was safe."

I glanced at Pike.

"See if she left anything."

Mrs. Hill waved the cane after him as he disappeared.

"Where's he going? What's he going to do?"

"Look around. It's a cop thing. We always look around."

She jabbed at the picture again.

"You better not be from the credit and lied to get in here. Jonna warned me the credit might send a man looking for her."

I kept my voice gentle, just like the smile.

"Did Jonna tell you she was hiding from a collection agency?"

"She got behind, is all. You know how these kids do with the plastic. She said they were getting mean about it and if anyone came I should say I don't know where she is and haven't heard from her."

Then she studied me as if realizing what she was saying.

"That isn't you, is it? If you're lying I'll get on the phone right now. I'll call the police."

"We're not from the credit."

"Then why do you want Jonna? She isn't in trouble, is she?"

"Yes, I think she is."

Sara clumped to the couch and eased herself down.

"Lord, please don't tell me that. She told me she had the credit problems, but now something like this."

I picked up the picture of Yvonne. Yvonne would have been five or six years older than Jonna, and though I could see a resemblance, they didn't look much alike. Even in high school, the woman I knew as Ivy Casik looked humorless and dark. Even then,

Yvonne's mouth had already curled into a knowing grin absent of innocence.

"Is this Jonna's sister?"

"I don't talk about that one. That's the bad one. She was always bad, and her bad ways caught up. I wouldn't even keep it up there if it wasn't for Jonna. She gets mad when I put it away."

"Her name was Yvonne."

Sara Hill was surprised.

"You knew her?"

"I worked on the case."

"She was a tramp. Wasn't no better than a cat in heat from when she was little."

My right eye ticked and I fought to control it. I put the picture back in its place.

"They had different fathers to go with the different last names?"

"The good one and the bad one, just like the girls, and the good one wasn't worth too damn much, either. He left like they all left, off to take up with tramps. Vonnie drove half of'm away, acting the tramp."

Pike reappeared. He shook his head, telling me he hadn't found anything. I sat beside Mrs. Hill.

"We need to find Jonna. She's got worse trouble than bad credit."

"Don't tell me she's turned into a whore. Jonna was always the good one, not like Yvonne. Just please don't tell me that."

"Remember Lionel Byrd?"

"I never heard of him."

"Lionel Byrd was charged with Yvonne's murder. You didn't know that?"

She twitched her cane as if she didn't give a damn either way.

"I washed my hands of all that. She was always bad, and her bad ways caught up to her. We parted company long before she was punished."

I wasn't quite sure what to say.

"You washed your hands."

"When the police called I told'm I wanted nothing to do with it. It liked to kill Jonna, though. My God, she carried on, going on and on about how this man got away with it, but I just wouldn't hear of it, all that sordid mess, and I said this must stop, Jonna, Yvonne isn't worth it. Yvonne has always been like this and she got what she deserved."

Pike said, "I'll wait outside."

Mrs. Hill frowned as he left.

I said, "Did Jonna want to punish the man who murdered Yvonne?"

She waved the cane again.

"Don't be silly. She got over all that, got herself a good job, and she's doing just fine, thank you very much. Jonna's my good baby. We don't talk about Yvonne. She knows I won't have it."

"Where is she?"

"I guess she's at home."

"We just left her place. It looked like she moved out."

Mrs. Hill seemed confused.

"Maybe she thought you were from the credit. She was here just a little while ago, and told me she was going right home."

Something in her casual certainty made me wonder if we were talking about the same thing.

"She went back to Hollywood?"

"What's down in Hollywood?"

"Her apartment."

"She doesn't live in Hollywood. She lives right over here by the reservoir."

I could see it in the clarity of her eyes. Sara Hill was telling me the absolute truth as she knew it. Her daughter had successfully lied to everyone.

Then her eyes grew smaller and blinked.

"You're not from the credit, are you? She was so afraid someone would come after her she thought she might have to hide."

I gave her a smile I did not feel.

"I'm not from the credit. Tell me where Jonna lives. I'll find out why she's afraid."

39

JONNA HILL had rented a small bungalow not much larger than Angel Tomaso's garage, less than a half-mile from her mother. Pike stayed with Sara to prevent her from warning her daughter, so I drove to Jonna's alone. I didn't know what I expected to find, but she was getting ready to leave.

The white Neon was parked at the side of the house with its trunk open like a hungry mouth. The woman I knew as Ivy Casik was carrying an armful of clothes toward the car when I pulled into her drive. She didn't recognize me at first because she stood with the clothes, staring, and then I got out.

"Hi, Jonna. Remember me?"

She dropped the clothes and ran toward her door. I closed on her fast, but she reached the door, and for no reason I knew then or now, she turned hard for the street. Maybe she was so scared all she thought was to run and keep running.

I tackled her in the front yard, and the two of us

tumbled into the baked earth and dead grass. She punched and gouged, pumping her knees to get away until I locked her elbow.

"Stop it, Jonna—stop!"

"I told the police about you! I'll call them again!"

"C'mon. I know you're Yvonne's sister. Stop."

She finally stopped, sucking air with a whimpering sound that wasn't quite crying.

I pulled her to her feet, then brought her inside, where she sat with her face in her hands. Several pictures of Yvonne Bennett were pushpinned to the wall, most showing the two of them as children together, Jonna much smaller because Yvonne was older, Jonna unsmiling even then, Yvonne with an arm protectively around her shoulders. Jonna had already taken down a few, but some were still up.

"Who helped you?"

"I don't know what you're talking about."

"Who helped you kill him?"

She shook her head.

"All I knew was Lonnie Jones. I didn't know who he was until I saw the paper."

"So Yvonne Bennett's sister just happened to rent a room across the street from the man who was accused of murdering her?"

"Shit happens."

"Where'd you get the pictures?"

"I don't know anything. I'm going to call the police."

Someone had given her the pictures. Someone had

told her where to find Lionel Byrd and had put the plan in her head and convinced her she could finally make the man who murdered her sister pay. Someone had used her, and I thought it might be Wilts. If Wilts wanted to set up Byrd to stop the Repko investigation, it had to be Wilts, but I didn't have proof.

"Was it Wilts?"

"What are you talking about?"

"Did Wilts give you the pictures?"

"I don't know what you're talking about."

Her eyes were clear and unafraid, and I knew she wasn't going to admit to any of it. I called Pike on my cell.

"She's here. I have her."

"I'm on my way."

I put away the phone, then looked through Jonna's things. I was mostly checking for a gun or knife or something she might kill me with, but I found a copy of Lionel Byrd's original arrest report and court documents relating to the dismissal of the charges against him.

I held them up to show her.

"This is what we call evidence."

She raised her middle finger.

"This is what we call the finger. You don't have shit."

Her wallet, keys, sunglasses, and two cell phones were on the kitchenette counter. I didn't pay attention to the phones at first, but one was familiar. It was a clunky, inexpensive knockoff, exactly the same phone pictured on the spec sheet I found in Marx's file.

When I picked up the phone, Jonna shifted uneasily.

"I don't know why you're doing this to me, but I'm going to have you arrested. That's no bullshit."

I touched a finger to my lips. "Shh."

"That isn't my phone. I found it."

"Shh."

The more I examined the phone, the more certain I became. Jonna's other phone was a nice little Motorola, but the Kyoto was identical to the disposable phone in Marx's file. Debra Repko had received six calls from a prepaid number assigned to the same model phone. She had called a similar phone on her PDA.

Pike turned into the drive behind the Neon and let himself through the door. He nodded when he entered, but said nothing. Jonna's eyes widened as if he were a cobra. I showed him the phone.

"Look familiar?"

"The disposable."

"Uh-huh."

I turned on the phone and watched the display as the phone found a signal. It took me a minute to figure out how to access the call list, then I scrolled through the outgoing calls. Maybe I smiled. All the outgoing calls had been placed to the same number, and it was a number I recognized.

Pike said, "What?"

"She's been calling the same number Debra Repko called. All the incoming calls were from the same number, too."

"Wilts?"

"Let's find out."

Jonna pushed up from the chair and tried to run, but Pike wrapped her in his arms. She kicked and whipped her head from side to side, but Pike held her close and covered her mouth. He squeezed just enough to make her stop squirming, then nodded at me.

I dialed the number, then waited through the rings. I didn't wait long.

A voice said, "Jonna? Jonna, where have you been? I've been calling—"

I held my breath, and wondered if he could hear the pulse pounding in my ear.

"Hello? Can you hear me?"

He raised his voice.

"Do we have a bad connection?"

I turned off the phone, then took a deep breath. I wanted to push it out and blow away all the terrible feelings, but I couldn't move.

Pike said, "Was it Wilts?"

I shook my head.

"No. Not Wilts. It was Alan Levy."

Part Four
RECIPROCITY

40

PIKE TIED her wrists with an extension cord. I put her cell phones in a paper grocery bag I found in the kitchen, but we left everything else as we found it. Marx would want the scene as undisturbed as possible for his detectives and criminalists. It was Marx's play and I should have left it to him, but didn't.

When Pike brought Jonna out to his Jeep, I called Bastilla. The only number I had was her cell, but she didn't answer. She was probably still angry, but she might have been working. Either way, I was glad she didn't answer. I left a message.

"Ivy Casik's real name is Jonna Hill. She is Yvonne Bennett's half-sister. Call Pike. She'll be with him."

I left Pike's number, then locked Jonna's house and joined them at the Jeep. I gave him the keys.

"The police will need these. I left word for Bastilla and gave her your number. They'll be calling."

Pike was going to hold Jonna and her mother at a safe location until we reached Marx.

Pike said, "You sure you don't want me along?"

"I'm good. I'll see you in a bit."

I watched them drive away, then glanced at Jonna's house. I studied it for a while, then considered the sky. The canopy overhead was empty of clouds or birds. I wanted something to be there, but the sky was a milky blue desert. I slipped into my car, studied the cell number Alan Levy had given to me, but I didn't want to speak to him over the phone. I called his office instead.

"Hi, Jacob. Is Alan there?"

"I'm sorry, no. Did he ever get back to you? I gave him your messages."

"Yeah, we spoke, but I need to find him again. He isn't in court, is he?"

"Oh, no. He cleared his calendar when all this started about Mr. Byrd. He hasn't been in for days."

"Ah, okay."

"I could page him again."

"No need. Listen, is he working at home?"

"I don't know, Mr. Cole. You know Alan. He might be writing a brief or doing research. He's hard to keep up with when he gets like this."

I hung up, then called a real estate agent I know who has access to the property tax rolls. Six minutes later I had Alan Levy's home address and was heading toward Santa Monica. It was afternoon when I arrived. I shouldn't have gone, but I did. I should have waited for the police, but I didn't.

The address brought me to a large two-story Cape

Cod home three blocks from the beach in a lovely residential area. It was a family neighborhood with curbed sidewalks, kids on skateboards, and a hybrid in every drive, but it was also near the beach in Santa Monica, which meant the families were rich. I parked across the street. Two kids roared past on skateboards and a woman who was probably someone's housekeeper stood on a nearby corner. Gardeners worked at several of the houses, but the Levy residence was still. A gate across the drive hid the garage, so I couldn't see if Alan's car was at home or not. This time of the summer his kids would be out of school, but I couldn't tell if anyone was home. Maybe they were away at camp, but maybe they were splashing and grab-assing in their pool, and Alan was splashing with them. Or maybe he was crouched inside the house, watching the street through a gap in the shades.

I took my gun from beneath the seat, wedged it under my shirt, then strolled up the sidewalk. My phone vibrated as I reached the curb, but it was Bastilla. I ignored her.

The front door was large and heavy as a coffin lid. I knocked politely, then rang the bell. No one came, so I climbed over the driveway gate into a spacious backyard featuring a beautiful pool with used-brick decking and a lovely rose garden. No kids were splashing. Levy's family wasn't enjoying the breathtaking summer day. A single leaf floated in the pool. The water was so clean it might have been floating on air.

I walked along the back of the house, rapping on

glass sliders and French doors, but nothing and no one moved.

"Hey, Alan, it's Elvis Cole. Anyone home?"

Not even a housekeeper.

I went to the garage. The garage door was down and the side door was locked. I didn't want to waste time picking the lock, so I returned to the French doors. I broke a pane, reached inside, and let myself in. I should have been holding my gun, but I put it away. I didn't want to scare his children. They might be inside, sleeping. Maybe all of them were sleeping.

"Is anyone here?"

I stood just inside the door, listening, but the house remained quiet. I called out still louder.

"Mrs. Levy? I work with Alan. Jacob told me he might be home."

My voice echoed as if their home was a cave. No magazines or DVDs littered the coffee table; no toys or video games cluttered the floor. The rooms were large and beautifully furnished, but lifeless in a way that made my scalp prickle.

"Hello?"

I crossed through the family room into the living room, then crept through a formal dining room as cold as a mausoleum. The table was lovely, the chairs lining its sides perfectly placed as if they had not been moved in years.

The dining room led into the kitchen, then the pantry. You have kids, you have food, but there was no cereal, no Pop-Tarts, no snack bars. The shelves were lined with cans of Dinty Moore beef stew. Only the stew. Empty vodka bottles lined the floor. The cans and bottles had been placed in perfect rows with their labels out, each label perfectly aligned. My underarms grew damp as I backed out of the pantry.

The refrigerator was loaded with take-out containers, soft drinks, and more vodka, but no juice or milk, no peanut butter or eggs. I took out my gun and held it along my leg, but knew I wasn't going to find anyone. Not Alan or anyone else. Not anyone alive.

My cell phone hummed again, as loud as a swarm of wasps. I didn't check. I muffled it with my hand, trying to hear past the swarm into the hidden reaches of the house. My breath grew shallow, and I wanted to crash through the door or dive out the window. I wanted to get out of this terrible house and into the light like a boy running from bees, but I didn't.

I trotted the length of the house. I had moved quietly before, but now I moved faster, hitting each door with the gun up and ready. I checked the master bedroom, then Alan's home office, where the walls bristled with citations and plaques. I jerked open doors, checked closets and bathrooms, then ran up the stairs three at a time. I was terrified by what I expected to find, but pushed harder to find it.

The children's bedrooms were on the second floor—everything perfect and neat, but somehow even more frightening than the rest of the house. Posters of fading celebrities and forgotten bands decorated their walls. Computers several generations behind the current models sat on their desks. The toothbrushes in their bathroom hadn't been used in years.

I almost fell as I ran down the stairs, racing back to the master bedroom. The master bath told the same story. The men's products had been recently used, but the women's products were dry and out of date, and no soiled female garments were waiting to be cleaned.

My heart punched hard in my chest as the silence roared like the ocean. It roared even louder as I ran. I ran back through the house and out the French doors and all the way back to my car. It roared until I realized my cell phone was vibrating again. Bastilla was trying again. This time I answered.

41

JONNA HILL sat in a pleasant beige room in the Mission Area Police Station at the top of the San Fernando Valley. She was as far from the eyes and ears downtown as Marx could hide her. It was a comfortable room with patterned wallpaper, where rape and abuse victims were interviewed. The feminine surroundings supposedly made it easier for victims to talk. We were watching her through a two-way mirror. She was alone now, toying with the cap from a water bottle. Jonna knew we were watching. Bastilla and Munson had spent almost two hours questioning her, but the pleasant surroundings hadn't helped. Jonna admitted nothing and refused to implicate Levy.

Munson rubbed his eyes, then leaned against the wall, frowning at me.

"Are you sure it was Levy?"

"Yes."

"Maybe it only sounded like Levy."

I said, "It was Levy, Munson. I know Levy's voice."

Our side of the glass didn't have patterned wallpaper or comforting decor. The observation room was battleship-grey with a work desk butting the glass, metal chairs, and recording equipment. Pike and I stayed with Munson when Bastilla left to pick up the original death album pictures. Marx was in and out, phoning his contacts at Barshop, Barshop. They were doing everything themselves in order to stay under the radar.

Marx returned a few minutes later, holding his cell phone as if it were hot. He glanced at Munson as he entered.

"She open up?"

"She's tough, man. Nothing."

Pike said, "She believes him."

Munson rolled his eyes.

"Oh, please, Pike. She's crazy."

I said, "She might be crazy, but she believes Levy helped her punish the man who murdered her sister. She thinks they're on the same side."

Yvonne Bennett's police record and files were spread across the worktable. The psychiatric evaluation ordered at the time of her first arrest described a pattern of sexual abuse by the men her mother brought home. If those men had felt free to abuse Yvonne, they had probably tried to abuse her younger sister. I wondered if Yvonne had protected Jonna by offering herself to them. I stared at the broken heart on Jonna's forearm and thought it might be true.

She was always bad, and her bad ways caught up. Wasn't no better than a cat in heat from when she was little. I wouldn't even keep her picture up there if it wasn't for Jonna. She gets mad when I put it away.

Munson didn't buy it.

"Well, it would be nice if she said something for the record. I still don't believe it. Wilts is our guy."

Marx jiggled the cell phone as if he was nervous, then crossed his arms.

"Maybe not. On or about the time Frostokovich was murdered, a partner at Barshop was raising money for Wilts's campaign. That's one. The hooker party Wilts threw a few years later was also attended by a couple of Barshop partners. The man I spoke with believes Levy attended. That's two. So it looks like Levy had access to these women through his firm."

I said, "Was Levy at the dinner for Wilts when Repko was murdered?"

"Someone is looking into it. He's going to call back."

Munson threw up his hands. The room was so small he almost hit Pike.

"So what the hell? Were we wrong about Wilts or is he still a suspect?"

"We'll know when she talks."

"Jesus. Could Levy be acting as an agent for Wilts?"

I shook my head.

"You don't share something like this. You do it yourself. If the pictures came from Levy, then Levy took the pictures."

Marx looked at Jonna, still spinning the cap.

"What's the last contact you had with him?"

"We spoke earlier this afternoon. He was pushing me to find her."

"Okay. Before that?"

"Yesterday. He came to my house. He was feeling me out about what you guys were doing and asking about the girl."

Munson grunted.

"Using you."

"Yeah, Munson, how about that?"

"I wasn't criticizing."

I turned back to Marx.

"My guess, he's looking to kill her. She hasn't been returning his calls, so she's probably thinking the same thing. That's probably why she went back to Sylmar."

Munson sighed.

"We should bag this guy, Tommy. Let's get him off the street."

"How? He could be halfway to China by now."

Pike shifted in the corner.

"No. He wants her. She's the loose end."

Marx didn't look convinced.

"If we make a play for him before she talks, all we'll do is warn him. We don't have anything. Even if this girl tells us everything she knows, unless she has something hard, it's her word against his. You know what Alan Levy would do with that."

Munson crossed his arms, looking sullen.

"He'll say she's harassing him because he defended the man who murdered her sister."

"That's it."

"That could be what we're looking at, anyway. We have her for forty-eight hours, then we arraign her or cut her loose. Either way, that's when Levy gets the word. We pick him up now, at least we catch him off guard."

"Pick him up where? He's not at the office. Cole says he isn't home. You think he's going to come in, we call him and ask?"

"Have Barshop, Barshop call him. Maybe someone at the firm."

Pike said, "He'll read it. He'll walk away from the phone, and you'll never see him again."

I was watching Jonna. On the other side of the glass, she was spinning the cap. The water bottle was empty, which meant pretty soon she would have to pee, but for now she spun the cap. I was watching the cap when she looked up as if she had felt the pressure of my gaze. She smiled as if she saw me, and I smiled back.

I said, "Levy thinks I'm looking for her. He wants me to find her and he's hoping I'll call. Let me call him."

"Where does that get us?"

"I can tell him I found her. I tell him where she is, he's going to show up."

"So we bag him. We still don't have a case."

"If she cooperated, we might be able to get him to incriminate himself. We get him on tape, you'll have the case."

Munson laughed, and swung his hands again. Pike stepped to the side.

"Wake up, Cole. Look at her. That girl is cold."

"Right now, she believes Byrd killed her sister. If we convince her it was Levy, she might change her mind."

Marx considered me for a moment, then looked at Jonna. She spun the cap. It skittered across the table, then arced into space.

Marx turned back to me.

"Let's figure this out."

42

I WAITED alone outside the interview room, sipping a thirty-five-cent cup of coffee I bought from a machine at the end of the hall. The coffee was bitter and so hot it blistered my tongue. I drank it anyway. The pain was a pleasant distraction.

Coins clattered into the machine and drew my attention. Marx fed in the money, then noticed me while he waited for the cup to fill. When he had the coffee, he walked over. He took a sip, then made a face.

"This is terrible."

"Pretty bad."

"I don't understand it. We have a machine at Central, makes the best cup of coffee in the world. Same machine, same thirty-five cents, that one's great, this is awful."

He had more of the coffee anyway. Like me, maybe he needed the distraction.

"We're on his house. No sign of him, like you said,

but the boys are watching. We'll keep her mother at Foothill Station for the night, then we'll have to put her up somewhere, a motel, I guess. We'll get the bastard."

He was just talking, but part of me needed it. Maybe he sensed why I was boiling my tongue. Marx suddenly lowered his voice.

"You weren't the only one. Imagine how all those hotshots at Barshop, Barshop are going to feel."

I laughed at his joke, and Marx's big face split into a grin. I had never seen him smile before and would have bet the two of us would never share a laugh.

I said, "You know what gets me the worst?"

"I can guess."

"Levy made me part of his play. Like his accomplice."

"You want to look at it that way, so was the judge, Crimmens, and everyone else, but that's bullshit. You were doing your jobs. Levy saw his opportunity and took it. This is one smart sonofabitch we're dealing with here. I'll bet you he's been planning this from the moment he heard someone was busted for Yvonne Bennett's murder."

"I hope we get the chance to ask him."

Marx was probably right. Yvonne Bennett was the fifth victim. Alan Levy had committed murder four prior times under circumstances where no arrests had been made, no one was charged, and where he was not a suspect. He must have have been pleased with himself. He almost certainly searched for news of the murders he committed, and probably made discreet inquiries from time to time as to the status of the various investigations. It made perfect sense—as a prominent defense attorney, Levy had contacts throughout the system. He was probably surprised when he learned someone named Lionel Byrd had been arrested. I wondered if he was amused someone else had taken the pop or pissed off because someone else was getting the credit. Maybe I would get a chance to ask him this, too. He probably first realized Lionel Byrd would make the perfect get-out-of-jail-free card when he examined Byrd's history and the shabby case Crimmens had filed. Once freed, Byrd would remain a suspected murderer—the man who had been charged with killing Yvonne Bennett and a potential ace up Alan Levy's sleeve. After all, if Byrd could be suspected once, he could be suspected again.

I was probably the extra added attraction, brought on because it made sense and looked right.

Marx said, "What are you smiling about?"

"I was wondering what Levy would have done if I had found out the truth when I was working on Bennett."

"He would have killed you. He probably had that part of it figured out, too."

I nodded, thinking if it had broken that way three years ago, both Lupe Escondido and Debra Repko would still be alive. Or maybe I would be dead.

Marx said, "It was the bomb tech, wasn't it?"

He was staring at me.

"What bomb tech? You mean Starkey?"

"Yeah. It was her helping you, wasn't it?"

"I don't know what you're talking about. Starkey didn't help me. Neither did Poitras. I had some inside help, yes, but not them."

"Starkey was pissed off we cut her out, so she helped you. I hear things, Cole. Just like you."

"Think what you want, but Starkey didn't have anything to do with it."

Marx started to say something more when his cell phone rang. He checked the incoming number, then raised a silencing finger.

"My guy at Barshop—"

Their conversation lasted less than a minute, then Marx put away his phone. He appeared pale in the harsh fluorescent light.

"Was Levy at the dinner?"

"Yeah. He wasn't expected, but he showed up early. Wasn't there more than fifteen or twenty minutes, then left before it got started. He appeared agitated."

"He wanted to see Debra."

"That's three for three, Cole. This thing is coming together."

Levy had probably been working himself up to kill her, but only Levy could tell us that now. Why had he chosen Debra Repko, and why all the others? What had compelled him to murder her that night, three months ahead of his typical schedule, when he had been so very careful in the past? I wanted to know.

The case against Levy might be coming together, but only if Jonna Hill went along.

Bastilla came around the corner with the pictures she had been preparing. Pike and Munson would be watching from the observation room.

Bastilla seemed taken aback when she saw Marx and me together, but then she focused on Marx.

"Ready when you are, Chief."

"Let's do it."

Bastilla stepped into the interview room. Marx started after her, then hesitated and turned back to me.

"For what it's worth, I'm glad you didn't back off, Cole."

"Thanks, Chief. Me, too."

"Or Starkey. Tell her I said that."

I nodded, and Marx pushed into the room.

43

JONNA LEANED back when we entered, and laced her fingers. She seemed completely at ease—not relaxed the way you're relaxed when you're just hanging around, but comfortable like an experienced athlete. Marx and Bastilla had agreed to let Bastilla do the talking, woman to woman. They wanted me in the room because Jonna and I had something in common. Her sister.

Bastilla and I sat, but Marx stood in the corner. Bastilla placed a brown manila envelope on the table, but did not open it.

Bastilla said, "How you doing?"

"Pretty well, considering."

"All right. You know Mr. Cole?"

"Yeah. He's the one who started all this."

"And Chief Marx?"

She nodded.

"You know this is being recorded?"

"I don't care. I didn't have anything to do with this.

I don't know what you're talking about."

Bastilla rested her palms on the envelope.

"Here you are, Yvonne Bennett's sister, and you just happened to get tight with the man who was accused of murdering her, just happened to use a false name while doing so, and just happened to do all this in the days immediately preceding his death. What are we supposed to think?"

"I can't help it if I knew the guy. I thought he was someone named Lonnie Jones."

Marx moved in the corner.

"You knew he was Lionel Byrd because Alan Levy told you."

"That isn't true."

"You hated Levy. Your mother told us you used to call his office and send him hate mail."

"She's old."

"So you were probably surprised when Levy contacted you. I'm thinking that's what happened, isn't it, Jonna? He probably told you how guilty he felt, how sorry he was, some bullshit like that—"

Jonna's face darkened, but the darkness was her only reaction.

"—how Byrd had fooled him back then, but now Byrd was out there killing people and he wanted to do something about it. Am I getting close here? Ten ring? The eight?"

Bastilla said, "Take it easy, Chief. C'mon."

Good cop, bad cop.

Bastilla took the pictures from the envelope. Each

picture was in a sealed plastic sleeve. They were the actual pictures from the album, still smudged from the SID work. Bastilla dealt them out one by one. Sondra Frostokovich. Janice Evansfield. Every victim except Yvonne Bennett.

Jonna barely glanced at them as Bastilla dealt them out.

"You know Byrd didn't take them because you gave them to him. You know the absolute truth about that. These pictures were taken by the person who murdered them. It couldn't have been any other way."

"You don't know. The police took them. They take pictures like this when people are murdered."

"Is that what Levy told you? Is that how he explained where he got them?"

Bastilla took a stapled report from the envelope and placed it in front of Jonna.

"This is the forensic analysis of the pictures. It explains how we determined when the pictures were taken. You can read it, if you want. If you don't understand it, we can have the SID people explain what it means. We're not lying to you about this."

Bastilla touched the picture of Janice Evansfield and pointed out the streamer of blood. She touched the drops that had fallen from Sondra Frostokovich's nose, then produced the coroner investigator's photograph showing a much larger puddle. While Bastilla was explaining these things, I slipped the CI's picture of Yvonne Bennett from the envelope and waited my turn.

Then I pushed aside the other pictures and put the Polaroid of Yvonne on the table. Jonna leaned forward when she saw her sister.

"Do you see this?"

I touched the blood bubble, then placed the CI's picture of Yvonne beside the Polaroid so she could see the difference.

"It was a bubble made in her blood. It formed as she died. It popped a few seconds later."

Jonna stared at the pictures, but I could tell she wasn't seeing them.

"You know I worked for Levy on behalf of Lionel Byrd?"

Her eyes came up, but they might have been focused on something a thousand yards away.

"Uh-huh."

Bastilla touched me under the table, and Marx smiled from the corner.

"Levy told you about me, didn't he?"

She shook her head vaguely, then went back to the pictures.

Bastilla said, "Cole's involvement was never mentioned on TV or in the papers. He never personally mentioned it to you, and we haven't talked about it with you or in your presence. You would have no other way to know that he worked for Alan Levy."

I said, "Jonna, look at me."

Her eyes came up again, but now they seemed dull and opaque.

"Levy used me the same way he used you, and I

never saw it coming. I worked with him, talked to him almost every day, and he totally played me. That's how good he is. Lionel Byrd didn't kill your sister. I know you believe he killed her, but he didn't. If Levy gave you the pictures, then Levy killed her, and now we have to prove it."

Jonna said, "Levy."

"Levy's been using me to find out what the police know. He's also been pushing me to find you. I believe he intends to kill you. We know from your phone he's been calling you a lot. We also know you haven't been answering his calls or calling him back. I think this is because you sense something is wrong with the guy."

Marx stepped out of the corner.

"We see you as a victim here, too. We want to handle it that way. I can't promise you won't pull some time, but we'll cut a good deal. Get you a reduced sentence and early parole if you cooperate."

She looked at Yvonne's picture again, the close-up showing the ugly red bubble of blood. She touched it, and her face settled into the same humorless, determined lines I had seen in her high-school portrait. She picked up the picture, kissed it, then dropped it with the others. She once more seemed at ease.

"What do you want?"

"A recorded admission of guilt."

"Okay. Whatever."

Bastilla shook her head.

"Not you. Levy. Your testimony won't be enough. We need him to acknowledge he gave you the pictures or helped plan the murder. All he has to do is indicate he had knowledge of these things, and that would be enough."

"You want me to call him?"

"Levy's too smart to make an incriminating statement over the phone, but we think Cole can bring him out."

I said, "If I find you, I'm supposed to call him."

"So he can kill me."

"That would be my guess. He will probably try to kill me, too."

Bastilla said, "We would pick a secure location. We would have plenty of protection, and—"

Jonna cut her off.

"I don't care. I want to go get him."

She said it without hesitation or remorse. Munson had been right. She was totally cold.

44

MARX COMMANDEERED a conference room, then called out an elite SWAT tactical team with supervisors and plus-one team leaders to plan the mission. They let me participate because my role was key—the task was not simply to capture Alan Levy, but to elicit a confession. They broke down a plan, selected a location, and deployed surveillance and tactical teams even before I made the call. We didn't know if Levy would agree to meet, but the SWAT boys wanted everyone in place asap. If the plan changed, they would roll with it. They were the best in the business.

A surveillance technician named Frank Kilane stuck his head into the room and gave us the thumbs-up. Marx patted me on the back.

"Ready to make the call?"

I grinned, but my grin was too large and strained.

"I live for making calls like this."

"Want some more of that coffee?"

"You trying to kill me?"

Marx grinned back with the same fractured leer.

"Not until after we get this bastard."

Nervous humor.

Pike and Munson were waiting in the interview room, but Bastilla had moved Jonna so they could continue the interview. Frank Kilane had wired my personal cell phone into a recording monitor through a hands-free jack. We were using my phone so Levy would recognize my incoming number.

Kilane gave me the phone.

"All you have to do is use the hands-free like you normally would. Don't worry about losing the signal. We have a pretty good signal here anyway, but I hooked you in with a booster."

Marx waved toward the two-way glass.

"Okay, then. Everybody out. Let's clear the room."

They left me alone to minimize background noise.

I took Jonna's seat. A yellow legal pad with Levy's number and the address of the location was on the table. I was glad they thought of it.

Marx's voice came over a hidden loudspeaker.

"Go when you're ready."

I dialed, and listened to the soft burring ring tone. The silence between each ring felt longer than usual, but Levy answered on the seventh ring. He sounded normal in every way.

"Hey, Alan, you still want to talk to Ivy Casik?"

"Fantastic. You found her?"

"Am I not the World's Greatest Detective?"

Mr. Just-Kidding-Around-Because-Nothing-Is-Out-of-the-Ordinary. Levy chuckled, showing me nothing was out of the ordinary with him, either.

"Ah, well, did you speak with her?"

"Uh-uh. I figured I would wait for you. I didn't want to spook her."

I gave him the address without waiting to be asked. It was an abandoned meth lab in a residential area. The SWAT guys selected it because the location offered cover for the surveillance teams and other advantages. The light traffic would make Levy easy to identify as he approached the location, and if he lost his resolve and departed without stopping, he would be easy to follow. If he left, we would let him. We didn't want him to know we were on to him until he had incriminated himself. I finished setting the stage.

"It's a little house at the bottom of Runyon Canyon. A dump, man. She appears to be alone."

He sounded hesitant for the first time.

"Okay, well, this is great work, Elvis, like always. You don't have to wait. I can't get over there until later."

I did my best to sound disappointed.

"Alan, your call, but I really busted my ass to find her. She didn't unpack her car. I don't know how long she will be here."

"Uh-huh, well, I have an appointment with some people at Leverage. They probably have more to offer about what Marx is up to than this girl."

"I can't watch her all day, Alan. I have things to do."

"It's all right, Elvis. Really. I have the address, but I have to see these people at Leverage first. Don't stay. If I get by to see her, I'll call you about it later."

"Whatever you want."

As soon as I turned off the phone, Marx pushed open the door.

"That bastard's going straight for the girl. Let's roll."

45

JONNA HILL stated during her taped interview that she did not shoot Lionel Byrd and was not present at the time of his death. This might or might not have been a lie. According to Jonna, Alan Levy provided the seven Polaroid pictures, the necessary information about Byrd, and cash to rent both the apartment near the Hollywood Bowl and the room across from Byrd on Anson Lane. He contacted her not long after the murder of Debra Repko, claiming to be racked by guilt for his role in freeing a man he subsequently learned was responsible for multiple homicides. Jonna found him easy to believe. He was so smart, she said. So convincing. She was a willing and enthusiastic participant. Levy taught her to mask her fingerprints with plastic-model glue and bind back her hair, and also provided the camera, film, and the *My Happy Memories* album. Her part was simple. Over the course of a three-week period, she befriended Lionel Byrd while posing as a writer, which had also been Levy's suggestion. She had Byrd handle the components of the death album to leave his finger-prints, then, on the night of his death, drugged his whiskey with the oxycodone, which Levy also provided. She stated for the record she was not witness to whatever happened after she left that night. This, too, might have been a lie, but it also might have been the truth.

We double-timed it out to the parking lot. Marx coordinated the roll through a SWAT plus-one as we trotted toward a surveillance van the size of a taco truck. The plus-one was a hard-looking guy with a blond crew cut. He glanced at Pike between orders.

"Aren't you Joe Pike?"

Pike nodded.

"You coming with us?"

Pike nodded again.

"Cool. I admire your work."

But when we reached the van, Munson stopped Pike.

"This is as far as you go."

I said, "He's part of this, too."

Marx considered Pike, then shook his head.

"We don't need more civilians. Sorry, Pike, but this is it."

The plus-one seemed disappointed.

"Bummer."

I shrugged at Joe.

"Don't sweat it, man. I'll see you on the other side."

Pike stared at me for a moment, then the corner of his mouth twitched.

"I'll see you."

Pike trotted away toward his Jeep as Marx waved me into the van.

"We gotta get you wired up. Get in there."

The van was walled with racks of surveillance equipment, recording devices, tools, and an ice chest so old the plastic was mildewed. Jonna and Bastilla were already inside. The space grew crowded as everyone piled aboard, and Kilane didn't like it.

"Jesus Christ, just sell tickets, why don't you?"

Jonna blinked at me.

"Are we going to ride together?"

"Looks like."

"Good. I'd like that."

Marx wedged his way up front with the driver, and we pulled out as soon as the door was closed.

Kilane fitted a wire microphone under Jonna's shirt as Bastilla asked her questions, like did Levy ever check her for mikes or feel up her boobs or search her. Jonna told her no, he never had, and seemed uninterested in what Kilane was doing.

I said, "You scared?"

Bastilla glanced over, irritated.

"Say something encouraging."

Jonna ignored her, and made a little shrug.

"I'm always scared."

"You hide it well."

"I know. I just look this way."

"Lift your arm, Jonna."

Jonna lifted her arm, but her attention was on me.

"I was thinking about what you said, how you never saw it coming. How does that make you feel?"

I realized why she had stared at me in the interview room and now wanted me in the van with her. She knew how I felt because she probably felt the same way.

"It made me feel like he owned me."

"Yvonne was a prostitute."

I nodded, not knowing what else to do.

"Do you have sibs?"

"No. I'm an only."

"Oh. That's too bad."

Jonna fell silent after that as Kilane finished his work and lowered the shirt. He turned to a bank of equipment and pulled on a headset.

"How's that feel?"

"Okay."

The tech raised a thumb. The mike was transmitting well. He pulled off the headset, then went to work strapping a similar mike to my chest.

Jonna looked around at the cramped quarters.

"Can I see how it feels when I move?"

"Sure."

Jonna twisted from side to side, then crabbed to the back of the van. Kilane, the plus-one, and I scrunched out of her way. She twisted some more, then stood as best she could with the low ceiling.

"Feels okay."

She waddled forward, but lost her balance and stumbled into the equipment rack. She made an *oof*-ing sound, tangled herself in a box of tools and wire, but managed to stay upright.

"I'm okay. Can you see it poking my shirt?"

Kilane laughed.

"Kid, your own mama couldn't see that mike."

Marx put away his phone, then climbed out of the passenger seat to join us. He glanced at me, but studied Jonna.

"We're ten minutes out. You remember what we talked about?"

"Sure."

"All you have to do is be visible. If Levy sees you and believes you're alone, he'll be more likely to stop. Once he's out of the car, you go into the house. Cole will carry the ball."

"I know."

Marx waved toward the equipment.

"We'll be able to hear everything you say. If you try to warn him, our deal goes out the window."

"I'm not going to warn him."

"So you know. We have your statement on tape now. We might not be able to convict Levy with it, but we'll sure as hell go after you. Get back in the house. An officer will be inside to take care of you."

"If I wanted to warn him I wouldn't have agreed to do this. Relax."

The plus-one laughed, but Marx ignored him.

"Something else I want you to know. Your safety is

my number one concern. You won't be able to see them, but we'll have three sniper teams watching every move Levy makes. We will be watching him. If he shows a weapon or makes a threatening move toward you, we will put him down. We won't give him a chance to hurt you."

"Everyone will be watching him."

"You can count on it."

"I am."

I patted her leg. The woman had committed murder with a cold-blooded obsession that had bought her a ticket to the psych ward, but I patted her leg. When I realized what I was doing, I stopped.

They let us out of the van in a Rite Aid parking lot in Hollywood not far from La Brea. Two men in civilian clothes who were probably D-team tactical operators were waiting in a green Chevy TrailBlazer.

Marx said, "That's your ride. We'll see you on the other side."

The TrailBlazer barreled up La Brea, then onto the residential streets twisting up into Runyon Canyon. Jonna did not seem nervous. She made a soft, breathy whistle, singing to herself. Da-da-daa, da-da-daa. Staring at nothing and singing until we reached the house.

46

THE SWAT planners had made a good choice. The house was an old canyon cabin isolated by a curve in the road. It had probably been built in the twenties as a hunting lodge and later expanded, but it hadn't been maintained in years. Jonna's white Neon was parked beside it. The man who brought it was inside the house, where Jonna would wait until Levy was spotted. When the surveillance elements identified Levy, they would radio the man in the house. Then it was up to Jonna. All she had to do was let Levy see her so he would know she was present. Once Jonna was safely back inside the house, the rest would be up to me.

They dropped us by the Neon, then quickly drove away.

I said, "Don't look around for the surveillance teams. You won't see them, but someone might see you looking for them."

"What happens if he doesn't come?"

"We'll be bored. You'd better get in the house. If he

sees me out here with you, we're screwed."

I waited until she was inside, then moved into a gnarled clump of scrub oak on the opposite side of her car. If Levy stopped anywhere at the front of the house, I would be able to approach him without being seen. I wanted to surprise him.

I settled in to wait. Levy would come or not. Might be ten minutes, or never. The occasional car passed without slowing. Local residents. Construction workers. First-time hikers trying to find the park who took the wrong turn. None of them was Levy. I listened to thrushes and mockingbirds. None of them was Levy, either.

The trees whispered behind me, followed by a voice that wasn't much louder.

Pike said, "Good spot."

He settled onto the earth beside me.

I said, "Marx is really pissed right now. I'm wired."

"You think I'm trusting someone else to cover your back?"

We fell silent. Marx would be cursing. He would be livid, but the blond plus-one would be trying not to laugh.

Jonna Hill stepped out of the house eight minutes later and went to the Neon. That was my signal and also the bait. A brown Dodge sedan crept around the curve, slowing to look. Levy was hunched over the wheel. He slowed even more when he saw Jonna, and stopped in the middle of the street. His head swiveled, searching the area.

Jonna stepped away from the Neon. She wasn't supposed to go into the house until he got out of his car, and didn't. Her lips moved as she studied the Dodge. She was singing again. Da-da-daa, da-da-daa.

The three sniper teams would be on him with telescopic sights, ready to rock if a gun appeared. If any of them saw a gun, that shooter would touch off a .30-caliber round traveling at 2600 feet per second. We didn't want him dead. We wanted him alive, but that's the way it would be if he made the wrong move.

The Dodge swung in a lazy arc and parked directly between Jonna and me. Levy got out, no more than a car length from her and two lengths from me. His coat and pants were wrinkled, as if he had been sleeping in them.

Pike sighed a whisper.

"Perfect."

Jonna did not return to the house. She should have immediately gone inside, but she didn't.

She said, "How did you find me?"

Levy responded as if this was the most natural moment in the world.

"You had me worried. Why didn't you answer?"

I slipped from the trees, and he didn't hear me until I was directly behind him.

I said, "Worried about what, Alan?"

He stumbled sideways so dramatically I thought he would fall, then spun in a panicked circle. I held up my hands, showing my palms and taking a step back.

"Don't have a stroke. Everything's cool. How'd it go at Leverage?"

When he realized he was still alive, he pulled himself together. He glanced past me to see if anyone else was coming, then at Jonna, then up and down the street. Frightened.

"The meeting got canceled."

"Good. We have a lot to talk about. Jonna, why don't you go inside, give us a chance to talk?"

Jonna said, "No."

Levy glanced at Jonna with bug eyes. Jonna had moved closer. She was staring at him, and I didn't like the way she was staring. Marx wouldn't like it, either. The snipers would have a more difficult time with Jonna outside.

Levy said, "I can talk to her alone. You didn't have to wait."

I edged toward Jonna, trying to put myself between her and Levy, but Levy backed away. He hooked his thumbs on his belt under his jacket. I didn't see a gun, but the shooters would be on high alert.

"Yeah, I did, Alan. My new best friend here, Jonna, and I have already talked. I know what happened."

Levy glanced at her again and continued backing away.

"I don't understand."

"Of course you do. Killing Lionel Byrd."

"I don't know what you're talking about."

"Alan, please. I caught you in one lie when you drove up. You told me you never met this girl, but you asked her why she hadn't answered, you told her she had you worried."

"I didn't say anything like that. You must have misheard."

Jonna said, "Yes, you did."

I took a step after him, trying to keep up the pressure. I wanted Levy focused on me, not her, and I was still trying to get between them.

"Here's what's going to happen—you can pay me to keep your filthy little secrets, or we'll go to the police. I'm thinking two million dollars, one for her, one for me. Sound good?"

Levy glanced up and down the street again as if he sensed the police were watching and knew he was being recorded.

"I don't know what you're talking about. I don't understand why you're trying to do this, but I'm leaving—"

He suddenly veered toward the Dodge, and then Jonna said something that stopped both of us.

"I taped you, Alan."

Fear played over his face as his eyes bulged.

"The day you gave me the pictures of the dead girls, I had a tape recorder under my shirt. I gave it to him. I let him listen."

Jonna pointed at me. She had never mentioned a recording, had not given a recording to me, and the police had not found such a recording in her possessions. I wondered if she knew she was lying. I wondered if she believed it.

"Go in the house, Jonna. Alan and I will work it out."

She didn't go into the house. She moved toward him.

"Two million dollars isn't enough."

Levy wet his lips. He looked from me to Jonna, then back to me, and his hands went back to his belt.

He said, "How much do you want?"

We had him with those words. Alan Levy had demonstrated knowledge and awareness of the pictures by negotiating with us. We had him, and Marx would now be issuing commands to effect the arrest, but then Jonna said something else.

"There isn't enough."

Jonna took a knee as if bending to tie her shoe, then came up like a sprinter out of the blocks with what we would later confirm was a rat-tail file she had palmed when she stumbled into the tool rack in the surveillance van. She went for his neck, hitting him so hard she knocked him backwards into the Dodge and onto the ground.

Everyone had been so concerned Levy might kill Jonna, it never occurred to us she would kill him.

The shooter teams crashed from their hides, but they were far away and unable to shoot with the three of us clumped together. Pike burst out of the trees. I grabbed Jonna from behind, but she had wrapped herself around Levy, stabbing him in the neck and the face and the head. I caught her arm to pry her away, but that's when I heard the popping, and then Joe Pike shouting.

"Gun!"

Levy had a small black pistol pressed deep into her belly and made a high, keening sound as he shot her. He pulled the trigger as fast as he could.

Jonna suddenly stepped back. I pushed her aside, then moved for the gun, but Levy had already dropped it. He was holding the bloody rag of his neck with both hands when Pike slammed into him.

Jonna stumbled backwards, sat down, then burped a red mist. I tore off my shirt and pressed it onto her belly as the SWAT guys swarmed over us.

"Hang on, Jonna. Hang on. Keep breathing."

I don't think she saw me. Her mouth was set in the determined line, but something in her eyes had changed. The seeds of anger were softer. I'm not sure, but I like to think so. I hope so.

Jonna Hill died as the paramedics arrived.

THE ROSE GARDEN

47

THE SANTA Monica sky was incandescent with shoreline haze, filling Alan Levy's backyard with light so bright the swimming pool sparkled. City Councilman Nobel Wilts and Chief Marx were standing beside me at the edge of the rose garden. Thirty-two varieties of roses had been carefully removed and heaped in a pile on the far side of the yard. They would not be replanted. When the city finished its work, the roses would be discarded.

Marx waved over Sharon Stivic, who was the chief coroner investigator overseeing the recovery.

"How much longer?"

"It's a big hole. You have to be careful with the soil. We don't want to miss something important."

The bodies were found using a gas sensor that detected the unusual concentrations of methane generated by decomposing flesh. A side-scanning sonar had then been employed to determine the exact locations, and now members of the medical examiner's office were scraping away the soil.

Wilts said, "Gotta be his wife and kids, right?"

Marx nodded. The sonar had defined their shapes and sizes.

"Won't know for sure until the identification, but yeah—it's an adult and two children."

"Jesus Christ, I met the woman. I'm pretty sure I met her. It was a while ago."

Wilts scrunched his face, trying to remember whether he had met Alan Levy's wife or not, but finally gave up. He mopped his brow, then scowled at the sky.

"Fuck this. I'm getting out of the sun."

We watched him walk to the house, which was swarming with criminalists, detectives, and reporters. Levy's street was crowded with so many news vans, coroner vehicles, and gawkers that I had parked three blocks away. None of the newspeople had showed up when Yvonne Bennett was murdered, but Yvonne had not been a downtown attorney who had murdered his family—Yvonne was only a nobody who had once protected her sister.

Marx had called early that morning, telling me the bodies had been located the night before. He had asked me to come to the recovery, so I did, though I had seen enough bodies. I didn't want to see more, but I was hoping for answers. Both for myself and the Repkos.

I gestured at the growing mound of dirt.

"Might find Debra Repko's PDA in there."

"Might."

"Or in the house."

"If we're lucky."

"Or more pictures."

"I hope to hell not."

"Levy's autopsy show anything?"

"Nothing. Brain was clear. No tumors, cysts, or lesions. No drugs. Blood chemistry looked fine. What can you say?"

"What about the people at his firm?"

"Stunned, like everyone else. Levy told them his wife left him and took the kids east. That was eight years ago, just before Frostokovich."

"Neighbors add anything?"

"Most of'm never met the man. We'll be reconstructing this mess for months."

There was nothing more to say. You want them alive to answer the questions. *Why did you do this? Were there only seven, or did you kill more?* Now we had questions that would never be answered. *Why had Jonna Hill done what she did?*

A booming laugh came from the house. Marx and I turned to see Wilts with a beautiful female reporter from one of the local television affiliates. Wilts was fingering her ass.

I said, "Does he know you suspected him?"

"Nah. I didn't see the point."

Marx had gone to the Repkos and the rest of the families to explain why he misled them, but had not told them his true suspect was Wilts. A fixer to the end, he kept Wilts out of it. I respected his courage for facing them.

Two men with blunt-nosed shovels were up to their thighs in a four-foot-by-eight-foot hole. They scraped the soil away one inch at a time. Both men stopped digging at the same time, then one stooped to touch something. They wore rubber gloves.

"I'm going to take off, Chief. I don't want to see this."

Marx stared at the ground for a moment.

"Do you think she taped him, the way she said? When he gave her the pictures?"

"She made it up. She made up a lot of things. Her sister was the same way."

"If that tape exists, I'd like to find it."

"You have her interview."

"Hearing that tape would help. Not just what he said, but how. You never know what the sonofabitch might have said. It could explain a lot. Might answer a lot of questions."

"If you find it, let me know."

I hoped he was right.

I left him standing by the grave in Alan Levy's backyard, and walked through the crowd to the street. The sky was a beautiful crystalline blue, as bright as any I had ever seen, but a certain darkness could blot the sky, even in the middle of the day.

Darkness had lived in Alan Levy. A dark shade touched Jonna Hill long before her sister was murdered. Debra Repko brushed darkness and never

384

returned. *Why had she gone for a walk with him?* *Why had he killed her on that night, and not another?* We would never know.

The darkness frightens me, but what it does to us frightens me even more. Maybe this is why I do what I do. I chase the darkness to make room for the light.